08851 6

C000154035

Aire

Something in the Aire

Stuart Campbell

© Stuart Campbell, 2014

Published by Wrymouth Publications

While the principal characters in this book are fictitious, they are set against certain historical facts, the description of conversations and events involving deceased persons being entirely from the imagination of the author.

A CIP catalogue record for this book is available from the British Library.

ISBN 978-0-9929894-0-8

Book layout and cover design by Clare Brayshaw
Cover photo © Davidmartyn | dreamstime.com

Prepared and printed by:

York Publishing Services Ltd
64 Hallfield Road
Layerthorpe
York YO31 7ZQ

Tel: 01904 431213

Website: www.yps-publishing.co.uk

For my family

About the author

Stuart Campbell was born in Bradford in 1938 and educated there and in Scotland. After military service, he spent eight years in provincial journalism before helping to establish one of the BBC's pioneering local radio stations at Durham and later as News Editor at Radio Carlisle. After ten years as Programme Organiser at Radio Leeds he retired from the BBC in 1989, taking up a new role as a career consultant. He is married with three sons and a daughter and lives in West Yorkshire.

Contents

Acknowledgements

To my wife Myra for her unstinting support and encouragement during this book's long gestation, my daughter Victoria for burning the midnight oil proof reading and copy editing my manuscripts, my editor Lorena Goldsmith and all those from whom I sought wise guidance including Bill Mason, Pat Jowett and Jennifer Grooby.

Thank you

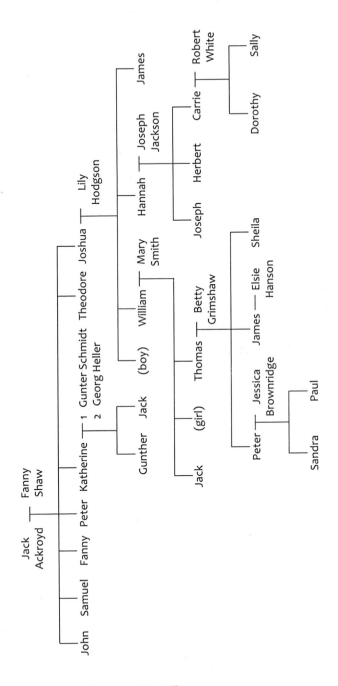

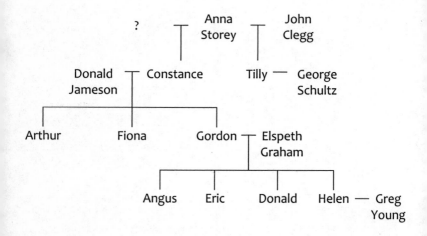

Bradford 1843

Jack Ackroyd yawned and pulled a cracked earthenware chamber pot from under the bed to relieve the pressure on his bladder. He shivered under his thick nightshirt, which gave little protection against the bitter cold that penetrated their small bedroom. Silver moonlight refracted through the icy panes of their one tiny window, faintly outlining features of the simple room with its rough wooden bed and washstand. Fanny, his wife, slept on beneath coarse woollen blankets, the moonlight highlighting silver strands in her hair, bearing witness to the seven children she had brought into the world. In the next room, four surviving Ackroyd children were still sleeping the sound sleep of the young.

Jack and Fanny fretted at the thought of seven-year-old Katherine still having to share a bedroom with their eldest son John, thirteen, and his brothers Theo, six, and Josh, four. They should be trying to find somewhere bigger, but still affordable, to rent in the industrial maelstrom that was Bradford in 1843. The wages Jack and his son brought home from the mill barely paid for their rent and food as it was. Before Christmas, mill owner Josiah Hudson appeared to promise Jack promotion in the weaving shed, but he had not said any more about it and Jack knew better than to ask for a wage increase. It was common knowledge that if you wanted to get on in the mill it was best to keep your head down and your mouth shut.

Anyroad, I haven't done that bad to get to overseer at forty-eight, mused Jack as he stretched and scratched, resigning himself to another long day in the shed. His big frame and lugubrious expression earned him an undeserved reputation as a hard taskmaster. But those who worked for him respected his hard work, fairness and loyalty to his mates. If there was a job to be done, Jack made sure it was done well and on time. But he never failed to ask about the families of the men who worked under him and was respected for the concern he showed for those falling on hard times.

From the street came the sound of shouts accompanied by a sharp tapping sound. These grew louder as the local knocker-up roused reluctant neighbours from their sleep with a long pole, shouting the time at each house at the top of his voice. Before the tap at his window, Jack was already pulling on hodden trousers reeking of grease from a thousand fleeces. He dressed quickly and, carrying his clogs, looked into the children's room to make sure John was awake and getting ready.

At one side of the bedroom, Jack could just make out the huddled shapes of Theo and Josh still sound asleep under their shared blanket. Katherine slept at the other side of the room behind a blanket screen. As usual, John was still in bed, needing a firm prod to make him put a reluctant foot on the cold boards. Like all boys of his age, he was loath to exchange his warm bed for the bitterly cold walk to the mill. But he knew he could not afford to risk a farthing of his meagre wages and threaten the family's wellbeing.

"I'll see you downstairs in five minutes, lad. You'd better look lively if you want something to eat," admonished Jack, starting to make his way down the steep, twisting stairs to their stone-flagged parlour. In one bare stone wall of the room that was the focus of all family activities, a slack-backed fire glowed dully through a black-leaded grate, radiating only a faint heat. Jack lit an oil lamp with a taper before mending the fire with more slack, sending greenish coils of smoke up the chimney, some whisps escaping into the room. He filled a sooty kettle from a pail and placed in on the grate.

The oil lamp cast its dull yellow glow across a scrubbed table and varnished chairs. Two high-backed ones, one resting on curved runners, faced the blackened range next to a tall, rustic dresser filled with plates, pots, pans and other kitchen essentials. Next to the dresser, a door covered by a blanket led to a tiny flagged larder-cum-scullery housing a deep stone sink. A bolted door led from the scullery into a narrow, flagged back yard with a midden privy in a corner.

Humble as it was, Jack and Fanny were proud of their mid-terrace house standing back to back with others on a steep rutted street overlooking the town centre. They considered themselves well off compared to some of the other millworkers who endured a miserable existence in hovels barely fit for human habitation. With new mills springing up all over town to cope with the insatiable demand for Bradford's worsted cloth, there were never enough houses for the constant stream of incomers seeking work. Until they found better, thought Jack, they would stay put.

He took a patterned tin from the dresser and was transferring two spoonfuls of tea to a brown teapot warming by the fire when John appeared, sleepy-eyed, at the foot of the stairs. In silence they ate thick wedges of bread smeared with dripping and drank tea from tin mugs, delaying to the last moment the time they would have to leave the relative warmth of the parlour.

John looked like a smaller version of his father. He was already starting to fill out into what promised to be a big frame and had the same large nose and shock of black hair hanging halfway down his forehead. Unlike Jack, he had benefitted from some elementary education at Sunday school before starting work at the mill when he was ten. He had hoped to go on to the new church school in John Street, but his father would not hear of it, telling his son that the family desperately needed his wages. In the dingy spaces he endured at work, John often daydreamed of escaping to the high moors, to the pure air and wide horizons that would liberate him from his incarceration of drudgery and tedium. He even thought about life at sea after his imagination was fired by the popular tale of desert island castaway Robinson Crusoe. But family loyalty dictated he submerge his dreams to meet the necessities of their very existence.

Like so many of his generation, Jack saw virtue in hard work rather than education, which could be a severe drain on a family's means. He had started work in one of the town's first mills at the age of eight, thirty years before an Act of Parliament outlawed the employment of children under nine. He began by collecting loose wool from the delivery bay, bundling it up for washing and combing with the rest. During the next forty years of grinding toil and long days, which had taken their toll on his health, Jack gradually worked his way up to his present position of weaving shed overseer.

He met and courted Fanny Shaw, a high-spirited twenty-one-year-old, when he was eight years her senior. Her parents, who ran a small alehouse in Bowling, were reluctant to approve their only daughter's involvement with a much older, uneducated millworker with uncertain prospects. But Fanny would not be denied this big, taciturn man with warm brown eyes, who had fallen head over heels for her. She wore down her parents' resistance until they agreed to her marriage to Jack in May 1829 in the new Christ Church at the top of Darley Street. The service was followed by a simple supper for both families and friends at the Shoulder of Mutton in Kirkgate.

That night a few of John's workmates and some hangers-on, fuelled by an evening of unaccustomed strong ale and revelry, brought a flush to Fanny's cheeks and scandalised her parents by accompanying the newly-weds the short distance to her home and noisily abetting successful consummation of their union. Successful it turned out to be, for Jack was to sire no fewer than five boys and two girls over the following ten years. Samuel, their second son, died in childbirth while Fanny, their eldest daughter, was killed by a runaway horse and cart on Stott Hill behind the Parish Church just after her fifth birthday. They had barely got over their grief for Fanny when Peter, their third son, was cut down by cholera emanating from the town's diseased waterways. He was just six years of age.

Devastated by their loss, Jack and Fanny added their support to the growing anger of townsfolk about the frequent outbreaks of cholera and typhoid adding to the toll of traditional diseases such as scarlet fever and smallpox. Their anger was fuelled by a report in the Bradford *Observer* that the town had one of the lowest life expectancies in the country at just over eighteen years. The newspaper reported that only a third of children born to textile workers in Bradford would reach their fifteenth birthday and children under five accounted for half of all deaths. One in five would not live beyond their first birthday.

"There's bread, cheese and pickle in the press for your bait. But you'd better shape up or we'll be late," Jack urged his sleepy son. John slowly folded his midday meal into a page from the *Observer* and, wrapped up against the bitter cold, father and son let themselves out on to the rutted street covered with ice and soot-stained snow. Daylight was still more than two hours away as they slipped and stumbled their way down the hill. Dark shapes of other muffled figures making their ritual early morning descent to the mill waved and exchanged muffled greetings. The usual clatter of wooden clogs was eerily muted on the dirty white carpet, which reflected shifting pools of yellow light from hand-held lanterns moving between the rows of dwellings. Here and there, light gleamed through chinks in curtained windows revealing stirrings inside. Otherwise, the pre-dawn darkness was still unchallenged by the newfangled gas lamps that had begun to appear on some streets in the centre. In common with many townsfolk, Jack did not trust the "smelly and dangerous" coal gas now being piped into some houses by

Bradford Gaslight Company. In spite of Fanny's enthusiasm for this modern convenience, he swore he would never welcome it inside their parlour.

The first of these bright street lamps came into view as they dropped down towards the grander buildings in Cheapside, behind which lay land earmarked by the Leeds and Bradford Railway Company for their terminus station. Winding its way through this expanding townscape but still out of sight, Bradford Beck lay partly frozen over, a condition townsfolk considered a blessing as it helped to mask the foul stench that in warmer weather emanated from the beck and the nearby canal basin it fed.

Jack and Fanny never ceased to mourn for Peter, an intelligent, mischievous child who regularly ignored his parents' instructions to keep away from the canal contaminated with raw sewage and industrial waste. There was too much fun to be had with the older boys, dropping lighted rags into the canal basin and watching blue flames flicker across the surface of the filthy water, igniting bubbles of marsh gas. When his sickness and diarrhoea grew acute and failed to respond to all the usual remedies, they realised Peter was desperately ill. As a last, expensive resort they called in a doctor, who told them he was spending many hours of his day tending to youngsters with symptoms like Peter's. He prescribed the only remedies he had to hand, advising Jack and Fanny to make sure their son drank as much clean water as possible. Peter died the next day.

These memories still haunted Jack as he and John crossed in front of the canal basin to join swelling ranks of millworkers clattering their way north along Canal Road. Soon most of the slow throng was crossing the beck by a substantial bridge into Mill Street and their eventual destination. The air was already thick with sulphurous smoke from a dozen coal-fired boiler houses as father and son turned between a pair of huge iron gates set in a high stone wall marking the boundary of Hudson's mill, their incarceration for the next twelve hours. It would be dark again before either of them would set foot outside the gates.

"I'll see you in the yard at home time then," said Jack in as hearty a voice as he could muster. John nodded his assent before plodding off across the yard with a heavy tread. Jack watched his son go, thinking about the contrast with Peter's derring-do character. He and Fanny had often tried to imagine what Peter would have been like as he grew into a young man. They had resolved to avenge the premature death of their son by joining the growing band of Bradford citizens vowing to rid themselves of the foul legacy as the most polluted town in Britain. Soon they would find themselves up against the vested interests of some of the most powerful businessmen in Bradford, who had no reputation for altruism when it came to civic matters. Among these men of wealth and influence was Josiah Hudson Esq., whose first-floor office window dominated the imposing mill entrance.

Trouble at Mill

Kathryn Hudson reviewed her new satin dress in the cheval glass. Smoothing it with her hands, she half turned this way and that before giving a little smile of approval at her reflection. She had chosen to wear three strands of pearls to complement her generous silver mane and majestic bosom. Joe's generosity had known no bounds when the mill had orders stretching weeks ahead. For once, she was actually looking forward to meeting the Ramsdens and the Priestleys without any feeling of inferiority. She crossed the landing to descend a wide marble and mahogany staircase, glancing sideways to admire again the new portrait of her husband that graced their circular entrance hall.

Josiah Hudson was already in their dining room when she entered. He was helping himself to breakfast from a series of silver tureens spread along a mahogany sideboard. The polished silver reflected the flames of a coal fire radiating only limited heat into the spacious room. Despite this, the mill owner was in shirtsleeves, his ample figure filling a generous worsted waistcoat hung with a heavy silver fob chain. His florid complexion and bulldog jowls beneath a full head of silver hair gave him a belligerent air, which he was suspected of cultivating to ward off unwelcome challenges to his authority.

He barely acknowledged his wife's arrival as he resumed his seat at the head of a long mahogany table with a second place set at the other end.

"Kedgeree's still warm, or there's scrambled eggs," he informed her without looking up. In almost the same breath he demanded, "Have you seen this damned report?" Gripping a folded newspaper in his left hand and a fork in his right, he read out loud:

'Commissioners in discussions to buy canal. New attempt to rid town of foul pestilence'.

"Damned insolence if you ask me. They're blaming *us* for polluting *their* canal. They should remember who creates the wealth in this town." His complexion began to take on a purplish hue as he continued, "We've no choice. We're forced to use canal water that's already full of filth from the beck. So the blame's on the Parish Vestry Surveyors. If they cared half as much about the town and its employers as preserving their civic status, they would have done something about this open sewer by now."

"Yes, dear," soothed his wife as she took her seat at the table, "but I'm sure Commissioner Priestley's got Bradford's best interests at heart. He's worried the canal could start a plague."

"And who's to blame for that? They talk about building a sewer to clean up the beck, but it's all just talk. They allow more houses to be built, which just adds to the problem. And where does all the filth from these streets end up? In the canal, that's where."

"Some of those terraces are for your own workers, Joe. I'm sure if you asked them they would say they hate living on filthy streets. But they've no choice. Anyway, I believe the canal company's breaking the law by taking water from the beck."

Unappreciative of his wife's reasoning, Josiah Hudson rose from his seat and strode to a bell-pull in the corner of the room to summon their elderly servant Preece. A bent figure shuffled arthritically into the room and was brusquely instructed to bring the carriage to the front door, as his employer was eager to leave for the mill. With a curt farewell to his wife, Josiah Hudson swept out of the dining room still nursing his anger at the "interfering busybodies" he feared were going to ruin his business. In the entrance hall, he was helped into his jacket and heavy black cloak, his top hat and silver-topped cane. On the snow-covered driveway he mounted the step of his carriage and settled back into the chilled leather upholstery for the mile-and-a-half journey into town.

Two chestnut horses snorted clouds of condensed breath into the freezing air as they pulled the carriage through rutted snow along Manningham Lane towards the town centre. Mansions set back behind tall banks of shrubbery soon began to give way to merchant townhouses, which in turn made way for rows of back-to-back millworkers' terraces on steep, narrow streets. Few carriages and horsedrawn wagons were braving the treacherous conditions. Most people seemed to be making their journey on foot, struggling to avoid falling on the compacted snow. Even the two horses, under the control of the shivering Preece, had difficulty keeping their footing down Cheapside and Kirkgate before reaching level ground as they crossed Bradford Beck and turned into Canal Road.

Josiah Hudson relished the acrid smell of coal smoke that began to permeate his carriage. Some medical practitioners were beginning to agitate for cleaner air, claiming it was unhealthy for children to breathe in the sulphurous fumes. He subscribed to popular opinion that not only was it not harmful to children, but it could be beneficial by helping them to fend off disease. Proponents of this theory sought further support by pointing out that smoke from the growing forest of chimneys had the additional benefit of masking the stench from the beck and canal basin in summer. As far as he and his fellow owners were concerned, it was reassuring proof that the mills had orders, cloth was being made and profits earned.

But with more and more mills starting up in town, Josiah Hudson faced growing competition. To stay ahead of his rivals, he felt justified using every means at his disposal to extract the most productivity from his workforce. If this meant working them the longest hours for the lowest wages and being able to take on or lay off workers as orders dictated, so be it. From his exalted position among the mill-owning elite, he was inured to the insecurity of his workers who suffered cruel conditions to keep their jobs and avoid the dreaded workhouse, the very last resort for families in trouble. He ensured that workers who cavilled at the inhumanity of the workplace were cast out as troublemakers and would soon find no one in Bradford willing to employ them. If they tried to unite with workers from other mills, he made sure they were ostracised as agitators and dangerous public enemies. But this only fuelled the determination of the more courageous and public-spirited activists, feeling they had little to lose and much to gain by organising gatherings and walkouts to force mill owners to meet their demands.

Jack Ackroyd was well aware of growing discontent among the workers at Hudson's mill and empathised with the married men whose ability to feed their families rested on the whim of the owner. This discontent was fuelled by already simmering unrest about the price of bread, a staple in the workers' diet, kept artificially high by the hated Corn Laws. As overseer, he knew he could not rely on the unquestioning loyalty of the men. Their resentment could boil over into a call for action that would inevitably drag him in. He needed to find out what was afoot by getting close to the ringleaders, treading a dangerous tightrope between them and the management. His opportunity came during an unexpected stoppage in the weaving shed when a drive belt snapped and needed to be replaced. He followed a group of weavers making their way into the yard to take advantage of the break for a quick pipe. Their conversation died away as Jack approached the huddle and all eyes turned towards him.

"Ay up, lads, be careful Mr. Hudson doesn't see you talking out here. He'll think you're up to no good, plotting behind his back," he told them with as much levity in his voice as he could summon up. The boldest of the group, a gaunt grey-haired weaver in his mid-thirties, but looking twenty years older, glanced around nervously before confiding, "There's trouble brewing, Jack. The lads say they've had enough and…" Before he could finish, all heads turned at the sound of approaching horses.

As his carriage turned into the cobbled yard past the huge iron entrance gates, Josiah Hudson caught site of the group of men slowly making their way back inside the weaving shed. He recognised one of the group as one of his overseers. Inside his oak-panelled office the owner shed his cloak and, warming himself in front of a blazing coal fire, summoned his head clerk. Jem Laker, a tall, servile individual wearing a high starched collar and pince-nez perched on a beak-shaped nose wasted no time responding to his master's call.

"A very good morning to you, Mr. Hudson. You called, sir?"

"There was a group of men talking in the yard when I arrived. They had a guilty look about them. I think one of them was Ackroyd, the weaving shed overseer. I want no trouble at this mill, Laker, so I'm relying on you to find out what they're up to." Minutes later, from his first-floor office window, Josiah Hudson watched his chief clerk cross the snow-covered cobbles and disappear into the weaving shed. If trouble was brewing, he wanted to be the first to know about it and who was responsible for stirring it up. I'll sack the ringleaders so the rest will fear for their jobs. *Pour encourager les autres*, he smiled grimly to himself.

* * *

In spite of a light frost and slush underfoot, Kirkgate was busy with townsfolk and horse-drawn traffic as Jack Ackroyd made his way to the entrance of the double, bow-fronted White Lion public house. A pale yellow glow and a hubbub

14

of voices filtered out of the front door into the dark street, silhouetting two figures lounging against the entrance lobby. The men were enjoying a coarse conversation punctuated by guttural laughter as they swigged from pewter tankards. Just inside the entrance, a low doorway led into a small parlour lined with wooden benches and lit by two hissing gas mantles. A moribund fire flickered in a tiny grate. In the opposite wall, a wooden hatch framed the round, florid face of the innkeeper, his visage completely framed by unkempt red hair.

"Ay up, Jack lad. It's a bit since you've been in. Is all well at home?"

"Can't complain, Bob. Much the same, but there's trouble at the mill. I'll have my usual."

Jack studied the faces of the half dozen drinkers deep in animated conversation around the smoke-filled room. To his relief, he realised he knew none of them and after giving him a cursory glance when he entered, each paid him no further attention. He took his tankard of ale and sat as far away as possible from the other drinkers, so his conversation would not be overheard. Soon a tall figure appeared in the doorway dressed in a black cape and wearing a wide-brimmed black hat pulled down over his forehead. His furtive entrance drew curious glances as he sank down on the bench next to Jack. Jem Laker declined a tankard of ale, settling instead for a glass of malmsey. He hoped the lack of his familiar pince-nez would foil recognition should any of the millworkers be there. But no one took any further interest in the two men as they got down to the purpose of their clandestine meeting.

The head clerk bent close to Jack's ear, "If there's trouble brewing at the mill, Jack, I need to know, or at least Mr. Hudson does. He saw the group in the yard and you there with them. He thought they had a shifty look about them, but he assumes you were just keeping your ear close to the ground."

"As they work in the shed, I wanted to know what they were talking about."

"Mr. Hudson's facing more competition, Jack. He can't afford any troublemaking at the mill. These men could threaten all our livelihoods. You know you can't afford to be out of work with all your family to feed. By the way, Mr Hudson says to tell you he hasn't forgotten about the promotion."

Jack let the implications of the head clerk's last words sink in as he fought with his conscience. His sympathies lay with men who lived and worked in terrible conditions without any guarantee of a job from week to week. But he had his own family to consider and, if he really was going to be promoted, shouldn't his loyalty be owed to the mill and its owner rather than to a few hotheaded troublemakers?

"I can't give you names, Jem, but I can tell you that some of the men are getting angry. They say that while the mill's still on full-time working, they're getting less wages for longer hours. Up to now, they've been scared to complain in case they lose their jobs. But some are saying enough is enough. I'm just telling you what I heard."

"But Mr. Hudson's laid no one off, Jack, not like some of the mills. They should at least be grateful for that."

"Well, it seems some of them feel it's time to take a stand. They say they've had enough of rotten wages for long hours and bringing up families in slum streets running with sewage. They say the mill owners only care about their profits, so they're talking about uniting with workers right across Bradford. They reckon that united they'll be strong enough to take on the owners. That's all I know, Jem."

"Well that's more than enough. Thank you, Jack," said Jem Laker with a thin smile. "Now we know what we're up against, we'll warn all the other owners to be on their guard. They'll be able to pick out the ringleaders who'll never work in Bradford again. This anarchy has been stirred up by the damned Chartists and has got to be stopped. They'll soon realise how well off they are. I'm obliged to you, Jack. Keep your ears open and let me know if you hear anything else. Mr Hudson will be pleased with your help today."

After Jem Laker's retreating black cape and broad-brimmed hat disappeared into the cold night, Jack had his tankard refilled while he considered his own position. If it came to a confrontation between the owners and the workers, he mused, where would that leave him? Could he trust Josiah Hudson to keep his word about promotion or was he just being fobbed off? Would he lose the trust of the men if he was seen to align himself too closely with the management? These thoughts continued to trouble his mind as he trudged home through the slush-covered streets, the smoke from a thousand coal fires turning the frosty air into a murky yellow fog that caught at his chest.

In the warmth of their kitchen, Fanny stood over a large cooking pot by the open fire, her face scarlet and shiny with effort. Strands of grey hair fell across her forehead as she prepared the evening meal. Theo and Josh played on the floor with sticks and bricks while Katherine sat on a stool, concentrating on her cross-stitch sampler. John hadn't returned from work. Jack took off his wet coat and hung it by the fire to dry, explaining to Fanny why he was home before John. She listened intently to the account of his conversation with the head clerk. "You've worked with some of those men for years," she protested. "I know you're due a promotion and we could do with the money, but it feels like you're betraying them. What else can they do to improve their lives?"

"I haven't betrayed anyone. I only told Laker what he is likely to find out for himself anyway. There's going to be trouble, that's for sure. Of course I worry how it will affect us if they go on strike and shut the mill down."

"Then you'll have to decide whose side you're on," said Fanny as the door opened and John stamped into the room followed by a trail of snow and a gust of freezing air.

"Get that coat off and warm yourself at the fire, son. We're ready to eat," she told him. "They say they're going to walk out," gasped John, giving a furtive glance towards his father. "I overheard men talking. They're calling a meeting with workers at all the other mills to decide on a strike. They're talking about getting together in some sort of union."

"Well, that's what I heard too," said his father. "Just keep your head down, son; get on with your job and don't get involved in it and you'll be right."

The family took their seats at the table as Fanny ladled stewed rabbit on to their plates. Jack said the simple

Grace that preceded all their meals, before dividing bread between them. As the conversation around the table drew on the various events of the day, Jack's mind was elsewhere, exploring the new situation at work that seemed to be opening up before him. There was no escaping the certainty that he would have to make a choice that could change their lives dramatically.

Unknown to his employer, he and Fanny had already become involved in the early struggle to clean up their town, starting with the polluted beck and canal. Because it was widely known what had happened to their son Peter, they had been approached by a small group of similarly bereaved parents determined to get action and not just words. Following a report in the *Observer*, this group resolved to add their weight to the plans to buy the canal and close it down. They would seek permission to attend a meeting of the commissioners to give their personal experience of disease and death spread by the stinking ditch. But the action group needed a leader and for that they turned to Jack.

Their meal finished, John went out to visit a friend along the street, while the younger children played in front of the fire.

"Well this is a right pickle," said Jack, helping Fanny to clear away the dishes. "It looks as if I'm between the devil and the deep blue sea in this trouble at the mill. And we're up to our necks in the clean-up group. If that gets back to Hudson, you can wave goodbye to my promotion. I'll be lucky to keep my job. Josiah Hudson is determined to keep the canal open as he reckons it's vital for the mill. He doesn't agree that the mills foul the canal. He says it's all the fault of the commissioners, for allowing the canal to be fed from the beck..."

"I'm certain it was disease in the canal that killed our Peter," interrupted Fanny. "It's high time the surveyors started building a sewer to clean up the beck. They just talk and do nothing while our children fall sick and die."

"Maybe we should be fighting for a sewer and not to close the canal. Then I won't upset Mr. Hudson and the other owners. Might even get that promotion after all, so long as he doesn't think I'm siding with the strikers. Look, I'll talk to the other parents and see if I can persuade them to change their demands. We might even petition the commissioners."

Fanny put her arm round her husband's broad shoulders as the flickering reflection of the coal fire lit up his determined features. She realised they were entering uncertain times that would make big demands of both of them. "You must do what you have to do, Jack. I've got every faith in you, but remember you have a family too."

* * *

With the deafening roar of weaving machinery ringing in his ears, Jack made his way down a flight of broad stone steps and through stout wooden doors into the mill's cobbled yard. Opposite was a squat stone boiler house dwarfed by the mill chimney from which a black column of smoke was rising vertically in the still, cold air this Saturday morning. A dun-coloured carthorse clattered its iron-shod hooves as it was led out of the shafts of a cart loaded with bales of raw wool, ready to be hooked and hauled three storeys up to the top floor. Jack exchanged greetings in the yard as he made his way between the huge iron gates into the street where more carts laden with woolsacks were waiting, their restless horses pawing the cobbles and snorting clouds of vapour into the frosty air. On the far side of the beck, snow-covered fields would soon become home to the new railway terminus. Not everyone viewed the coming of the railway with enthusiasm, especially the canal owners who regarded it as unwelcome competition. But the mill owners were beginning to think that the railway could be a way of liberating themselves from the constant carping about their alleged pollution of the canal. All these sceptical entrepreneurs needed was proof that the railway offered a quicker and more cost-effective way of despatching their cloth to the markets and docks.

Across Church Bridge, halfway along Kirkgate and opposite the White Lion Hotel, a group of men and women muffled in thick winter shawls stood in the doorway of the old Shoulder of Mutton Inn. They greeted Jack, following him inside and up a rickety staircase to a small room on the top floor, lit by two smoky oil lamps. They pulled six chairs into a circle and one of the men produced a copy of the *Observer* reporting the commissioners' intention to buy the canal.

"But that's not going to solve our problem," protested a swarthy, middle-aged woman with a strong Irish accent. "I say we should organise a rally to support closing it. I'll be able to get plenty of people out on the street. That will show we mean business." As she spoke she swept the group with piercing dark eyes, seeking support for her proposal.

Jack realised he needed to head off this radical approach before it took hold in the meeting; he cleared his throat to get their attention. "I've a different suggestion. If we just call for it to be shut down, we're going to make enemies of the mill owners. They still see it as essential to their trade."

"Until the railway comes," interjected one of the men.

"Yes, but they need to be sure the railway is going to be profitable for them. Until then, they are for the canal staying open," said Jack.

"So what's your idea then?" challenged the man.

"Well, the commissioners want to close it down because of its reputation for causing so much illness, leading to many deaths. We know some of its pollution comes from the mills, but much worse is the sewage that runs down our streets into the beck that feeds the canal."

"Aye, it's a bloody disgrace and it's getting worse with all these new houses going up," protested another member of the group. "It's about time they did something about it."

"Well, that's my point," said Jack. "For ages we've been promised a sewer to take the muck away from the town centre, but nothing's been done about it. If you ask me, no one wants to pay for it. I think if we could gather enough support for a campaign we could force the surveyors to build it. Given the choice between that and closing the canal, I reckon we might even get the support of the mill owners as well."

"As long as they don't have to dip their hands in their own pockets," said the owner of the newspaper. "They complain long and hard about the state of the town until they have to cough up some brass. Then they can't afford it because profits won't allow. That's why nothing ever gets done."

"Look, I don't disagree with you, but there's never been a campaign by the people for a sewer. Now is a good time to put pressure on the commissioners, who must be getting more and more embarrassed by Bradford's bad name for disease and squalor."

After a few moments of thoughtful silence, it was proposed that support for Jack's campaign for a sewer be put to a vote. All but the Irish woman raised their hands in support. After an excited discussion about how the campaign should be mounted, Jack called for a volunteer to draft a suitable bill calling townspeople to a rally. "The *Observer* and the commissioners will take notice if we get lots of people out, say up at St Peter's Church. The mill owners won't be able to shut the Press up then and might even see it in their interest to support us."

"That'll be the day," said the Irish woman. "Look, I'm not saying I agree with you, Jack, but I accept the vote of the meeting. I'll volunteer to write the bill and make sure it goes up all over town. We need a date, time and place. I'll find out if the vicar has any objections to us having the rally outside St. Peter's."

"Let's meet here again in a week," said Jack. "Then we can agree the wording of the bill and arrangements for the rally. Now let's get some ale in and talk about the details."

As he was about to descend the narrow, wooden steps to the bar, he was met by his eldest son, out of breath, taking them two at a time. "There's trouble at Hudson's," John managed to blurt out, having run all the way from the mill. "They've sacked the men who were talking about starting a union and now everyone's going on strike. Management's calling it a lockout, but the men are blocking the gates and won't let anyone in or out."

Jack and two other members of the group who also worked at Hudson's, abandoned ideas of a drink and set off through the twilight towards Canal Street. On the way they overtook a company of soldiers, resplendent in scarlet jackets and white webbing, marching towards distant angry shouts and a babble of voices. Word of the lockout seemed to have spread rapidly to nearby mills and the Hudson's men were being joined by other groups of discontented workers. As Jack neared the edge of the jostling crowd surrounding the gates, he could just discern, at a first-floor window, the face of head clerk Jem Laker. At a tall window in his office above the main entrance stood Josiah Hudson, scarlet-faced and implacable.

The soldiers of the 15th Hussars arrived and began to take up positions in the road. Unable to reach the mill gates through the dense throng, the captain in charge appealed to the workers to disperse. His voice was drowned out by jeers and whistles. Somebody threw a stone, which bounced off a soldier's helmet, drawing more jeers and laughter. The captain drew his pistol and fired a warning shot in the air, creating an immediate hush. He produced and proceeded to read a copy of the Riot Act, warning the men and the few women present to disperse or face the consequences. The soldiers formed up into a semi-circle facing the strikers, to be met by taunts of "traitors" and "mill owners' lackeys", but the threat was enough to cause the strikers to start drifting away. The stone thrower was identified and pulled out of the dispersing crowd. Two others who tried to protest at his detention were apprehended and also placed under arrest. All three were branded as ringleaders and handed over to constables who had been watching from a safe distance behind the soldiers. The three men were manhandled roughly as they were marched off towards the town lock-up to await trial for causing an affray, leading to almost certain imprisonment. Jack, who had left the mill earlier in the day before the trouble erupted, decided to keep a low profile as he mingled with the stragglers on their way home along Canal Street. Men in small groups loudly voiced their anger and frustration as they moved along the dimly lit street.

"Hudson has not heard the last of this," one of the men shouted at Jack when he was recognised among the crowd. "We'll be back tomorrow and the day after. He'll soon learn he can't bully us if we stand together." But Jack knew much of this anger would evaporate in the face of their wives' anxiety and distress at losing their regular income, however meagre.

Fanny was waiting at the door as father and son emerged through the gloom. "I heard the shot, what happened? Are you both all right?" she enquired, grabbing Jack by the sleeve and pulling him round to face her. Fear distorted her features as she stared wide-eyed at her husband, waiting for him to give her news about the disturbance.

"The men went on strike and blocked the mill entrance so they sent for the soldiers to break it up. It's over for now. Three of them were taken away. I reckon Hudson's going to lock the strikers out until they agree to go back on his terms. But if he tries to take on other workers to fill their places, there will be a proper riot, no fear."

"What about you and John? Are you both locked out as well? What will we do about money? I need to buy food before the week's out. What are we going to do?"

"It's best if John stays at home for now, love, but I'll go back in tomorrow to find out what's happening. Jem Laker knows I wasn't part of the strike, so I should be able to get into the yard unless the strikers stop me. Anyroad, I was expecting something like this to happen and I reckon it could spread, considering the mood the men are in. God knows what will become of us then."

The Go Between

Steel-rimmed wheels crackled the ice-rutted surface of Manningham Lane as a coach and pair, bearing Commissioner William Priestley and his wife, swung between wrought iron gates into the driveway to the Hudsons' gritstone mansion. The horses maintained a more sure-footed plod along the curving gravel driveway, bordered by the brooding dark shapes of mature rhododendron bushes. Two acetylene coach lamps barely penetrated the dark driveway, leaving it to the welcoming glow from the porch to guide the coachman to their destination. The hunched figure of Preece, dressed from head to toe in black, stepped forward to open the coach door and deploy the step. Welcoming the Priestleys to Royd Hall, he offered his arm to assist Mary Priestley from the coach and bade them accompany him into the gaslit entrance hall.

Commissioner Priestley, a short stocky man with receding grey hair and hooded watery eyes, exuded an air of authority in keeping with his exalted status in the town. His eyes seemed constantly on the move as he cast off his heavy cloak to reveal a significant corporation crossed by a heavy gold chain, hung with a fob watch and enamelled medallions. His wife, a slight, birdlike woman, was relieved of her cloak to reveal the latest in ladies' fashion, rather over-ornamented with expensive jewellery.

"Thank you for coming out on such a night, William," greeted Josiah Hudson, extending a hand to his guest before guiding him by the elbow into the warmth of the library. Kathryn Hudson greeted her opposite number and together they followed the men to comfortable seats by a blazing coal fire. "You are the first to arrive. I'm sure you would welcome a warming glass before dinner," recommended their host, gesturing to the hovering Preece.

"The Ramsdens and Cartwrights are sharing a carriage as they live close by each other off the High Street; though I doubt they will be able to use Church Bank in this weather," said William Priestley. "That could mean a lengthy detour. The beck's been frozen over for a week, but the canal never seems to freeze no matter how cold it gets. I don't know how we would get our cloth away if it did."

"Well, there's all this talk about the railway," added Josiah Hudson. "If it provides half of what its sponsors say it will, we'll have the fastest means of transporting our goods."

"Ah, but at what cost? The market is becoming more congested and we just can't afford to pay fancy prices to the railway company the way things are," cautioned William Priestley. The sound of voices in the entrance hall heralded the arrival of the other dinner guests. Josiah Hudson excused himself to greet two couples enveloped in a draught of frosty air and stamping their feet against the cold. Herbert Ramsden blew on his hands before removing a copious black cape to reveal an almost spherical figure topped by a wide face with huge eyebrows above penetrating dark eyes and a hooked nose. His wife, equally rotund, was dressed all in silk, her long auburn hair framing an expression of permanent disdain. Meredith Cartwright cut an altogether more commanding figure. Standing more than six feet tall, an aquiline nose and military bearing gave him an air of superiority, reinforced by his habit of looking down at those around him. His wife, a good foot shorter than her husband, emerged from several layers of outer clothing, which had given her a dumpy appearance to go with her generous, motherly figure.

"Welcome to The Larches on a night I wouldn't put a dog out," greeted Josiah Hudson, steering the new arrivals towards the warmth of the library and his first guests. Greetings were exchanged and glasses of sherry filled and refilled to general small talk before Kathryn Hudson invited them all into the wood-panelled dining room to take their places at a table laid with crystal glasses and silver cutlery reflecting guttering flames from two dozen candles placed along its length and around the walls. A coal fire in a grand marble fireplace created dancing shadows on the moulded plaster ceiling. On each elaborate place mat, a hand printed menu promised a meal of seven courses including fish, fowl and venison and accompanied by white and red wine.

When his guests were seated, Josiah Hudson intoned a short grace before opening the conversation. "I expect you'll be pleased Parliament's going to give commissioners greater powers, William, although much will depend on what you do with these powers. It could get expensive for the rest of us," he added, to laughter from the others.

"Bradford needs the status of a Borough with its own Mayor and Town Council, so we can get things done," said William Priestley rising to the bait. "Of course we will have to raise money through local precept and that includes local industry. But there will be a huge benefit to the town in the long run."

"As long as the begging bowl doesn't stop at the mills," said their host. "We provide jobs and wages for the townsfolk and now we're going to be taxed by Parliament. We don't have a bottomless pit."

"Did you read in *The Times* that William Wordsworth is to be the new Poet Laureate?" asked Meredith Cartwright, changing the subject. "I'm shocked, given his sympathy for the barbaric regicide in France fifty years ago."

"Not only that, but he's been trying to stir up support for public assistance for the unemployed," said Herbert Ramsden. "We'll be expected to pay for that with this new income tax, I suppose. It will just encourage indolence among the working classes. Why would anybody want to work if they can get paid for doing nothing?"

"These are the policies that inflame the likes of the Anti-Corn Law League," said Josiah Hudson. "They and the Chartists are bent on destroying our traditional way of life. And they're encouraged by Robert Peel and his pals in Parliament."

"Well I don't know much about Parliament," interrupted Kathryn Hudson in an attempt to lighten the conversation, "but I think young Victoria will bang Conservative and Whig heads together if she has to. After only six years on the throne, she seems to know her own mind."

"Or she's being well advised by Albert," said Meredith Cartwright. His following observation that "our royal family could do with a bit of Teutonic common sense" triggered a spirited discussion about the merits of the crowned heads of Europe that lasted until the end of the meal. Taking her cue as the port decanter was transferred from the sideboard to the table, Kathryn Hudson addressed the wives, "Ladies, shall we withdraw for coffee and let these men talk about their boring politics?"

Josiah Hudson passed round the port and circulated Havana cigars before starting the discussion by condemning the strikers who had brought his mill to a standstill and were threatening to keep his looms idle unless their demands were met.

"It's the French disease that has crossed the Channel, infecting the minds of these so-called Chartists," he declared. "Equality and liberty? No, what they really want is anarchy. They must be put in their place. We create the wealth so they have jobs and food on the table. Let's see how they get on when they're out on the street. They won't be so keen to riot then. Anyway, I'll have no hesitation calling in the Hussars again if I have to."

The other three nodded their assent, only Herbert Ramsden adding, "Yes, we've got to keep order, but we can't afford our mills to stand idle for long. Competitors will steal our customers. New mills are springing up all across the West Riding and they're taking on Irish workers, who'll work for less money."

"Maybe that's the answer," said Meredith Cartwright. "We should replace the strikers with Irish immigrants."

Commissioner Priestley, who had been listening intently, cautioned against starting a long-running feud with the strikers. "They have the skills. We would have to train these Irish, who have never worked in a mill in their lives, and that costs time and money. We should try to calm things down by listening to the strike leaders. At least it will buy time so we can consider our next move."

"Listen to people who could put us out of business?" exploded Josiah Hudson, his face turning from crimson to purple.

William Priestley held up his hand. "I only said listen, Josiah. What we do afterwards will be our decision. We will still be in control."

"I will not sit in the same room as these bloody anarchists," replied Josiah Hudson.

"Is there anyone at your mill you can trust as an intermediary?" asked Herbert Ramsden. "Someone who is trusted by both the strikers and yourself and who knows what's going on?"

Silence descended on the room, punctuated by the ticking of a large case clock. Josiah Hudson leaned back in his chair and took a sip of port, candlelight glinting on the medalled silver chain straddling his ample stomach. "There is one man I can think of," he said at last. "He's an overseer in the weaving shed. My chief clerk met him to find out what's going on. I think he has the respect of the men for all he's known as a hard taskmaster. If they let him speak for them, I'll listen to him. But that is all. *Listen*, I'm making no concessions. It's my bloody mill and I set the rules, so they had better be prepared to listen themselves and listen well."

"I think this business has been brewing for some time," said Meredith Cartwright. "There's growing anger in the town about the amount of disease. So many children have died. The new general infirmary is already dealing with more cases of cholera, believed to have come from the beck and the canal. Streets are running with sewage, which has nowhere to go but into the beck. I think the sackings at your mill, Josiah, may just have been the spark to light the bonfire…"

"Which brings me to my next point," broke in William Priestley to head off another explosive outburst from their host. "As a commissioner I've been asked to look at the feasibility of building a sewer to take the filth away from the town centre. Some say it should also remove the mill waste that's adding to pollution in the canal."

"And who's going to pay for that?" asked Josiah Hudson, rhetorically. "The put-upon mill owners, of course. Well, they needn't come knocking on my door with their hands out."

"It will have to come out of the local precept we were talking about earlier," said Herbert Ramsden. "Maybe that will be one of the first tasks for the town council when it comes into being. Mill owners can't be expected to bear the entire cost."

"Or even any of it," added Josiah Hudson. "We have enough of a problem trying to make a decent profit in these difficult times as it is."

"Well, as I said, we are only carrying out a preliminary study," continued William Priestley. "First surveys show the sewer will have to follow the line of the beck. As Bradford sits inside a semicircle of hills, the beck has only one way to go and that's north, by way of Frizinghall to Shipley, where it enters the River Aire. We are required by Parliament to act to end Bradford's unfortunate reputation. Things have got so bad there are moves to relocate mills well outside the town. Titus Salt is planning to build a new mill complex on the banks of the river at Shipley to give his workers healthier working and living conditions. Gentlemen, we need your co-operation for the benefit of mill owners and citizens of Bradford alike."

Only the sputtering of blazing coals casting dancing shadows across the patterned walls and the ticking of the long case clock broke the ruminative silence as four of Bradford's wealthiest entrepreneurs tried to grasp the implications of the emerging social changes that offered the greatest challenge to their established way of life.

The following day, a handful of men were standing around the gates when Jack Ackroyd arrived at the mill, summoned to an early meeting in the presence of the owner. A thaw had set in, the snow turning to wet slush underfoot as he crossed the cobbled street to face his fellow workers.

"Ay up, Jack. You're not going in to work I hope," shouted one of the men. "He'll be on his own if he does," said another.

"Don't let us down, lad. We've got to stand together in this. It affects you as well as us," said a third.

"I'll not let you down," Jack told them. "Management want to know why you're on strike, so I'm going to tell them. I'll let you know what they say. If I can persuade them you've got a genuine grievance, we might find some common ground. Anyroad, what we all want is to get back to work."

"Give nothing away, Jack. We'll listen to what they've got to say, but we're making a stand. We want action this time, not empty promises."

Jack crossed the yard leaving the knot of animated strikers being joined by more workers outside the gates. Through the main entrance doors and up a wide flight of stairs, he was ushered into the spacious office of Josiah Hudson, seated behind a deep mahogany desk. He was flanked by his general manager, Charles Lister, and chief clerk, Jem Laker. Jack was not invited to sit down as Josiah Hudson launched into a strident denunciation of the strikers.

"I'll not stand by and see this mill destroyed by a bunch of anarchists," he roared. "Don't they know textiles are going through hard times? I don't have the money to increase their wages; they're lucky to have a job at all, the way things are. I'll see them starve before I give an inch to them."

Jack felt his stomach tighten as he absorbed this bellicose opening salvo from his intimidating employer. His tongue stuck to the roof of his mouth as he began to explain the strikers' concerns.

"They've asked me to say they are not anarchists or revolutionaries," Mr. Hudson. "They are just ordinary working men and women who find it increasingly difficult to feed their families on the wages they get, in spite of the long hours they're having to work."

Josiah Hudson fixed Jack with an unblinking stare while Jem Laker scratched in a large ledger with a quill pen.

Charles Lister, pale and languid, coughed consumptively into a stained kerchief and leaned forward to address Jack.

"Am I to understand these strikers will go back to work if the sacked men get their jobs back?"

"I would have to check that with them. But the men say they want a meeting with the management first to put their demands…"

"Demands! Demands!" roared Josiah Hudson. "I'll give then demands. We'll not talk to strikers and that's that. Any talking will start only after they return to work. And there must be no more of this talk about forming a union. I'll not have a union in my mill…"

He was interrupted by the sound of pounding feet on the stairs, followed by the door bursting open. Everyone in the room looked round. A breathless girl clerk from the office below apologised for disturbing them, saying she had an urgent message for Mr. Ackroyd.

"Can't you see we are in a meeting?" bellowed Josiah Hudson. "It can wait. Get out."

In spite of her terror at her employer's outburst, the girl stood her ground, blurting out, "It's his boy sir. He's been taken badly and he's in the infirmary. Mrs. Ackroyd is there with him. She says it's serious and she wants Mr. Ackroyd to go up to the infirmary, sir. I'm very sorry, sir."

Flustered and on the verge of tears, the girl backed out through the door and ran down the stairs as Jack Ackroyd excused himself from the meeting, strode quickly out and took the stairs two at a time. At the gate he paused only to explain briefly to the curious strikers about his family crisis.

He promised to meet their leaders as soon as possible to explain what had transpired at the meeting.

Unaware of the stares towards his running figure, Jack kept up a steady pace into Canal Road and Well Street, across Church Bridge spanning the thawing beck and up Kirkgate to the clean frontage of the new infirmary in Westgate. "Not another, please God not another," he kept repeating to himself as he covered the three-quarters-of-a-mile in just six minutes. Were he and Fanny having to suffer the pain and agony of a fourth child dying in less than ten years, he agonised, and none of them having enjoyed more than six short years of life? In the entrance hall an orderly directed him down a long, wide corridor to a half-open door at the end. Inside the bare ward, below tall windows, two rows of cots bore a shrill of crying infants. A group of mothers stood about the ward clutching babies and toddlers to them, some children crying pitifully, some lying limp and pale against their mother's chest.

Jack spotted Fanny stooped over a cot towards the end of the ward and rushed to her side. He could tell at once from her tear-stained face that whatever it was, it was serious. "It's the same as our Peter," she sobbed. "I went to get him up and he'd been sick all over the bed. He's got the runs bad as well. He's had nothing proper to eat since last night. He just keeps moaning and groaning."

Jack was shocked to see Josh, his normally mischievous four-year-old son, lying so still and deathly pale. The boy did not seem aware of anyone around him, just staring blankly ahead.

"He can't keep anything down. They're just giving him water. They think it's what our Peter had and we can only pray and hope."

Fearing the worst, Jack put his arm round his wife's shoulders to comfort her in her distress and offered what hope he could. "The strong ones pull through and he's a strong little lad, so we must put our faith in God," he told her with as much conviction as he was able to summon up in this ward full of very sick children and anguished parents. "How are Katherine and Theo?"

"They're not showing any signs yet. I'll have to boil up the bedclothes and scrub the kitchen like we did with our Peter. Oh Jack, why us? It's like a curse..."

"No, I won't have any of that, Fanny love. It's not a curse, it's that filthy beck and canal. They're full of disease and the little lad's probably been playing down there even though we told him to keep away. It's a bloody disgrace and I'm damned if I'll keep quiet any longer while the commissioners and mill owners do nothing about it. We've got our meeting next week to launch the campaign for a sewer and I'm determined to get all the townsfolk behind us."

"You'll put your own job at risk, Jack. You know Hudson won't have any agitators in his mill, especially among the overseers."

"Look, I've got to do this for Peter and Josh. Someone's got to take a stand. How many more children have to die before something's done? It's time to act and I'm going to see it through no matter what. Nothing could be worse than doing nothing. Anyroad, I've got to get back to the yard now, love, to talk to the lads. I think there's a chance the management might be prepared to have talks if the strikers go back." Taking a last look at his ailing son, Jack kissed Fanny on the cheek and strode off down the ward, acknowledging some of the mothers he recognised from his street.

Back at the mill a sizeable group of strikers was still gathered outside the gates, watched nervously by the same constables from the previous day's riot. Jack singled out the self-appointed leader of the strike and beckoned to him. This met with some barracking from the others. The two men walked to a quieter spot where Jack reported the bones of his meeting with the management.

"They will only talk to you if you go back to work first. Only then will they discuss the sacked men. But you would have to drop any talk of a union; Hudson simply will not have it."

The strike leader bridled at Hudson's reported intransigence and reminded Jack that their strike was a last resort. "If we give in now we'll have achieved nothing. We'll have no weapons left to fight the exploitation and indifference of this mill owner and many others across town."

"I understand the feelings of the lads," said Jack. "They've been pushed to the limit and they want change. So do I, but I think change will be best achieved by talking. You can use the threat to strike as a bargaining point."

"Are you with us or with them, Jack?"

"I just want to end this standoff for the benefit of us all," replied Jack, who went on to relate the events of the afternoon and his renewed commitment to lead the campaigners for a sewer. "I'm just as much a victim of the blind pursuit of profit and heads in sand as everyone here. But it's easier to fight for change on a full stomach, don't you think?"

Jack's reasoning was having the desired effect on the strike leader who, after mulling over their conversation for a few moments, said, "All right, I'll call a meeting of the lads and put to them what you've told me. It's up to them to decide. I know you'll want to be with your family tonight Jack, so I'll call at your house later and let you know our decision."

Out of the corner of his eye Jack caught sight of John who had been unable to resist coming to see the trouble at the mill. Jack called his son over, "Let's go home, lad. Your brother's been taken badly and we need to help your mother clean the house. They won't miss you here."

Later that evening, Jack answered a knock on the door to find the strike leader on his doorstep and invited him to come inside.

"Nay, I'll stay outside Jack, if you don't mind. I've just come to tell you the lads decided to go back. But it was a close do and the sacked men must be taken back. The lads will strike again if the bosses aren't prepared to listen to our grievances. So you can tell Hudson we'll be back at work as soon as they've got steam up. I'll bid you goodnight Jack and, by the way, the lads asked me to say they're praying for your little lad."

Jack thanked the strike leader and closed the door feeling a huge sense of relief having obtained the result he had hoped for, but not really expected. His relief was tempered by the realisation that this was just the beginning of what promised to be a long and hard-fought battle to achieve decent working and living conditions for the workers in Bradford's burgeoning woollen mills. Alongside this was his personal commitment to the campaign to rid Bradford of its terrible legacy.

* * *

Josiah Hudson hung back as the parish church slowly disgorged worshippers after the morning service. He wanted the ear of the vicar who was shaking hands with members of his congregation as they filed past him at the main door. Wealthy parishioners received a particularly warm handshake from the tall, balding clergyman with the cherubic countenance. This contrasted with his cursory acknowledgement of many who occupied pews at the rear of the church. It required all his diplomatic skills to disengage himself from an elderly lady parishioner who complained loudly about a shameless new book she had been given by her daughter. Her disgust at the story of *Jane Eyre* was compounded when she learned that the writer, Charlotte Brontë, was a daughter of the church in the same diocese.

"It's a matter of public decency and should be raised with the Bishop," she insisted. The vicar said he had not read the book, but the Reverend Patrick Brontë was highly respected in the remote moorland village of Haworth.

After the last member of the congregation had departed, the vicar invited Josiah Hudson to join him in the privacy of the vestry, where the mill owner solicitously enquired about the health of the incumbent and his family. "I trust you have sufficient coal to ward off winter's chills in your draughty vicarage. If not, I'll see to it they drop off some cuttings to see you right."

"That's very kind of you, Josiah. Please pass my blessings on to your dear wife...er, you wished to speak?"

"Yes, I've heard that some of the townspeople are planning to hold a rally about the canal and they want to hold it in the church grounds on the Sabbath. Well that's sacrilege in my book and I hope in yours as well, vicar. We can't agree to such profanity, can we?"

"Absolutely not, Josiah," replied the flustered vicar. "It's not God's business, is it, so there's no reason for them to meet here. This is what happens when these Chartists start to inflame people. I said it would give them ideas above their station. These simple folk think they can run things, which should be left to their elders and betters. I'll tell them they can't meet here as it's on consecrated ground, so don't worry about that."

"Good man, good man. We've got to take a stand against these anarchists or there will be revolution before we know it. People infected with lies put about fifty years ago are using these naive townsfolk for their own ends. There has got to be law and order."

"Absolutely, Josiah, although I think some of the townspeople have got genuine concerns about the state of the beck and the canal," ventured the vicar, casting a nervous glance at Josiah Hudson's florid complexion. "They are pretty sure pollution is the source of the disease that has caused so much illness and death in the town."

"There's no evidence to say the canal is the source of the illness. These people create the filth so they have only themselves to blame if it makes them ill. The canal is our lifeline. They can't see it provides the wealth that pays their wages? Anyway, I'll be looking to you to stay firmly on our side, vicar. Remember who pays for the upkeep of this church and how that money is made – the wool trade, that's how. I'll bid you good day, sir." Josiah Hudson strode from the vestry and made his way out of the church, leaving the vicar wrestling with his conscience about the wellbeing of his flock.

Later that day, Jack answered a knock at his door to find the Irish woman from the White Lion meeting standing breathless and agitated. "Vicar's banned us from holding the rally anywhere near his church. I reckon he's been leaned on because he's a bit sheepish about it. Said he's got no choice as it isn't a religious event."

"The vicar's not such a bad sort, but it's difficult for him," said Jack. "He has to keep on the right side of those who pay for his living. Anyroad, I've been thinking, what about the new Mechanics Institute at the bottom of Leeds Road? They might let us hold the rally there."

"Well, that's where I've just come from, as it happens, and they agreed, provided the rally is for Bradford folk only. They don't want troublemakers from other parts. I suppose they mean travelling Chartists. I said we would make sure it was orderly and I booked it for Sunday after next."

Jack thanked her, inviting her into the parlour to discuss the bill she had designed and how it should be displayed across the town. He offered to get in touch with the *Observer* who, he thought, would probably want to send along a reporter. "We'll put our own people on the doors to keep out anyone intent on causing trouble. We don't want to give the constables any excuse to shut us down."

Fanny had been listening to the conversation from the scullery. Drying her hands on a towel, she stepped into the parlour with a worried expression. "They'll think of ways to shut you down as soon as they get wind of it – the mill owners, I mean. They think we're trying to close the canal and make them pay for a sewer."

"We've got to go ahead for Josh's sake, love," Jack reassured her. "We have to force change."

As the days passed, the rally became the main topic of conversation in Bradford's homes and taverns. Several of Jack's workmates and men from other mills volunteered to act as stewards on the day. Others helped to stick up bills advertising the rally. Jack was surprised he had heard nothing from the mill owners or commissioners who seemed to be keeping a low profile. They would have seen the article in the local Press, which was careful to take a neutral stance to avoid upsetting friends of its wealthy proprietor. The paper could not ignore however, nor fail to print, a letter from one of Bradford's most high profile employers. Titus Salt, who had taken over the running of the family textile firm, Daniel Salt and Son, ten years earlier, was known for his concerns about the prevalence of cholera and eye-stinging boiler smoke in the town centre. In a characteristic act of altruism, he even installed special equipment in his own mill chimneys to try to reduce the amount of air pollution. He supported the aims of the rally.

The day dawned with strong winds gusting around the bowl of hills cradling the town. Heavy rain showers proved no deterrent to the three hundred or so men, women and children who converged on the Mechanics Institute, erected just three years earlier under Titus Salt's patronage to provide working men with a basic education. Inside, Jack and members of the original White Lion group arranged themselves on chairs across a raised platform, while the rows of seats in the main hall gradually filled with damp townsfolk engaging in an excited hubbub. At the appointed time Jack rose to his feet and welcomed everybody to the hall, setting out the reasons for the rally and what they hoped to achieve by it.

Reading from a carefully prepared script, he began. "Let me say at the outset that we have no quarrel with the powers that be, the commissioners and the mill owners. The message we want to send from this rally today is that something has got to be done, and done soon, to clean up this town of ours. We must end unnecessary deaths from that deadliest of diseases – cholera. As I speak I have a little lad in hospital fighting for his life and too many of you have lost loved ones, many at the beginning of their lives. We believe the disease comes from the town beck and the canal, which is fed by the beck, making them little more than open sewers. We say the time is long overdue to rid them of the polluting filth flowing into them from our streets. At the moment, human waste has nowhere else to go, but if we can persuade the authorities to build a sewer to carry it away from the town centre, we believe we will see the health of Bradford transformed. That is our case, so now we want to take views from the hall."

Jack's last words were almost drowned out by enthusiastic shouts and hand clapping as he sat down. In the middle of the hall, an elderly man in a brown cape rose to ask, "How do we know they will pay any attention to anything we say here today?"

The Irish woman, dressed in a green shawl, leaned forward in her seat next to Jack to reply, "Because this will be reported in the *Observer* and soon we will have most of the townsfolk with us. They'll have to take notice then."

"There's nothing to stop us organising a petition for a sewer," added Jack. "But first, we want to know if there is general support for what we are proposing."

"Wouldn't it be cheaper to close down the canal?" asked a man towards the back of the hall.

"That wouldn't solve the problem of sewage in our streets and the beck," Jack replied. "And the canal is important for transporting woollen goods to market and the docks."

A young woman cradling a baby in a grey blanket got to her feet on the front row and asked, "Who will pay for the sewer?"

As Jack rose to answer, a sudden stirring at the back of the hall caused people to look round to see two constables striding down the centre aisle. They divided and climbed each side of the platform before flanking Jack. Their red-faced, bewhiskered leader grabbed one of Jack's arms and announced that he was being arrested for sedition. As the shock of this unexpected turn of events sank in, people in the hall began to protest loudly. A group of men began moving menacingly towards the platform shouting, "Let him go" and "get off the stage". The constables drew their truncheons and warned the men of the consequences of starting a riot.

"This meeting is over and everyone must leave the hall immediately," one of them announced, hauling Jack to his feet and steering him towards the side of the platform. At this point, a shouted command was heard above the melee. The commanding voice of Commissioner Priestley ordered the constables to release Jack. They complied at once and retreated to the back of the stage, cowed by the advancing figure of authority in a green frock coat and black riding boots. From the centre of the platform, William Priestley held up a hand urging the still-angry townsfolk to resume their seats.

"There has been a misunderstanding, which I am sure these constables will wish to acquaint themselves with. Let me just say to you all that urgent steps are being taken to address your concerns about the pollution of the beck and canal. Unfortunately, this rally was seen principally as a threat to the canal. I shall put the record straight that you people, led by the group on this platform, simply wish to solve the pollution problem by the building of a sewer. Well, so do I and we have already embarked on a feasibility study to look at the geological problems and probable cost of such a project. Now, I am happy answer one or two of your questions before asking you all to leave in an orderly fashion so I can discuss with Jack Ackroyd and his group how they will be able to help us in our important endeavour."

The young woman cradling a baby got back on her feet in the front row to demand again, "Who is going to pay for this sewer? Most people in this hall can barely make ends meet as it is," she asserted, to murmurings of assent from those around her.

"Everyone will be asked to contribute what they can, according to their means," replied William Priestley. "After all, a sewer will benefit the whole community."

"Especially the mill owners," shouted a man at the back of the hall. "Where there's muck..."

"As I said, everyone will be asked to contribute, including all the businesses in town," interrupted William Priestley to a frisson of cynical laughter. "It is as much in the interests of the mill owners that Bradford is cleaned up as it is for everyone else. You can rest assured they will pay their fair share."

"Well, we'll believe that when we see it," responded the interlocutor as William Priestley raised his arms to bring the meeting to an end. A rumble of conversation filled the hall as people slowly left their seats and filed out into the street followed by the two constables, still grasping their truncheons as a visible warning against any threat to their persons.

"Titus thought you might have trouble," William Priestley told the bemused group on the platform, "so he suggested I should attend the meeting. Sorry I was a bit late, but all's well that ends well. I will arrange for you to meet the rest of the planners, Jack, then we can decide how best to use your energies in this enterprise."

As Jack made his way from the hall, heading for the General Infirmary, he mulled over the extraordinary events of the day. Had he burnt his boats with Josiah Hudson or would William Priestley and Titus Salt be his insurance against the opprobrium of his employer, he wondered. Whatever his situation, there could be no turning back, the die was cast. History was in the making and for better or worse, he was in the thick of it.

Fanny met him at the entrance to their son's ward and exultantly relayed the news that Josh was rallying and showing definite signs of recovery. "Then God has answered our prayers, lass," said Jack, embracing his wife. "He must need our Josh for some divine plan of his. Let's tell the boy he's coming home."

In spite of William Priestley's patronage, Jack Ackroyd still worried that his central role at the rally might have jeopardised his position at work once Josiah Hudson got to hear about it. He was unaware that the commissioner had portrayed him as the man who had saved the hour by steering the townsfolk away from wanting to close the canal towards support for a sewer. Jack's subsequent invitation to meetings of the commissioners and surveyors, as a representative of the townsfolk, did not escape the attention of Josiah Hudson, who calculated that his overseer was someone to keep close in turbulent times. He decided to reward Jack's loyalty in helping to head off a crippling, long-term strike at the mill by giving him the long-promised promotion to foreman. Fanny immediately wanted to know how much extra would be in his wage packet at the end of the week and when told, replied, "We'll be able to afford a better place to live now. I've always fancied up by St Peter's. Can we start looking right away?"

Within a few months, Jack and Fanny had relocated their family to a bigger terrace house in John Street, just behind the Parish Church, affording Katherine her own bedroom for the first time. Along with younger brother Theo, she attended the nearby Sunday school to receive tuition in the three Rs. Josh, who had regained his health, demonstrated a thirst for learning, which placed huge pressure on his parents. They were relieved when he secured a place at Stott Hill School, the first member of his family to attend a day school. Jack was happy for his youngest son to receive the education he never had, but believed Josh should still start work at the bottom like John before him. So at the age of ten, Josh joined his father and brother at Hudson's mill. He hated the twelve-hour days doing repetitive, mind-numbing tasks in cold, damp rooms, attracting hard treatment from an overseer determined that he should not be privileged because of his father's position. The boy received little sympathy from Jack, whose usual response to any complaint was that it was much worse in his day and, anyway, it would make a man of him.

Josh was unaware of the relentless campaigning by Leeds reformer Richard Oastler to end the brutal conditions endured by children in textile mills, leading to the passing of the Ten Hours Act. This law, limiting daily working hours for children, made it on to the statute book against intense opposition from mill owners such as Josiah Hudson, who argued that youngsters actually benefitted from long hours in the mill as part of growing up.

Although he gradually worked his way out of the most demeaning jobs at the mill, Josh never became reconciled to the textile industry and continued to look for an apprenticeship in a skilled trade. Craft apprenticeships were hard to find, demanding an initial payment to the employer, and were self-supporting. He would face an uphill task persuading his father and mother to pay for his keep for the requisite number of years in training. But it was Jack who was to provide his son with an escape route from the mill. From a casual conversation with another churchgoer after morning service at St. Peters, he learned that a builder was looking for bright lads to train as masons for Titus Salt's massive mills and housing complex at Shipley. Realising Josh would never be happy in textiles, Jack took him for an interview, which Josh passed with flying colours. Shedding tears of relief and gratitude, he embraced Jack with the promise that one day he would make him a very proud father. "Just make sure you're the best at whatever you do," said an embarrassed Jack. "Just good enough won't do."

Josh loved the mason's craft, learning about different types of stone and working it into shapes and patterns to suit the prevailing architectural tastes of the day. Over months and years he applied his increasing skills, helping to realise Titus Salt's remarkable vision of a self-contained textile community free from waterborne disease and vice. Even Jack and Fanny were caught up in their son's unflagging enthusiasm, agreeing that their additional financial burden was worth his obvious new happiness.

Meanwhile, along the course of Bradford Beck, from the town centre to Frizinghall, residents and passers-by became used to seeing groups of men wielding measuring instruments. They were advance parties surveying the line of the main sewer designed to relieve Bradford Beck, and ultimately the River Aire, of its daily burden of sewage and industrial waste. In the popular view, this would be a problem solved. No one could have imagined that it would take half a century more before Bradford would come close to ridding itself of its unenviable reputation.

New Dawn

A billow of steam, oil and smoke enveloped Josh in a writhing white mantle as the six-forty-five passed under the bridge and slowed to a stop at the platform to shouts of "Saltaire for Salts Mill". The clatter of iron-shod clogs on stone flags sounded the arrival of dozens of men and women, boys and girls as they stepped down from the carriages, forming an untidy stream up the steps and out of the station towards the towering mill buildings across Victoria Road. Their lives had been transformed by a man with a vision of happy workers living on clean streets, spending their days in a healthy environment. Appalled by the disease and squalor of early Victorian Bradford, Titus Salt belied the common caricature of a ruthless wool magnate by his sincere search for a solution to the town's pollution, deciding his only recourse was to move his mills and workforce well away from toxic smoke and filthy streets. He bought Dixon's Mill on the south bank of the River Aire, three miles north of the town, from landowner William Rookes Crompton Stansfield of Esholt Hall, whose heirs would play a decisive role in releasing Bradford from its squalor.

The last doors slammed; the guard blew his whistle and climbed aboard as the train eased forward out of the station, resuming its journey up the Aire valley. Josh continued down Victoria Road, turning into the driveway leading to the Classical frontage of the new Congregational church, sited to be a constant reminder of God's presence within this modern edifice to mammon. He felt proud to be finishing the stonework of the ornate clock tower on this architectural gem at the heart of Titus Salt's model village. It was his reward for the long, hard hours spent learning the craft of masonry to become a Journeyman under the direction of Lockwood and Mawson, Bradford's most respected architects.

Although it had been against Jack's early ambition for his son, Josh did not regret turning his back on his family's traditional employment in the woollen industry. Textile manufacture had slumped due to increased competition and worker unrest, leading many to envy Josh's trade in Bradford's seemingly unstoppable building boom. Newly hired as a builder's mate at Saltaire, he had witnessed the procession of civic dignitaries, led by the great man himself, who attended the official opening of the first huge mill building. In the following years Josh would help to build houses for the mill workers in terraced rows behind the mill. His outgoing personality and agile mind made up for what he lacked in physical stature, gaining him a reputation as a quick learner and conscientious worker.

Many workers had already moved out of Bradford for the enviable living conditions at Saltaire, to be replaced in town by Irish immigrant workers fleeing the potato famine at home. Dozens of Salts workers now made the daily return trip to Saltaire by train. Josh had grown tired of this ritual and left the family home for the convenience of lodging with a Shipley family in a humble back-to-back a few minutes walk from the mill. His father and mother had been sad to see him go, but happy he had escaped the life-threatening disease that killed his older brother.

Jack's health began to deteriorate, worsened by news that their son, Theo, who took the King's shilling as a boy soldier, had lost his life in the Crimea. In the same year, their remaining daughter, Katherine, married the son of an immigrant German family and moved to live in the textile town of Aachen on the border with Belgium. Fanny was forced to go out to work as a housemaid at one of the big houses in Manningham to make ends meet.

Josh was concerned about his parents, but considered that John, being closest, would let him know if he was needed. This thought comforted him as he put on the rough apron of his trade, took up his bag of tools and climbed a steep ladder to the roof of the church, where he got to work bedding down lead flashing. Shafts of sunlight lit the wooded slopes and heather moorland across the river. On the canal below, barges swollen with coal for the mills were tying up to be offloaded. Across the canal bridge, horses pulling clattering carts loaded with woolsacks headed down Victoria Road and into the bustling mill yard. He could think of nowhere he would rather work. Tomorrow, the Lord's day, would find Josh striding out along Otley Road across the canal and river, eventually turning upstream and climbing the steep escarpment to Shipley Glen. Here among the heather and outcrops of rock, families spent precious hours together enjoying the fresh moorland air in blissful idleness before beginning another week of heavy toil.

* * *

High above Baildon Moor a skylark trilled a fluttering vigil over a patch of heather a hundred feet below. White clouds drifted across an azure sky creating moving shadows across the boulder-strewn plateau of Shipley Glen. Families in their Sunday best tried to keep boisterous children in order as young couples made their conspiratorial trysts away from prying ears and eyes. Josh loved the glen in April, sensing the renewal of life all about him. He found his favourite rock outcrop and extracted a copy of the *Observer* from his knapsack to settle down for a read. Once again the editorial was railing against the pitiful lack of progress in tacking Bradford's terrible health record. It had been six years since the Borough Surveyors had drawn up plans for a sewer, but town council inertia and opposition from mill owners was being blamed for holding up the scheme. A devastating report detailing the filthy state of Bradford, which led to the Public Health Act of 1848, was beginning to exert new pressure on the councillors, forcing them to meet in emergency session in the fire station house in Swain Street.

A commotion at the edge of the plateau, where outcrops formed a low cliff above a beck, caused Josh's gaze to focus on a woman frantically signalling to a group of young men. Two began running towards her and Josh, sensing his help might be needed, joined in. As they reached the cliff edge, a cry of pain drew their eyes to a ledge halfway down. A small boy lay there clutching at heather to prevent him falling any further. "It's my little lad. He's fallen over and can't stand up," sobbed the woman hysterically.

Between them, they formed a rescue chain and Josh gently lifted the boy back up to the plateau. One of his legs was bent awkwardly and he was bleeding from a gash on his forehead. Josh volunteered to run to the nearest houses to find something to serve as a stretcher while the crying boy was alternately scolded and comforted by his mother and older sister. After some minutes, Josh returned with a handcart and its owner. Between them they lifted the boy on to the cart for the mile-and-a-half journey to Otley Road and a doctor's surgery.

"I warned him about going on them rocks. I just took my eyes off him for two seconds," sobbed the distraught mother as she struggled to keep up with the cart. "And where were you?" she asked, directing her guilt and anxiety at her daughter, a pretty auburn–haired girl who was trying to comfort her younger brother, holding his hand as the cart bounced over uneven ground. The girl cast a nervous glance at Josh, as if seeking his support. This created in him an unsettling sensation. He wanted to go on looking into those flecked irises, which now turned shyly away as the girl's cheeks flushed pink. "Daydreaming, as usual," accused her mother as Josh and the other man steered the cart down a steep incline towards the river.

At the main road a passerby directed them towards a large stone house standing in its own grounds. A polished brass plate on a gatepost bore the inscription *Doctor J.P. Illingworth M.D.* The boy whimpered with pain as he was lifted from the cart and carried towards the front door where his mother was tugging at a brass bell pull. A maid opened the door and, after a brief explanation, ushered them into a high-ceilinged consulting room where Josh laid the boy on an examination bench. They were soon joined by the tall, ascetic doctor, called from his afternoon nap, irritably polishing steel-framed spectacles.

"He fell up at the glen," explained the boy's mother. "I think he's broken his leg." After a brief inspection of the boy's injuries, Dr. Illingworth demanded, "Everyone apart from the mother please leave the consulting room."

Outside in the road they thanked the owner of the handcart for his help, waving him away back up the hill. Josh's attention now returned to the girl whose eyes had met his at the glen.

"Do you live near here," he asked in a gauche attempt at opening a conversation with her.

"Windhill," she told him. "My dad will go mad when he hears about Sammy. I should have been minding him." Josh put a comforting arm around her shoulders, suddenly realising he was enjoying one of the best moments of his life.

"It was an accident," he reassured her. "You weren't to blame. He's mischievous, that's all, like all boys of his age, what, eleven, twelve?"

"Sammy's thirteen and a half. He's small for his age, but he's a handful."

"Lily, come and give us a hand," commanded her mother from the doctor's front door. Then, turning to Josh, "And thank you kindly, young man. You're welcome to call on us, if you'd like – to see the boy's right. The name's Hodgson and we live at 5 Hall Lane, that's Windhill Bottom. Happen next Sunday if that's all right. About twelve, say. You'll stay for a bite to eat?"

"Thank you, Mrs. Hodgson, I will," replied Josh, scarcely able to believe his good fortune at being given the perfect excuse to see Lily Hodgson again. He suddenly needed to know a lot more about this tantalising girl, who seemed to have dropped out of the sky into his life and awakened feelings in him essential to his very existence. The walk back to his lodgings on winged feet had never seemed more agreeable or the street of back-to-back houses so welcoming.

Josh let himself into his lodgings to find a message waiting for him on the table in the kitchen: it urged him to go home as soon as possible as his father was seriously ill. Coming down to earth with a bump, he reckoned there would be a train to Bradford in about twenty minutes, just enough time to cut himself a piece of cheese and drink a mug of tea before setting off for the station. The fifteen-minute train journey and seven-minute walk to his parent's house should get him there just before five o'clock when his parents usually ate.

He was shocked by the frail appearance of his mother when she opened the front door. She seemed to have aged ten years, her hair now completely white and her face deeply lined, with dark patches under her eyes. She embraced her son warmly and ushered him into the parlour where an ashen-faced and emaciated Jack Ackroyd sat in front of the fire, clutching a bloodstained cloth to his lips. A spasm of racking coughs convulsed Jack's body as Josh moved to lay a comforting hand on his father.

"I can't get him to go to bed," complained Josh's distraught mother. "He just sits there and says if he goes to bed, it'll be the end of him. There's the sanatorium, but he won't hear tell of it. I really don't know what to do any more." She pulled Josh by the arm to a corner of the room and whispered so that her husband would not hear. "The doctor says he hasn't long. That's why I wanted you home today. John's been a brick, but Katherine's too far away to come home."

Josh put an arm round his father's shoulders, alarmed by the feel of the skeletal body fighting for breath. He felt confused by this new turn in his life – unabridged joy one minute and deep sorrow the next. He decided it was a conundrum only God could answer.

* * *

Faced with scepticism from some business leaders and civic elders, the commissioners invited medical experts to address them about the latest research into water-borne diseases. The commissioners were told it was beyond reasonable doubt that the beck and canal were the source of cholera, but it remained uncertain how it was caught and if it could be transmitted between people. The biggest obstacle to tackling the problem, they were told, was complacency and parsimony. This was partly solved by the Public Health Act of 1848 allowing public money to be raised for a sewer. But it was the cholera outbreak the following year claiming more than four hundred lives that spurred town councillors, serving the new Borough of Bradford under their Mayor Titus Salt, to take action. The line of the first sewer was established in 1853.

Meanwhile, set amid green fields and clean air alongside the river that gave it its name, Saltaire provided working and living conditions hitherto undreamed of by families living in Bradford. Six years after its foundation, its huge sandstone chimney reflecting spring sunshine proudly announced the arrival of one man's idealistic vision. The bulk of the first four-storey mill towered over a disparate landscape of rising buildings and an emerging grid of terrace houses, the whole scene reminiscent of a mother surrounded by her orderly progeny.

Josh felt a mixture of elation and anxiety as he surveyed sunlit Baildon Moor beyond the mill, mulling over events of the previous weekend. He had made a real effort for this visit to Lily's family, even persuading his landlady to let him take a bath, his second in a fortnight. Dressed in clothes he reserved for high days and holy days, he made his way down steep, cobbled streets lined with stone cottages, under a railway bridge and over the Bradford canal to reach his destination in Hall Lane. A face at a cottage window revealed Lily's anxious anticipation. She drew back quickly when she spotted his approaching figure. As he reached the front door, it was pulled open by a tall, broad-shouldered man with thick sandy hair and a concerned expression. He offered his hand. "Happen you'll be the young man who rescued our lad. Well, I thank you for that. Little bugger broke his leg so he'll not be climbing any rocks up at the Glen for a bit. Come on in."

Lily's father moved back inside and Josh followed him into a narrow passage with doors leading off to the left and right. From a door at the end of the passage came the sound of clattering tins and the smell of hot cabbage. He was waved through a door to his left into a low parlour filled with black lustrous furniture and richly patterned wallpaper backing black-framed prints and photographs. His heart leapt when he saw Lily seated by a generous fire, her eyes demurely cast down, her hands resting in her lap. She was wearing a green dress to compliment her auburn hair tied with silk ribbons. Brother Sam, on the opposite side of the fire, sat with his plastered left leg straight out in front of him. He gave Josh a cheeky grin and thanked him again for his rescue.

"Do you like to go bird-nesting?" he asked. "We can go nesting up on the moor, if you'd like. I've got a grand collection, but I'm still trying to find a lark's nest..."

"Go and help in the kitchen," cut in Lily, feeling upstaged by her little brother. Sam reluctantly eased himself from his chair and, with the aid of a crutch and a wink at Josh, limped out of the room.

"Don't mind him," said Lily, looking directly at Josh for the first time. "He's always getting into trouble one way or another. It was lucky you were there. Thank you for looking after him...er...I'm sorry, I've forgotten your name."

"Josh. Josh Ackroyd. I'm a Journeyman mason at Salts. I'm just about to start work on the houses as the church is all but finished."

"It is lovely. You must be proud to work on such a grand building."

"Well, yes, I suppose so. But I like most things I do. And you?"

"I work at Salts, on the looms. I'll be eighteen next birthday and they'll let me take over a section. That'll mean more brass for the family. Dad looks after the horses down there."

"And Sam? Does he work yet?"

"Yes, he's apprenticed at the smithy. Then there's Albert, my older brother. He lives in Bradford and he's going to be working on the new sewer tunnel. Albert says it's dirty, dangerous work, but it's good brass."

"My mam and dad live in Bradford with my older brother," Josh told her. "But dad's very ill with consumption. I think I'll have to go back home to help look after him. They need my brass, so I've no choice really. I don't fancy travelling to Saltaire every day, so I'm looking for work back in town." Fearful that he might be giving the wrong impression, Josh added hastily, "But I'll always get over at weekends because I love the glen." Lily's eyes met his in silent confirmation that weekend visits would be most welcome and Josh felt the same strange sensation he felt on first meeting her gaze on the moor.

"It's ready – Oh, hello again, er..." Lily's mother interrupted, as she poked her head round the door."

"It's Josh," helped Lily.

"Righto, Josh, come and sit yourself down and Lily, you can help with the plates."

Josh found himself the object of curiosity throughout the meal of spicy offal, mashed potatoes and buttered cabbage. He answered a succession of questions about himself and his family, noting Lily's satisfied smile when he said he was nineteen last birthday. He wondered if he was being sized up as a likely suitor. If so, he encouraged his interrogators enthusiastically, having decided there could be none other than Lily in his life from now on. He was tortured by not knowing if she felt the same about him, but was determined to find out at the earliest opportunity.

The sound of heavy footsteps in the passage heralded the late arrival of Albert, a chip off the old block and glowing happily from his traditional Sunday visit to the pub at the bottom of Thackley Road. He was introduced to Josh and endured an affectionate scolding from his mother, who busied herself getting his meal.

"Josh is a stonemason at Salts," Lily told her brother. "But he's looking for work in Bradford. I told him you'd been taken on to work on the new tunnel."

"I don't know if there's any work there at the moment," confessed Albert, "but they were looking for skilled masons for the tunnel lining last month. I'll ask for you, if you like."

Josh thanked Albert who promised to send word back through Lily. Another strand in the web, mused Josh who was now thoroughly relaxed into the lively conversation and banter that obviously characterised the family's Sunday get-together. When it came time to leave, Lily accompanied him to the front door where he thanked Mr. and Mrs. Hodgson for their hospitality and promised to take young Sam up on the moor bird-nesting when his leg was better. Lily stepped outside with him, half shutting the door behind her to avoid prying ears.

"Next Sunday then?" asked Josh.

"Yes, but it will have to be here. My dad won't let me walk out until I'm eighteen. It'll be all right if Sammy's with us, just up there by the hall; it's not far."

"Three o'clock Sunday then. I'm really looking forward to seeing you again."

"Me too, but I'd best go in now."

Instead of going directly to his lodgings to inform his landlady of his intended move back to town, Josh climbed to the top of Wrose Hill from where he had a panoramic view of Titus Salt's mills and the expanding village below. If he had to return to his parents' home in disease-ridden Bradford, so be it. But nothing could dampen his spirit now he had found the special person with whom he intended to spend the rest of his life.

* * *

A cold wind played with the woollen shawls of mothers and daughters moving in slow groups to join a growing throng of millworkers at the bottom of Victoria Road. Menfolk exchanged rough greetings, cursing intermittent showers of rain that turned the cobbles into a slick reflection of the weak April sunshine. In spite of the weather, the men, women and children were animated and excited at the prospect of seeing the great man and his entourage. At the sound of approaching horses, all heads turned to watch the arrival of a closed carriage carrying Titus Salt and his family, followed by more lacquered carriages filled with top-hatted dignitaries and their crinolined ladies. The procession turned into the driveway leading to the striking Classical façade of the new

Congregational Church, where the proud mill owner stepped down to enthusiastic cheers and applause from the crowd. In the porticoed entrance, he was greeted by the minister and sidesmen as a peel of bells rang out from the ornate tower. Titus Salt and his family were followed into the church by the civic dignitaries, mill managers with their spouses and, lastly, employees invited to fill the back of the church, all dressed in their finest.

Across Victoria Road, at the rear of the pressing throng, Josh held on to Lily's hand as they clung to railings on a low wall, straining to get a better view over the heads of the crowd. He was elated to feel her return his hold and he put a protective arm round her waist to steady her in the buffeting wind.

"I've told the lodgings I'm moving back home. Next week it'll be, but I'll still get over on Sundays."

"Yes, I'd like that and we could take Sammy up the glen. My dad will let me go as long as we're with Sammy. His leg is..." She never finished the sentence as she spotted a face in the crowd and froze into silence.

"What's the matter, Lily? Who've you seen?" asked Josh, feeling sudden tension in her grip.

"I'll have to go. Walk me home, Josh, now, please."

"Tell me what you've seen, Lily," he insisted, alarmed by the fear in her voice.

"It's just a lad I know. He works at the mill and he's been following me about. Keeps trying to get me to walk out with him, said he won't give up. I'm scared what he might do."

Josh followed her frightened stare to a group of youths.

One of them was looking menacingly at them across the heads of the crowd.

"They're far enough away, they can't get to us," he reassured her. "Don't worry, you're quite safe with me." She kept a firm grip of his hand as they pushed their way through the crowd up Victoria Road on their way back to Windhill. Josh felt proud that Lily was relying on him for protection against this unwanted attention.

"Like you were saying, I'd like to go with you and Sammy up the glen next Sunday if his leg's better. What do you think?"

"Well, his leg's healing, but he'll have to wait a bit longer before he can go nesting. If he's not right, you can still come over, though, and we can take a walk up to the hall at the end of our street."

Josh reluctantly let go of Lily's hand as they approached the house in case her father was watching. He said goodbye at the front door and returned Sam's wave at a window before striding off in the direction of his lodgings. Feeling as light as air, reflecting on his good fortune at meeting Lily, he was making his way along Briggate towards Kirkgate when he suddenly sensed danger. A group of youths was blocking the narrow alleyway ahead. He recognised the menacing face he had seen among the crowd at the mill, the face that had frightened Lily. Josh slackened his pace, giving him time to appraise the situation. He could turn round and go back the way he had come, but that might seem like he was running away He decided to continue on his way even though the gang seemed be looking for trouble under the leadership of the menacing one, who stood out as their leader.

"Going somewhere?" he asked Josh with a sneer, standing in the middle of the alleyway, thumbs hooked into his waistcoat and displaying a mouthful of decaying teeth. His sniggering friends watched Josh like feral dogs waiting for an order to pounce.

"I'm going home, as if that's of any interest to you. So if you don't mind…"

The leader continued to block his way. "What were you doing with my lass down there? You're not from round here. Who the hell do you think you are walking out with my lass? I reckon he needs to be taught a lesson, eh lads?"

"She says she's not your lass and she was happy to be with me," said Josh.

"Ah, so you was talking about me behind my back, was you? You're a big man when you're with her, aren't you? Let's see how big you are now." With that he lunged at Josh, who hadn't noticed one of the gang crouched behind him. As he moved back, he fell over the crouching youth and two others closed in to begin kicking him, as he lay curled up on the ground. Fending off the blows as best he could, Josh managed to struggle to his feet only to be doubled up with a punch to the stomach and a knee in his face. With blood streaming from his nose, he staggered back against a wall waiting for the next onslaught. None came and when he opened his eyes the alleyway was empty of his assailants who were in full flight. They were being pursued by two men whose womenfolk hovered over Josh, anxiously examining his damaged face. One offered him a kerchief to stem the flow of blood. Eventually, the two men gave up the chase and breathlessly returned to the alleyway.

"You all right lad?" enquired one of the men. "He's a right bad 'un, him and his gang. Best get yourself home and keep away from them lads in future. They're just trouble." Josh thanked the men for rescuing him and limped the rest of the way to his lodging in some pain.

"What on earth...?" gasped his landlady, studying his swollen, bloodstained face. Josh explained what had happened as she fussed about him with warm water and a towel. "That'll be the Rosse Street gang," she told him. "He'll end up in Armley that one. See, I'll make you some tea and there's fresh bread."

"I don't want any more trouble. I think it's best if I move my things back home today." said Josh. "I'll pay to the end of the week to give you time to find another lodger."

He slept for most of the short train journey to Bradford, waking in familiar surroundings as his carriage juddered to a halt in the Leeds and Bradford Railway terminus. Old remembered smells and sounds accompanied his walk up steep streets to his terrace home where the front door stood half open. Fanny looked up from kneading bread dough on the parlour table, shocked to see the injuries to her youngest son's face. Josh embraced her with a brief explanation reassuring her it was only superficial and told her that he would be living at home from now on. "And the best news of all," he continued, "is that I've got a lass. I can't wait for you to meet her. Her name's Lily Hodgson."

"It must be serious then," was his mother's only reply as she dabbed at his face with a damp cloth before turning her attention back to the dough with even greater pumelling from her strong, flour-covered arms. "Your dad's in bed. Be careful not to wake him if he's asleep." Josh mounted the steep wooden stairs quietly and eased open the door to his parents' bedroom. He was shocked to see the deathly pallor of his father's sunken face as Jack struggled for each breath in his shallow sleep. Was this the way it had to end after a life of continuous struggle to survive? he mused. It all seemed so cruel and pointless.

Her dough prepared and placed by the fire, Fanny climbed the stairs and resumed her vigil at her husband's bedside. She whispered in Josh's ear, "There's no point calling the doctor again. He's already said there is nothing more he can do; it's just a matter of time. Go down and get yourself something to eat. I'll keep watch here."

With the first light of dawn penetrating the bedroom window, Fanny woke with a start in the armchair next to Jack's bed. Instead of his laboured breathing, there was a stillness about the room that told her the vigil was over. She kissed the pallid forehead of her life's companion and whispered, "God bless, my love. You can rest in peace now."

A surprising number of townsfolk and former workmates stood in the pews of Christ Church as Jack Ackroyd's coffin was carried in followed by Fanny, dressed from head to toe in black and accompanied by her two sons. Josiah Hudson sent along Jem Laker with strict instructions to be no longer than an hour away from his desk. In thirty minutes the coffin was on its way back out of the church for the short journey to a company grave in Undercliffe Cemetery overlooking the town. As the horse-drawn hearse passed an almost complete, highly ornate mausoleum for a newly deceased mill owner, a mason was busy chiselling into the stone lintel the legend *'sic gloria transit mundi'*.

* * *

Josh lowered himself through the manhole, feeling with the toe of his boot for the first of the iron hoops to take him down into the tunnel. His topcoat was soaked from the constant heavy rain in that spring of 1863, and he groaned as his boots splashed down into ankle-deep icy water. Sometimes he wondered whether he had made a mistake coming to work on the sewer, but it paid good money and he was determined to save enough for his wedding to Lily in the summer.

In spite of the doubters, who described sewers as a waste of the rates, the first mile of Bradford's sewerage system had been completed the previous year. Even the most devoted supporters of the undertaking agreed that it was simply transferring the town's waste problem further downstream to enter the beck at Frizinghall; the beck still emptied into the River Aire. But town councillors had been forced to act with the threat of legal action hanging over them if they failed to clean up their town. Powerful voices were lined up against council inertia. At his rural Esholt estate bordered by the river, William Rookes Crompton Stansfield complained loudly and often about the polluted water that, he claimed, made the Aire little more than an open sewer. During warm weather he was dissuaded from opening windows or venturing across his extensive riverside lawns due to noxious odours wafting up from the river. Other campaigners agreed that the sewerage system was only part of the answer to Bradford's problem. As their torch-bearer, Jack Ackroyd had achieved his first objective by getting human waste away from the town centre. But since his death, activists insisted the canal basin was still no better than a stinking pool of industrial waste and should be filled in.

Josh, meanwhile, continued to work alongside some of the hardest men he had ever encountered, building sewers branching down from Horton, Lister Hill, and Whetley in the West and Leeds Road in the East. His ears had become attuned to the broad Irish brogue that echoed through the tunnels from men who had fled the potato famine fifteen years before. These highly valued workers had left their native shore, probably for good, and were marrying local girls. They matched hard work with hard drinking that kept the cells of the new police force fully occupied and the town's magistrates in regular business. For all that, Josh enjoyed their raucous good humour and tall tales of the old country.

A dim, yellow glow in the gloom ahead barely illuminated the series of wooden props and planks that secured the top and sides of the tunnel before it was lined with hardened bricks. This was the job Josh would spend the next ten hours doing, with only a short break for his bait and not a breath of fresh air. He was teamed up with a jolly giant from Wexford called Pat Brady, who stood six foot two in his boots, sporting a head of bushy red hair and a ready smile. His job was to keep Josh supplied with bricks and mortar, a job that he carried out willingly and with good humour in spite of the arduous conditions. His smile only faded when he told Josh harrowing tales of starvation back home and of how he had seen whole families crowded on to boats bound for America to escape what they feared would otherwise be a lingering death. He sent most of his wages home for his ageing mother and father who had survived the famine, but who were in poor health as a result of being on a subsistence diet for four years.

Josh stumbled forward between rusting rails towards the flickering oil lamps where he had finished work the previous evening. A buzz of voices and the sound of picks biting into stone told him how far the tunnellers had progressed ahead of him. Scooping up a trowelful of mortar, he coated a brick and placed it at the base of the curved wall next to yesterday's lining. He repeated the action, which was slowly extending the lined tunnel forwards. With three hundred yards completed and a thousand to go, his robotic movements allowed him to fall into a reverie, producing treasured images of his beloved Lily who had accepted his proposal of marriage with the blessing of her mother and father. She obtained special permission for the service in the very Saltaire church he had helped to build. In just six weeks, he mused, they would be walking down the aisle, arm-in-arm, man and wife. He had already agreed to rent a terrace house only five streets away from his mother and brother John and planned to move in soon to prepare it for his bride-to-be.

A shout from farther up the tunnel, "Man hurt here, coming through," broke his reverie. Two tunnellers stumbled forward pushing a flatbed trolley carrying the limp body of a third man stretched out on his back. "Sure, a rock fell on him, knocked him cold," explained one of the men as they squeezed past Josh heading for the manhole. "He'll be right with some fresh air." After they passed, everyone fell back into the rhythm of work, serious injuries or even death barely slowing the pace in this harsh environment.

Because Lily considered his job too dangerous, Josh kept news of such mishaps to himself. She begged him to find other work, but he persuaded her they needed the money for a good start to their married life. He promised he would look for another job after the wedding, in the hope she wouldn't hold him to it. But this didn't appease Lily who wanted her man alive and well. She had already had a scare when she learned, many days later, about his encounter with the Rosse Street gang. She was so terrified they would attack him again, she had her father report the matter to the local police, who issued the ringleader with a warning that one more incident would find him up before the magistrates with a likely spell in Armley prison.

Even prison could not be any worse than working in the wet and dimly lit confines of the sewer, mused Josh. It was the lure of good wages that brought men into such an inhospitable environment, risking life-threatening and long-term illness. Working for months in a space barely big enough to stand up in, drove some men mad. But there was no shortage of volunteers to take the place of anyone who left the job, a fact frequently voiced by the bull-headed overseer who daily cajoled the men into greater effort. His employers had contracted to finish the job by the end of the year and any delay would cost them money. Josh realised his status as a skilled journeyman put him among the elite in that particular workforce, earning him greater respect from the overseer. He kept on the man's good side by pulling his weight and not getting involved in any griping by the navvies. Lily was his life and future now and he would endure any hardship to achieve their dream.

Pressure Grows

Outside the main entrance to St.George's Hall, a group of middle-aged gentlemen stood talking in the late September sunshine. Their top hats and gold chains stretched across ample corporations were evidence of Bradford's rising prosperity and status. Flat northern vowels were interspersed with the more guttural voices of two Germans struggling with the English language. Any early xenophobia triggered by the influx of these immigrant wool merchants had soon given way to a cautious welcome as the town discovered how much trade these recent arrivals generated with European countries. The Germans were establishing their colony of tall stone buildings in an area of steep streets a stone's throw from St. Peter's Church, introducing new business and cultural ideas, which were gaining wider interest.

All heads turned to watch the arrival of a liveried coach pulled by a pair of greys. The coachman climbed down, opened a door emblazoned with the initials WRCS and secured the step affording the owner of Esholt Hall access to the pavement. The group parted instinctively to allow William Stansfield to stride into the building without stopping to pass the time of day with his fellow mill owners.

After a few moments they followed him to join thirty or so councillors, clergymen and the town's Member of Parliament towards the front of the main hall. Last to take his seat on the stage was the Mayor of Bradford, resplendent in a scarlet robe trimmed with ermine. To his right the Town Clerk, an austere figure dressed in a black frock coat, adjusted his pince-nez as he rose to his feet with a cough to attract the attention of the citizenry filling every seat from the floor to the balconies. He addressed his opening remarks to the dignitaries immediately in front of him.

"Gentlemen, I welcome you to this extraordinary meeting of the town council, which has been called by popular demand to gain the views of citizens affected by our polluted beck and canal. I now call upon the Mayor to address you on behalf of the council."

The Mayor glanced nervously in the direction of William Stansfield who had fixed him with an unflinching stare. Rising slowly to his feet, the leading citizen cleared his throat and began by welcoming the landowner to the meeting.

"It is indeed an honour to have among us today Mr. William Stansfield, whose generous and public-spirited action facilitated the building of Titus Salt's remarkable mills on part of his Esholt estate." Hoping his emollient opening remarks were having the desired effect, the Mayor was disconcerted to meet again the unyielding stare of the landowner. He continued, "As many of you know, we have implemented the plans of our Borough Surveyor and completed the first stage of his sewerage system for the town. This work is ongoing and will eventually lead to the clean up of the beck and the canal basin, which have been identified as the source of so much disease in recent years."

"Humbug," shouted William Stansfield, to the shock and surprise of those sitting near him. The Mayor, caught off guard, promptly sat down as the landowner rose to his feet and addressed the platform. "This is pure self-interest. It may well sweeten your beck and canal basin in the town centre, but where is all that sewage and mill waste going to end up? I'll tell you where, lower down the beck. From there it has nowhere else to go but into the river that bounds my estate. So the river will continue to be an open sewer for the filth of Bradford. Its stinking mix threatens my health and the health of my family. I want to know what plans this council has to rid the river of this noxious effluent."

The Mayor, looking thoroughly discomforted, stayed rooted to his seat as he sought the support of his councillors. But it was the Member of Parliament who rose to say that Bradford's problems were also causing much concern in Parliament. "Many members have been influenced by the words of Mr. Charles Dickens, who visited Bradford ten years ago and was appalled by what he witnessed," said the MP. "There are increasing calls for more to be done to rid this town of the squalor and disease that has brought misery and grief into so many homes. The sewers are a start, but there is still much to be done."

"So what *is* your answer?" asked William Stansfield. "There had better be an answer or I will be seeking satisfaction through the courts."

"It is too early to give you a definitive answer," replied the Borough Surveyor, rising from his seat clutching a sheaf of papers. "There have been experiments in other parts of the country to eradicate human and industrial waste, none of which has been entirely successful..."

"Experiments which we will be expected to pay for, I suppose," contributed Josiah Hudson, who had been growing redder in the face and more agitated as the meeting progressed. His sideburns bristling with indignation, he challenged the claim that mill waste was at all to blame. "It's just wool washings and they're natural, not pollution. It's sewage from the streets that's been the problem, fouling the water we take from the canal. If this sewer gets rid of the human waste from our beck and canal basin, then it might just be worth the extortionate amount we are being asked to pay for it. Just remember, the wealth of this town is built on wool. Anyway, our mills are a good three miles from the river, so I don't see that as our problem."

"Then I will make it your problem," roared William Stansfield. "You will be hearing from my lawyer." With that he left his seat and strode from the hall, loudly summoning his coachman as he pushed through the double exit doors.

After a stunned pause while all present absorbed the last engagement, the Borough Surveyor regained his feet and continued, "What I was going to add was that Bradford has two unique problems in dealing with its waste. The first is topography: the town sits in a crescent of hills to the south, which means the beck can only flow in a northerly direction, making the river the inevitable receptacle for our raw waste. Secondly, we are noticing a marked increase in the volume of grease from wool washings as a proportion of the sewage. This makes it harder to deal with at our proposed treatment works at Frizinghall where the sewer tunnel ends. Much will depend on the outcome of current research."

The Mayor, relieved that the meeting had avoided turning into a shouting match, invited further comments from the hall. These followed traditional lines: councillors and clergymen expressing concern, mill owners urging caution in case they were expected to dip into their own pockets to fund costly experiments and some townsfolk demanding that the canal basin be closed. Little further consideration was given to the plight of William Stansfield, whose estate lay a good three miles downstream from where the beck entered the river. It was simply a case of out of sight, out of mind.

By early evening the meeting place had been transformed back into a concert hall, the stage set out with a grand piano and music stands. Josh felt proud to be accompanying Lily to what, in his eyes, was a posh event, although he knew next to nothing about the works of Beethoven. He hoped their companion for the evening, Georg Heller, a German who had befriended his sister and brother-in-law in Aachen, would be their musical guide. In return, Georg was grateful for the help he was receiving from Josh and Lily to find his feet in the town that was to become his home, and where he planned to make his fortune trading in wool. Tall and angular with a full head of straight blond hair above a fresh, honest face, Georg brightened up any company he was with. He talked incessantly, if allowed, singing the praises of his newly adopted country and the business opportunities it was providing him. Like all his compatriots, he was a hard worker, still enjoying the freedom afforded by bachelorhood.

He assuaged any feelings of homesickness by keeping in touch with other German expatriates in the town such as Julius Delius, originally from Bielefeld in Northern Germany where Georg grew up and was educated before moving to Aachen. An occasional guest at the home of Julius and Elise Delius, he had joined in celebrations at the birth of their fourth son, Fritz, the previous year. Georg's enthusiasm for life in his adopted Yorkshire was not mirrored by Josh's sister Katherine, now married to Gunter Schmidt and happily settled in a town free of Bradford's squalor. She had resisted all entreaties to return to her birthplace, even for a short visit, but said she would make an exception for the wedding of her youngest brother at Saltaire, well away, she hoped, from harmful contagion.

The rousing presto of Beethoven's 14th Sonata reverberated around the galleried hall, casting its liquid spell over the two young people holding hands and enjoying the power and emotion of the music. Georg allowed himself a smile of satisfaction that his two English companions were so moved by their first encounter with the genius of his fellow countryman, whose life had ended just thirty-six years earlier.

"That was grand. We'll have to do this again," enthused Josh to an entranced Lily over a cacophony of applause.

"We will," she replied, "when we're married."

* * *

It seemed like all the residents of Hall Lane had turned out to watch Lily step from her front door in a billow of white organdie, carrying a posy of freesias. She acknowledged the cheers and shouted good wishes of her neighbours as she was helped into an open carriage by her father for the short journey to Victoria Road. Steel-shod hooves found their grip on shining wet cobbles as the sun began to regain mastery over a cloud-dappled sky. A puckish breeze played with her veil and the elegant white plumes topping the collar of the bay mare as the carriage set off along Saltaire Road.

"I expect Albert will be in church already," she told her father as they passed between the first of Titus Salt's new workers' houses. "It's good of him to bring Josh and his family all the way from Bradford."

"Aye, lass, it's grand our families get on," replied her father as the carriage turned down Victoria Road. "He'll make a good son-in-law, will Josh."

Next to the stables, where Lily's father spent his working life, they wheeled into the church approach and drew to a halt before the ornate building. He stepped down to offer a supporting hand to his only daughter, marvelling how radiant she looked on her wedding day. Lily took her father's arm as they made their way through the colonnaded entrance into the bright interior. Two dozen family and friends filled pews on both sides as they made their way to join Josh in front of the altar table. To the right sat his mother, brother John and sister Katherine and her husband Gunther from Germany. Side by side the betrothed pair made their solemn vows and had no difficulty pledging mutual, lifelong fidelity. The short service over, the bride and groom returned blinking into bright sunlight outside to be greeted by a small crowd of wellwishers.

As they turned out of the drive into Victoria Road, Josh felt Lily's hand on his arm tighten suddenly and her step falter momentarily. She nodded towards a group of lads on the railway bridge gathered round her stalker and Josh's assailant.

"Never mind him, there's nothing he can do to us now," Josh reassured her. "We'll be living in Bradford miles away from here. Anyroad, he's had an official warning, so any more trouble from him and he'll be up in front of the beak." It was only a short walk from there to the mill dining room next to Saltaire railway station, where the wedding guests were served a simple meal seated at two rows of trestle tables. Afterwards, toasts were proposed, good fortune wished and laughter and tears evoked in equal measure by John's portrayal of his younger brother and regret at the absence of their father. A particular welcome was reserved for Katherine and the new German dimension in the persons of her husband Gunter and friend Georg. John concluded by calling for a toast to the new bond forged that day between the Ackroyds and Hodgsons.Soon it was time for Albert to take his new in-laws, including the newlyweds, back to Bradford, where Josh had booked a room for the night at the White Lion Hotel in Kirkgate. "Tomorrow," he promised Lily, "you'll have the trip of a lifetime for our weekend honeymoon far away from here."

"So where are you taking me?" she pressed him as their carriage headed off at a brisk pace towards Manningham.

"All I'm going to say is that you'll be making a train journey," he confided. "You said you'd never been on a train, so this is part of your treat. You'll see where you are when we get there," he teased, earning him a playful jab in the ribs.

"You told me there'd be no secrets in our marriage," she laughed. "We're not married a day yet and you're keeping things from me already."

"Honeymoon apart, you just make sure he does keep his promises," advised Fanny Ackroyd weakly, with a wink in Lily's direction.

"Or he'll have me to answer to," added Katherine, to general amusement.

"I'm being ganged up on by the women," protested Josh. "What say you, John?"

"If it's good enough for our mam, it's good enough for me. I know which side my bread's buttered on," copped out his brother.

Passers-by in Kirkgate stopped and shouted good wishes as Josh helped his bride from the carriage, to the accompaniment of her mother's stern advice to Lily to keep warm and eat well. Josh smiled at this implied preparation for motherhood and caught the glint of a tear as Lily returned the promise, waving goodbye to her new in-laws. She comforted herself with the thought that not only had she gained the husband of her choice, but she also had the proximity of his mother and brother to help her cope with her new life in this unfamiliar urban environment. Intuiting Lily's thinking, Josh put a comforting arm round her, steering her towards the gaslit entrance to the hotel. He was confident she would soon feel comfortable at the prospect of life together in their own home.

"Good evening Mr. and Mrs. Ackroyd," greeted the publican in an unnecessarily loud voice, attracting the curious glances of regular patrons as the newlyweds stepped into the warm interior. "These are on the house," he said, handing each a glass of warm spiced wine. "I expect you'll be tired after your busy day," he ventured mischievously, turning to wink at a group of men standing at the bar. "Happen we can delay breakfast in the morning, if you like."

"We have to be at the station for half past eight, so I would be obliged for an early call for breakfast at seven thirty," replied Josh, noting Lily's scarlet cheeks. "We'll enjoy these in our room, thank you."

At first light the next morning, after a plain breakfast brought up to their room, Josh and Lily made their way down Kirkgate, the short distance to the railway terminus. Josh bought two tickets and steered Lily towards the seven-coach train waiting at platform one, helping her into an empty third-class compartment. A few minutes later, two blasts on a whistle, a hiss of escaping steam and a quickening series of percussive exhausts of sulphurous smoke signalled the start of their journey. Drab townscape gave way to flat green meadows with the promise of distant moorland as the train steamed along the Aire valley towards the wide uplands of the Dales. After Skipton, each country station seemed more remote than the last, every variation in the Pennine landscape exciting childlike delight and wonder in Lily. Almost two hours after leaving Bradford, the train steamed into Clapham station, opened fourteen years earlier by the North Western Railway Company. In bright sunshine, under scudding white clouds, the honeymooners were greeted by and squeezed into the only available transport, a mud-spattered dog cart pulled by an ancient piebald pony. They set off up the mile-long lane to the village, seated behind the broad back of the taciturn, incurious driver. As grey stone houses came into view, Josh and Lily marvelled at the sweetness of the air and freshness of the countryside where they were to spend the next three days, among limestone crags and grassy escarpments.

That evening, well fed on the landlady's mutton stew and dumplings, the honeymooners sat side by side on a high-backed settle, their faces contentedly reflecting the blazing logs in a high limestone fireplace.

"This is the best thing that's ever happened to me," she said, squeezing Josh's hand. "But I want you to promise me one thing. I want you to get out of that dangerous tunnelling job when we get back."

"I'll see what I can do, love," Josh demurred, "just as long as we've enough brass to keep us going."

* * *

William Stansfield took shelter beneath the branches of a weeping willow on the banks of the river as a fine drizzle drifted across his close-cut lawn, which sloped up to the grand frontage of Esholt Hall. Cooler weather had reduced the stench given off by the turgid brown current flowing past the last exposed remnants of a Cistercian nunnery, dissolved by Henry VIII in the sixteenth century. The ruins, and the hall built over them, occupied land that once belonged to Norman immigrants, the de Brus family of Guisborough in North Yorkshire, progenitors of Scotland's Robert the Bruce.

The current landowner began to pace the riverbank, seething inwardly at his apparent impotence to staunch the foul invasion of his estate. He vowed to maintain his pressure on the town council and carry the fight to the highest courts in the land if necessary. To achieve his aim, William, being childless, needed the unwavering support of his nephew and heir to the estate to continue the fight after his succession. Colonel Henry Crompton Stansfield, a frequent visitor to the hall with his wife and three daughters, was a hero of the Crimean war and a respected figure in West Riding society. He projected a military mien with considerable charm, which he directed especially at young attractive women who happened to catch his eye. His presence at the hall always caused a frisson of excitement among the female servants, who vied with each other to get his attention.

In his struggle with the town council, William Stansfield realised his influence would depend to a considerable extent on his family's high social position and good name in county circles as both a land and mill owner. A good name within the aristocracy had more weight in straight-laced Victorian society than new-found wealth. Adding to his current agitation was concern that his standing could have been seriously compromised by his nephew's ill-judged act of kindness towards a member of the household staff.

Anna Storey, a seventeen-year-old chambermaid, was distraught when her life suddenly unravelled on the disappearance of the man who had promised her a gold ring and a white wedding. Henry Stansfield, happening across the girl sobbing inconsolably behind some rhododendron bushes in the hall gardens, sought to calm her with a comforting arm around her shoulders and an imprecation on her treacherous suitor. She could leave her duties early and he would drive her the half mile to her home in Esholt Village to save her a walk in the dark and rain. It was some time later that Anna was delivered to the door of her parents' cottage in style and much to the family's embarrassment that she should have so inconvenienced her employer. And that might have been an end to the matter had Anna's middle not begun to swell, causing tongues to wag and eyebrows to rise. She refused to identify the creator of her condition, which only added fuel to the fire of village gossip. Enemies of the Stansfields, of whom there were a number in the neighbourhood, took advantage of the situation to spread malicious rumours that were neither confirmed nor denied by the girl and were totally ignored at the hall where Anna's employment was terminated peremptorily. From that day on she was no longer seen about the village and it was some weeks later that a villager happened across her in Rodley, where she was staying with one of her father's unmarried sisters.

The intensity of the scandal had subsided by the time Anna returned, heartbroken and alone, to her family home at Esholt some six months later. Gossip over the bar of the Commercial now focussed on the fortunes of the baby girl, left to be raised by her aunt. As days went by, Anna never ceased to pine for her child and, despite agreeing to give her up, she returned to Rodley to reclaim her baby, ignoring her parent's dire warnings of public ostracism if she tried to bring her illegitimate daughter up on her own. Rejected by her aunt and shunned by her parents, she found a room to share in Keighley. After walking the streets for a day and a half and visiting numerous establishments, she was given a job in a back street haberdashery. The owner, who had once been in a similar position, took pity on Anna, allowing her to take little Constance to work with her during the daytime. Her wage was barely enough to pay for the rent and food for herself and the baby, but she considered the sacrifice was worth it for them to be together.

Henry Stansfield felt a twinge of conscience when he learned through another of the chambermaids about Anna's struggle to keep her independence with her baby daughter in Keighley. His uncle had insisted that Anna leave the hall so precipitately and Henry wished to find a way to ease her burden. But it would have to be done anonymously. He instructed his solicitor to make the sum of two pounds a month available to Anna through a West Riding Penny Savings Bank account, with the strict proviso that she must never know the identity of her benefactor. The payments were to continue until the child reached the age of sixteen, but would cease if Anna married. If the Stansfield name was ever linked to the gratuity, it was to be vigorously denied.

Anna could hardly take in what she was reading, although the letter seemed genuine enough. It was from the recently opened Keighley branch of the bank, telling her she now had her own savings account, which would receive a monthly sum of two pounds. The first amount was entered in the accompanying bank book with her name on the cover. She could withdraw as much or as as little of the money she required, provided she did not try to draw out more than was in her book. The bank disclosed no further information as to the source of the money. She suddenly felt the need to sit down at her kitchen table and re-read the letter carefully in case she had not fully understood its contents the first time. At last she understood that her money worries were over and she would be able to find a better place to bring up her baby daughter.

"Connie, my love," she said, jogging the little girl up and down in her outstretched arms, "we're in luck, you and me. And that's the way we're going to stay, if I've anything to do with it." She promised God she would to go to church on Sunday to thank Him for His beneficence – and for their benefactor, whoever it was.

*　*　*

By the spring of 1870 dozens of German companies were adding to the growing wealth of Bradford, by now England's most important wool processing centre. Families crossing the North Sea to formalise their settlement brought disturbing news about rising political tensions between their homeland and France. Prussia, under the scheming Otto von Bismarck, was conscripting a formidable force to oppose Napoleon III. Georg Heller was first to hear that Gunter Schmidt had been called up into the 16th Infantry Division and sent to the German Frontier town of Saarbrucken. There he became one of the earliest casualties of the bitter seven-month conflict when French forces, in a pre-emptive strike, overran and occupied the town. Napoleon paid dearly for his hubris, having to surrender to the conquering Prussian army just two months later.

Josh received confirmation of his brother-in-law's death in a letter from his distraught sister, Katherine. 'I can no longer see how to provide for myself and my two boys in a country where I am still considered a foreigner in the eyes of the local population,' she wrote. 'Much as I hate to do so, I feel I have no option but to return to England to be near my family in Yorkshire. Our mother's ill health is probably proving too much of a burden for John, who would welcome my help to look after her. The family home might be small, but there should be enough room for all of us. I have enjoyed my time in Aachen, but too many things here remind me of my beloved husband, whom I miss terribly. His parents live too far away to be of any real help, so I feel it is time to make a break with the past and build a new life in Bradford. As soon as I have settled my affairs, I will make my way through Belgium to Ostend to board a packet for England.'

Josh read and re-read the letter, reflecting that fate had played yet another bad hand for his family. Lily had given birth to their first baby, a boy, who had only lived for a few hours. They would try for more children, but Lily would find it hard to get over her first bitter disappointment. He had agreed with John not to tell their widowed sister that Fanny might have only weeks to live; it would only add to her distress. They resolved to welcome her back into the bosom of her family and give her all possible support to bring up her fatherless children.

"Katherine might feel a stranger in her own town now with so much change – all these mill buildings going up and all," suggested Lily. "At least they've shut and emptied the canal. She'll notice there's less of a stink in the town centre these days."

"Aye, they only shut it because a court ordered the canal company to stop taking water from the beck," said Josh. "But Stansfield's still creating hell about the beck putting filth in the river in spite of court orders. The council will be forced to build a treatment works at the end of the sewer at Frizinghall before allowing anything to get near the beck and the river. Happen I might apply for a job there myself."

"Well, it's six years since you worked like a mole in a hole all day. I was really scared then. I was relieved when you got the Wool Exchange job."

"The new Mechanics Institute will be topping out soon, so Frizinghall could be the next big job. Although, how you treat sewage, I can't imagine. It'll be a bit smelly, but council wages are always good."

"And if you don't get a job there?"

"Well, then there's all these schools the *Telegraph* says they're going to build under the Education Act. They'll need lots of masons for that, so I don't think I'll be out of work whatever happens."

Three weeks later, John and Josh waited near the platform barrier of the North Western Railway terminus as the four twenty from London drew to a halt under the glazed canopy. All along the train, doors swung open and crumpled passengers stepped out to be greeted by tactile adults and excited children. They soon spotted Katherine, who engaged a porter to wheel her sea trunks and cases from the guard's van to where her brothers were waiting. With tears in her eyes she embraced each in turn before introducing her wide-eyed boys, Gunther aged nine and seven-year-old Jack, to the uncles they had never seen.

"Welcome back to Bradford, lass, though I wish it was happier times," said John. "We've got a trap outside. Your cases will be sent on."

"I'll look after the porter; you just go with John," said Josh.

Soon they were moving to the metallic clop of hooves on granite cobbles along narrow streets of smoke-blackened terrace houses until they reached Katherine's new home.

"Doctor told our mam to stay in bed, so she won't be at the door," warned John. "She might not know you at first because she's taken a bit of a funny turn."

Katherine was shocked to see how much her mother had changed. White-haired, pale and desperately thin, she sat propped up in bed seemingly unaware of her surroundings. Katherine held her mother's frail hand and kissed her translucent cheek. "I'm home, mam, and I'm staying to look after you now."

"I want my tea," said Fanny Ackroyd. "Will you get it for me?"

"She's forgotten she's had it," said John. "We'll just make her another cup. The boys will be hungry, so you sit with her and we'll look after it."

Later, in the warmth of a generously stacked coal fire, the brothers and sister sat around the parlour table exchanging news and gossip while the children explored their surroundings in this strange town where everyone seemed to speak the same language as their mother.

"I've got some money, but I'll need to find work of some sort," said Katherine, to the relief of John, who worried that his wage from Hudson's mill would not be enough to keep them all.

"Happen they'll need someone up at the big houses in Manningham," volunteered Josh. "Or you could try Salts, if you don't mind the journey. I know they're taking people on."

"It's a lot better place for children, with green fields to run about in instead of filthy streets," said John. "You might even get the chance for one of the houses," he added, reckoning that his thirty-four-year-old, newly widowed sister was still young enough, even with two children, to attract another husband.

"Lily worked at Salts until we were wed," said Josh. "She'll be happy to go with you, if you'd like."

"It's all very new; I need some time to settle in," said his sister. Thank you both for thinking of me and making me feel so much at home. I'll let you know when I've had chance to think it over."

What Katherine could not foresee was that events would very soon precipitate her decision. Fanny Ackroyd's health worsened rapidly from the day her daughter arrived back in Bradford. Within a month she had drawn her last breath with her sons and daughter at her bedside. She was buried next to Jack after a short service attended by her family and a handful of mourners. At the graveside, the sun's rays fought to penetrate the town's mantle of choking grey smoke that was evidence of the increasing prosperity and privileged indifference of this epitome of northern industrial progress.

If the ailing Esholt estate owner recognised the irony of his position, as a mill owner, using all legal and political means to stop Bradford pouring industrial waste into the River Aire, it did not for a moment seem to embarrass him. Pollution continued unabated as mills sluiced away increasing quantities of grease and dirt from thousands of washed fleeces, more than three quarters of the total amount of wool being processed in England at that time. It required heavy rainfall on the hills above and beyond Skipton to flush out the fetid river as it curved past Esholt Hall. At all other times, the stench was intolerable to the Stansfields, who were growing increasingly angry and litigious in the face of the corporation's apparent inertia. When William Stansfield's 1869 interim injunction failed to stem the pollution, the Court of Chancery was invoked to put an end to the nuisance on pain of heavy fines. The following year, with the situation largely unchanged, Bradford was ordered to find a practical solution to the problem by early 1872.

The Council found itself trapped in the jaws of a slowly tightening vice between the foot-dragging mill owners on one hand and the legally backed persistence of William Stansfield and militant townsfolk on the other. Heated debates produced entrenched opinions on both sides leading to stalemate, until the results of trials taking place elsewhere to find an effective treatment pointed to the possibility of a solution. This broke the impasse and resulted in the building of an experimental treatment works at Frizinghall.

Bradford's unique position, nestling within a crescent of hills three miles up a narrow, southerly spur of the Aire valley, dictated the line of its trunk sewer into which all others fed. The obvious place for an experimental treatment plant was at the end of this newly constructed tunnel, where the untreated waste continued to flow into the beck at its lowest point in the borough. Eleven acres of land were purchased at Frizinghall and plans drawn up for the construction of a number of sunken brick-lined tanks containing a variety of permeable materials to filter out solid waste, allowing only purified liquid to be released into the beck. Early in 1871 Josh joined a group of men queuing in the hope of a job with the private company contracted to build the plant. Some of the men had worked with him on the main sewer.

"So you've come to join the shit shifters again," joked Lily's brother, Albert, standing near the front of the queue. "Bit of a come down after the wool exchange isn't it?"

"One job's like another," Josh laughed. "Anyroad, I reckon I'll be well away before the muck flows down here. They say it'll be two years before it's finished. Smell from the beck's a bit strong, though. I reckon Lily's going to be keeping the washtub busy if I get taken on."

"We're only looking for skilled masons and bricklayers just now," said the foreman as Josh reached the front of the queue at a green corrugated iron shed belonging to the Peat Engineering Company.

"That's me," said Josh, offering evidence of his skills. The engineer was satisfied with Josh's journeyman's certificate and account of his work experience and told him to turn up with his mason's tools to start work the following week.

Back at his own front door, the enticing aroma of newly baked bread greeted him as he stepped into the warm parlour. Lily emerged from the pantry carrying a tankard of ale as he shrugged off his coat.

"What's this, love? Celebrating my new job, are we? Aren't you going to join me then, a drink to our continuing prosperity?"

Lily thrust the tankard into her husband's hand. "I'll not be having any," she blushed. "Not right now, at any rate," she added, fixing him with a cheeky grin. It took a few seconds for the penny to drop.

"You're not, are you, love?"

"Yes, isn't it wonderful? I reckon it's near enough two months. I didn't let on because I wanted to be sure. My mam doesn't know yet, I can't wait to tell her."

Josh drank a toast to his son or daughter-to-be and took Lily in his arms. "This one's going to be alright, lass, you'll see. Now, you just take it easy."

"Stop your fussing, Josh. I'll be right as rain so long as I don't have to go back on the looms. And your new job's taken care of that. Anyroad, I'll have your Katherine to help. This new job won't be as dangerous as the sewer, will it?"

"No, love. This time I'll be working in the open and it looks like I'll have your Albert for company again. He was in front of me. It might be a bit smelly, but they pay well and it looks like we're going to need it. Anyroad, I was thinking, why don't we ask our Katherine and the boys to join us for a picnic in Peel Park on Sunday? It can be our celebration.

Your Albert and Sam might like to come an all. I'd ask our John, but I know he's got a meeting at the temperance."

"They don't allow anyone to lark about in Peel Park on Sundays," Lily reminded him. "Why don't we take the train to Shipley and walk up the glen. You've never taken our Sammy nesting, like you promised, and he's twenty-five now. But Katherine's lads will love it and Sammy can show them his favourite nesting spots."

"Then we'll call on your mam and dad. She'll never forgive us if you don't tell her about the baby first."

Many parents with children, all in their Sunday best, made their way down Victoria Road past silent mill buildings and across the river bridge leading to the new park gifted by Titus Salt to his workers for their health and recreation. Gunther and Jack ran ahead as Josh and Lily, Katherine, Albert and Sam weaved their way between happy family groups strolling across the grassy expanse and headed up a long wooded incline to the heather covered glen. At the top a short walk brought them to the rocky crags that served as picnic tables, affording fine views over the sunlit valley.

"You'll be a bit more careful on the rocks this time, eh Sam?" joked Josh.

"Didn't do you much harm, anyroad," replied his brother-in-law. "You wouldn't have met our lass if I hadn't broken my leg. Now then lads," he shouted to Gunther and Jack, "let's see if we can find a lark's nest in the heather. First one that finds eggs gets a treat. You coming, Albert?"

Josh stayed to help Lily and Katherine set out their picnic, recalling the delight of Lily's mother and father on hearing their news. "I've got a good feeling about this one, love," he told her.

"I hope you're right, Josh. There's been too much sorrow for all of us lately. Let's hope our luck's turned at last."

"I found one! I found one!" shouted Gunther excitedly twenty minutes later, running ahead of his brother and uncles. Panting for breath as he arrived at the picnic rock, he opened a fist to disclose a perfect brown-grey skylark egg. "I only took one; there were more in the nest," he confided. "Do I get my treat now?"

"After our sandwiches," Katherine said.

All except Lily helped themselves to a bottle of ale, Albert raising his to head height for a toast. "Congratulations to our clever sister, not forgetting her husband, of course. It's a great day for the Ackroyds and Hodgsons."

"I'll drink to that, and it's even better for having my big sister and her boys here with us," said Josh, raising his bottle to Katherine standing with her arm protectively round Lily's shoulders.

Barely seven months later, Bradford was to see the very public departure of one of its most prominent citizens and the very private arrival of another, spanning three centuries of growth from a small rural village to a prosperous bustling town. Curtains remained drawn at Esholt Hall as a sign of mourning for eighty-one-year-old William Stansfield by his widow, nephew and wife and their three daughters. Meanwhile, at a humble terrace cottage in town, an elderly neighbour had barely entered the front door when she was calling for warm water and clean cloths. Katherine anxiously set about collecting all the necessary requisites, while listening intently for any sounds from upstairs. She had summoned the neighbour, recognised by everyone in the street as their redoubtable and trusty midwife, as soon as her sister-in-law's waters broke as she boiled clothes in the old copper. Carrying a basin with the cloths tucked under an arm, Katherine had just begun to mount the stairs when Lily's sharp cries announced the imminent arrival of her baby. Katherine held Lily's hand as her sister-in-law strained and pushed on the low bed, the neighbour providing a second by second account of her progress until she was able to hold the tiny body in her hands. A lusty cry almost drowned out the joyful exclamation. "It's a boy!"

"He's a big 'un," said Katherine as Lily reached out to cradle her brand-new son. "Look, he's already got lots of hair," said Lily, just like his dad. "We're going to call him William. He's my boy Bill."

"William Ackroyd, that's a fine name," said Katherine, "but he'll get Bill, apart from Sundays."

"Right then, let's get him cleaned up and have a cup of tea to celebrate," said the neighbour. "We want him looking his best for your Josh."

"He'll be right glad it's a boy," said Lily. "He always said he had a good feeling about this one."

* * *

Josh Ackroyd wrapped his pie and pickles lunch in a page of the *Telegraph* and nestled it among the trowels, plumb bob and levels in his satchel. Hoisting the leather bag on to his right shoulder, he kissed his wife goodbye and stepped through the front door of their cottage to begin the mile-and-a-half walk to work. He could smell fresh grass in the breeze from the surrounding hills on this bright summer morning, a measure of the council's success in reducing smoke pollution in the town. He knew it would be different in winter, however, with every house burning coal.

His daily walk along the canal towpath to Frizinghall was a pleasure since the canal company drained the cut in compliance with an order to stop using water from the polluted beck. In the absence of an alternative source of water, the company had no option but to leave the canal high and dry at the risk of losing business to the thriving Midland Railway Company. All that remained of the formerly busy waterway was a narrow strip of stagnant water between sloping banks of black mud, already home to colonies of weeds and discarded household refuse. The canal wharf and warehouse near St.Peter's Church were long gone, with the canal filled in as far down as Wapping. New buildings were transforming that part of Bradford into a modern urban landscape where only fifty years before there were farms and green fields.

Josh was often joined by fellow workers on his daily walks to and from the new sewage treatment works nearing completion in the shadow of the steep hill marking Bolton's lofty perch. Large sunken brick-lined tanks were already filled with a variety of experimental filtering materials, a channel directing a steady flow of waste material into them. A private company was running the plant in partnership with the council. They planned to purify the waste sufficiently to return clean water to the beck and sell the solid matter to local farmers to use as manure. Unfortunately, the plan came unstuck when it was discovered the solid matter would not dry out because it contained so much wool grease. Eventually the company admitted defeat and the experiment was declared a failure. Raw sewage and industrial waste from Bradford sewers continued to flow into the River Aire.

Fearing his skills would soon be no longer required at the treatment works, Josh had called in at the Midland Railway terminus to seek out anyone responsible for hiring workers for the new Frizinghall railway station. All the jobs were taken, but he knew there would be plenty of other work for him in Bradford, where civic and private buildings were being erected with alacrity. He resolved to pay a visit to a few sites, such as the new town hall and the huge mill development at Manningham.

These thoughts were still uppermost in his mind when, at the end of a tiring day, he made his way back along the tow-path and up the steep cobbled street to his home. He was greeted by little William toddling towards him with outstretched arms. In the doorway Lily, already showing signs of a new baby, cautioned her young son to be careful as Katherine took her leave of Gunther and Jack.

"Not staying then?" called Josh as he swept his son up into his arms.

"Not tonight, Josh. I'm walking out and Lily's looking after the boys."

"So you've found a man?" laughed Josh. "About time too, lass. You shouldn't be on the shelf at your age."

"Who says I'm on the shelf, you cheeky bugger. Anyway, for that I'll keep you guessing. See you tomorrow." She reminded each of her boys to be good for their aunt and uncle and made her happy departure on this warm summer evening with the sun still high above the horizon.

Lily beckoned Josh into the house while the boys played in the yard. "I didn't want to say anything in front of Katherine, but your John's in trouble. He's in the Bridewell. One of his mates from Hudson's came to tell me the police took him in after a fight at the Cock and Bottle up the High Street last night. It seems John got right mad when someone called him a coward for not going to the Crimea. He walloped him; knocked him clean out and the man banged his head when he fell. They say he's still out cold in the infirmary. It's probably one of them as had a lucky escape out there, and it's made him bitter. Anyroad, you'll need to see what you can do to get John out."

"The Crimea, that's nearly twenty years ago. The man must be out of his mind."

"Well, he certainly was, taking on your brother, the size of him. Anyroad, I've got your meal ready and you can go after that."

"He'll come to no harm in the Bridewell. It'll give him time to sober up. John's been supping a lot at the Cock and Bottle since our mam died. He'll lose his job at Hudson's if he doesn't buck up."

From a black cooking pot nestling by the fire, Lily tipped two ladles of steaming stew into her husband's plate and cut two thick slices of bread. "I had mine with Katherine and the boys earlier," she said. "But what you said about your John, I reckon he regrets not getting wed so he could look after his mam. He probably thinks he's missed his chance, so he's drowning his sorrows, so to speak."

"It's the mill that gets him down," said Josh. "He always wanted to find a way out, but now it's too late. Anyroad, they might let him out of the Bridewell if we promise to look after him. We haven't got room for him here unless Katherine goes to stay in his house for a couple of nights."

In a cold, damp cell behind Bradford's main police station, Josh found his chastened elder brother suffering a bad hangover from the night before. He said he had no memory of his alleged assault on a fellow drinker.

"The other chap's conscious now so your brother can go with you, but make sure he doesn't go near a pub," the duty sergeant told Josh. "He'll likely be up in front of the beak, so he'd better keep out of trouble or he'll find himself back here, quick as a flash."

Josh gave the necessary assurances and walked John back to the cottage, where Lily offered him a bowlful of stew, seasoned with pithy sisterly advice.

"I know, I know, you probably want me to sign the pledge," John groaned, feeling sorry for himself. "I've been in such a bad way, maybe I should. But it's easier if you've got someone to keep you on the straight and narrow. You're the lucky one, Josh. I only wish lady luck would smile on me."

"It's never too late," comforted Josh, not really believing in his own words. He was very concerned to see his brother in such a low state and wondered how they would be able to keep an eye on him from now on.

Just over a mile away in Lister Park, two lovers walk arm in arm in the gathering twilight. A warm summer breeze carries the low sound of two voices conversing in German, one more fluent than the other, as Georg steers Katherine towards a bench surrounded by tall rhododendron bushes. There, she allows him to take her in his arms and returns his ardent kiss with a breathless, "Ich liebe dich". Her fears about being five years older than Georg and the mother of two children are swept away by the evidence of his feelings for her. As they kiss and caress in the fading light, Katherine looks forward with renewed optimism to a future in this town where both nationalities are engaged in creating wealth from wool.

* * *

There was no dispute as to what happened in the Cock and Bottle the night John Ackroyd struck the man he thought had rudely questioned his courage. Several witnesses testified to John's hitherto good character, saying he had been goaded into retaliating. It was just bad luck his victim had hit his head on a fender as he fell and spent two weeks in hospital with a cracked skull. He was now back home and likely to make a full recovery.

From his lofty position in the wood-panelled courtroom, flanked by three of the town's eminent citizens, magistrate Pickles addressed the smartly dressed accused standing nervously in the dock before him. He acknowledged John's previous unblemished record and the testimonials to his good character. However, he took into consideration that excessive drinking had played a large part in the assault. He admonished John for succumbing to the "demon drink" and advised him strongly to change his ways if he was to avoid further appearances before the Bench. "Taking everything into consideration, I am going to fine you thirty shillings, to be paid in full by the end of this quarter." With that, the magistrate brought down his gavel with a sharp crack, gathered up his robe and retired through a door at the rear of the courtroom.

John, dazed and abashed by the experience, was helped down from the dock by a policeman to join Josh, Lily, Katherine and Georg who, with other well wishers, escorted him out into the street. "I'd suggest going for an ale to celebrate, but I don't think that's a good idea in the circumstances," quipped Josh. "Let's go back to our house for a cup of tea and some of Lily's baking".

Back in his brother's parlour, John found his voice to thank them all for supporting him in court. "It's been a right nasty do, but I suppose I've only got myself to blame, so I'll think on."

"Well now, Georg and I have got plans," said Katherine to lighten the mood. And we'd like to include you in them too, John." All eyes turned on the pair as she announced, "Georg and I have known each other for many years, since we lived in Germany in fact. It's just wonderful that we've found each other again here in Bradford. What I really mean to say is..."

"...we want to get married," interrupted Georg, sensing Katherine's sudden shyness in front of her family, "and soon. We've discussed it and we'd like John to stay with us until he gets himself straight, so to speak. There's a job going at Delius's," Georg continued, and turning to John. "I can put in a good word for you, if you'd like."

"It'll give you a new start, John," urged his sister.

As everyone in the room expressed their congratulations and appreciation of the generous offer, John, looking almost as dazed as when he left court, struggled to come to terms with the unexpected turn of events. With all eyes on him, he studied dancing yellow flames for a full half minute before making his characteristically taciturn response. "Firstly, congratulations – and thank you, both. I'll think on and let you have my reply tomorrow. I don't want to seem ungrateful, but I just need time to think it through. Thank you again, both of you," he concluded, shaking Georg's hand and giving his sister a kiss.

The mood in the room changed again as the outside door swung open and a lively not too clean four-year-old bounded in, followed closely behind by his younger sister, who promptly ran up to sit on her Uncle John's knee.

"This is going to be your new uncle, Uncle Georg," Katherine informed Bill and Hannah, who were attracted to their mother's baking laid out invitingly on the parlour table. "The new Board school will help to keep these two out of mischief," she told the room. "But they'll have to be watched now there's water in the canal again. At least it's a lot cleaner since they stopped the beck pouring into it."

"Now you mention it, the council's had to take over from the contractors at Frizinghall and sewage is just going back into the beck there," said Josh. "William Stansfield must be turning in his grave. His nephew's living at the hall now, and says he's going to keep fighting."

"They're trying to get a court injunction to stop the corporation putting sewage in the river, according to the *Observer*. That should put a rat among the kittens in the new Town Hall," contributed Georg, who had not quite mastered colloquial English. "But we have a clean canal at last."

"They say canal can't compete with the railway," put in John. "They reckon canal's finished, or soon will be. Hudson's not moving with the times sticking with it. Other mills are moving cloth faster in railway wagons, so I reckon he'll have to change his ways before long."

"There seems to be nothing but change these days," said Josh. "Anyone who left Bradford five years ago wouldn't recognise it if they came back now. Everyone's in such a scramble."

"Yes, but Bradford's becoming a wealthy town," Georg countered.

"All right for them as has the brass," said Josh.

"But we've got the new parks for picnicking and children to run about in and there are railway excursions to the countryside," said Georg. "We've got Forster's new Board schools, cleaner streets and gas lamps and they're even talking of having tramcars pulled by horses. It's all got to be paid for and it's the woollen mills that are making the money the council spends."

"Then they should spend some of it building better houses for their workers," objected Lily. "Some of the cottages are little better than hovels compared to the fancy houses in Manningham, where most of the owners live."

"It will all change for the better – it just takes time," Georg insisted. "We'll all benefit from Bradford's growing prosperity in the long run."

"Well I hope you're right," said John. "It's us that makes the prosperity and we're entitled to a decent share of it."

To change the subject away from contentious politics, Josh announced that he also had something to tell them. "I intended to keep it a secret a bit longer, but while I was working on the Piece Hall, I dropped into The Swan on the other side of Market Street for a pint. I got talking to the owner who said he was looking for a new landlord. Well, I've always quite fancied the idea of running a pub," he beamed, to gasps of surprise from his in-laws. "How much brass it makes is up to me. Lily's not too sure, but I'm thinking of taking it on. There's no house attached, so we'll go on living here and if I don't like it I can always go back to my trade."

The irony of Josh's announcement in view of his brother's recent drinking problem was not lost on the others who were searching for something to say. It was Katherine who spoke up for her brother. "Well, why not give it a try? It's a nice little pub, right in the centre of town and not far from here. And, as you say, if it's not right, you can always go back to the building work." No one in the room was prepared to articulate, there and then, what was going through their mind – that Josh would be in a better position to keep a careful eye on him if brother John could be persuaded to make The Swan his regular instead of the Cock and Bottle.

Many Bradfordians felt that a remarkable era in the modern history of the town had ended with the death of Sir Titus Salt, leaving an indelible legacy on the banks of the river at Saltaire for the wonderment of future generations. Such was his stature that special trains ferried hundreds of mourners from Bradford to pay their respects at his last resting place in the family mausoleum next to his beloved church.

In London, the seeds of even more dramatic change for Bradford were being sown with the granting of a perpetual injunction to Esholt Hall, prohibiting the council from discharging untreated sewage into the beck and consequently into the River Aire. The move came as the new network of sewers was delivering more than 30,000 gallons an hour to the still inefficient Frizinghall treatment plant. For the council, it was a problem destined to grow in proportion to the town's expansion. For the Stansfield sisters, the injunction would prove to be a Pyrrhic victory with far reaching consequences for their privileged way of life.

Greener Grass

Anna Storey checked her hair in the hall mirror one more time before letting herself out into the street and locking the front door behind her. Light was just starting to fade on this mild autumn evening as she made her way along the row of terrace houses towards Keighley railway station. The years since leaving service at Esholt Hall had not been kind to Anna. Her five-year marriage to John Clegg, a brewery drayman, had produced a second daughter, Tilly, but had proved to be a disaster since her husband turned out to be a drunkard and a wife-beater. She remembered with horror that any night of the week might find him staggering home late and demanding to be fed.

"I did cook a meal for you, John, but it spoilt when you weren't back."

"Don't give me excuses, woman. Get me some food and quick about it," he said, grabbing her by the hair and pushing her towards the kitchen sink.

"And I don't have any money to buy food 'cos you spend it down the pub," she pleaded, protecting her head with a raised arm as he rained blows on her back.

"Don't be gobby with me, woman," he said, punching her on the side of the head. "If you think I spend it down the pub then I might as well prove you right." With that, he would leave, slamming the front door and frightening the children out of their sleep. Only his sudden but, to her relief, timely death under a full cask of ale had relieved her of the beatings and abuse that had characterised her life for so long. She took the blows to protect her two young daughters and rescue what little wages she could after her husband's drunken forays.

The gratuity from her secret benefactor ceased when she married and for the past five years the three of them had been living in near penury. Desperate to provide for Constance and Tilly, she had resorted to making money on the streets when the pot on the mantelpiece was empty. With her growing daughters placing greater demands on her purse, Anna resorted more frequently to selling her body for a reward she could not match in the normal workplace. She chose to pursue her business well away from home, travelling by train as far as Bradford where she felt anonymous among the other unfortunates whose lives had been blighted by misdemeanour or misfortune. Despite looking a good ten years older than her thirty-four years, Anna still cut a good figure and never failed to attract customers prepared to pay for her services in a convenient close or stairwell. Any romantic flames were quickly doused however, and would-be suitors sternly rebuffed to avoid unwanted male involvement in her life. For Anna, it was a case of once bitten, twice shy as far as men were concerned.

Constance, now a pretty sixteen-year-old with chestnut curls, blue eyes and a coquettish smile, looked after her younger sister during her mother's absences, but felt that life was passing her by. She yearned for adventure away from the grim terraces of her hometown and often put herself at risk by roaming the streets as public houses turned out in the hope of meeting the person who would transform her life. Outside the Queens Head in Cavendish Street, it was the sight of a scarlet uniform and the handsome young soldier inside it that took her fancy. Eavesdropping on their conversation, she discovered that Harry Pratt was home on leave from his regiment in the Borders and enjoying a drink with his pals. Constance snared him with her eyes, edged herself closer and asked, "When do you have to go back?

Harry Pratt had noticed this attractive young woman taking an interest in him and decided to test it out. "I've still got two days left," he told her, ignoring the taunts of his pals. "If you can get out, I could meet you at the market tomorrow morning."

"I'll see you just inside at ten o'clock, then," she told him, feeling slightly breathless. At dizzying speed, Constance had lost her heart to the eighteen-year-old soldier. As she made her way home, she was already scheming to follow him back north, where she would find work and shelter near his barracks. In the meantime, it would remain her secret.

The following two days passed in a whirlwind of brief assignations as the lovers grew to know each other, Constance keen to avoid raising the suspicions of her mother by staying out of the house too long. She was torn between betraying her mother's love and pursuing what she considered to be her true path to happiness. Then one evening, Anna arrived home to find a note waiting for her on the kitchen table. Tears of frustration and betrayal wet her cheeks as she read that her eldest daughter had left home, saying she did not want to be a financial burden. She had left Tilly with the next-door neighbour. Constance added that she really was in love and asked her mother to forgive her for leaving like this, but she felt it was for the best. She loved them both and would write.

Resettled in temporary lodgings in Berwick-on-Tweed, Constance soon made friends with Jenny Smith, a girl of the same age working as a live-in lady's maid in a large baronial mansion, a mile from Harry Pratt's barracks. Jenny put in a good word for her new friend at the mansion, securing her a housekeeping job. Constance felt she had never been happier, having found the love of her life and grasped her freedom away from the misery and grime of the West Riding. At every opportunity she met Harry for long walks along the sea shore and it was on one of these romantic rambles that he broke the news of his regiment's impending departure for the Far East.

"I'll be away for maybe a year at most," he told her, feeling in his pocket for a tiny, square box. "But I'll be thinking of you all the time. Will you wait for me?"

"Yes, of course I will, Harry my love. I'll miss you more than you know. I just want you back as soon as possible and in one piece."

That evening, his last before embarking for Burma with his regiment, Harry Pratt shared a high-backed settle in front of a cheery log fire in the snug of the Red Lion Inn in Castlegate. He extracted the tiny box from his pocket and managed to force out the question he had been rehearsing all day. "Connie, my love, will you accept this ring as a token of our engagement?"

Laughing with relief and pleasure, she offered him her left hand. "Oh yes, I will, Harry. I do."

Later that evening, just out of sight of the guardhouse, Constance bade a tearful farewell to her soldier with a lingering kiss and the whispered words, "Come home soon. I love you."

* * *

In Bradford, passers-by still checked their stride to gaze up at the ornate, gilded bell tower that soared above the magnificent Venetian Gothic Town Hall opened a decade earlier. If they happened to be in the vicinity at midday, they slowed to listen as a thirteen-bell carillon sent the notes of a well-known hymn tune floating across the rooftops. This magnificent status symbol confirmed for its citizens that Bradford could at last rival the brio of its nearest neighbour Leeds. No amount of civic pride or pomp, however, could disguise the nagging fact that Bradford was still one of the worst polluting boroughs in the country. Inside the decorous council chamber anxious voices of the great and the good thrashed out the vexing question of how to deal with an ever-increasing volume of raw sewage, mixed with wool scourings, pouring into the River Aire at Shipley. The council remained under constant pressure to mitigate the problem, but so far had only resorted to expanding the

Frizinghall sewage treatment works to cope with the flow. It could not keep pace with Bradford's expanding woollen industry and had no answer for the grease-contaminated sewage that defied all known attempts to deal with it.

Back working at Frizinghall, a visibly aged and greyer Josh often looked back on one of the most enjoyable times of his life, as landlord of The Swan public house in Market Street. He and Lily worked long hours to learn the trade and provide a welcome that was to attract many new regulars over the years. They were not successful in moderating John's drinking, which was thought to be partly responsible for his death, officially ascribed to chronic emphysema brought on by a life of unrelenting toil in unhealthy environments. He was laid to rest next to his mother and father in a simple ceremony attended by family and a few workmates.

The bitter blow that changed Josh from God-fearing to a cynical, God-baiting agnostic was the premature death of the love of his life, Lily, who failed to survive a stillbirth at the end of an unplanned pregnancy. Her funeral at Undercliffe was attended by one of the biggest turnouts seen there in recent memory, a testament to her popularity among The Swan regulars.

Josh stayed on at the pub for a few more years, but his heart was no longer in it. Without Lily at his side, he found it difficult to play the cheerful mine host and his regulars began to melt away. He increasingly found common cause with the hustlers and other petty criminals who increasingly frequented his bar until the owner announced the pub was to be closed and demolished to make way for a large Market Street development.

Left on his own, he was grateful for the help of sister Katherine and her husband Georg in helping to bring up his three children. Bill, then a strapping fourteen-year-old, played his part in looking after siblings Hannah and brother James, but was actively seeking a job to ease the family's fortunes. He was fascinated by new horse-drawn trams that were proving a very popular form of public transport. Because they could be a problem on some steep inclines out of the town centre, the council was investigating powering the trams with electricity like the ones newly introduced to Blackpool promenade. Young Bill wanted to be part of this cutting-edge transport, even if, initially, it meant working with squads of navvies setting rails into cobbled streets and helping to erect wire-supporting stanchions. He applied for and gained an apprenticeship working out of the Manningham Lane depot and by his eighteenth birthday, was helping to lay tracks for the electric extension to Bolton Junction. By now, his eyes were firmly focussed on his ultimate ambition – to become a tram driver.

Meanwhile, less than a mile to the west in the valley bottom, a main sewer poured out a constant flow of foul-smelling effluent, most of which still found its way, untreated, into the beck and thence to the River Aire. At Esholt Hall, Henry Stansfield and his daughters vowed to take Bradford to the highest authority in the land, if necessary, to rid themselves of the waterborne ordure that so afflicted their otherwise privileged lives.

* * *

Constance Storey grew increasingly frustrated by the lack of news from Burma, tearfully confiding to Jenny Smith that she had not heard from Harry for over a month. She could gain little information from his regiment, which took the view that it only needed to inform next of kin. Girls claiming to be engaged to soldiers were dismissed as unimportant camp followers. Along with other lovelorn females, she took to hanging around the barracks in an evening in the hope of picking up any titbit of news about her betrothed. Any rumours rapidly grew into facts among the desperate assembly, leaving Constance poised between hope and despair. Then, after several weeks without any news, she returned to her lodgings one evening to find a letter waiting for her from Harry Pratt's parents. In the belief that she already shared their knowledge, the letter commiserated with her on the death in action of her fiancé. The news hit her like a punch in the stomach. With tears streaming down her cheeks, she read and re-read the fateful words to try to make sense of what they were telling her.

Unable to eat or sleep in her grief, Constance cried on and off for a whole day and night while Jenny did her best to comfort her. "I might as well go back to Keighley," she sobbed. "There's nothing for me here now."

"You always said you were glad to come north to escape the smoke and grime of Yorkshire," Jenny reminded her. "Look, I've applied for a more senior position at Floors Castle and I would love you to come with me. I'll put in a good word for you there and we can share lodgings again. Do say you'll come."

After a week grieving for her lost love, Constance gave notice to her employer and moved with her friend to the Scottish Borders town of Kelso, where she soon found employment as a maid at the grand home of the Duke of Roxburghe.

At first she immersed herself in long hours of hard work at the huge castle as a way of blunting the pain of her loss. Eventually, the spirited eighteen-year-old began to re-emerge and took every opportunity to enjoy the limited pleasures of the agricultural community. It was not long before she caught the eye of a young stockman as she and Jenny sauntered by the livestock market, sizing up likely suitors. Donald Jameson, four years her senior, would not ordinarily have got a second glance from her. Dressed in a hodden jacket and trousers, dung-covered boots and a lovat cap, he had an unruly ginger beard and weather-reddened cheeks. Perhaps it was his startling blue eyes that revived a forgotten and rather pleasant feeling in her.

"Who's he staring at," asked Jenny as they leaned on railings surrounding the auction ring. "Not me, I hope, cheeky beggar."

"It's interesting; let's just watch this sale," replied Constance, not realising her future was being determined within the uneven dun-coloured stones of the noisy enclosure, stuffy from jostling beasts and encircling farmers. "I wonder if he's married."

"If it's Donald you're wondering about, he's as free as the air," said a man to her left, to Constance's intense embarrassment. Her question answered, Constance persuaded Jenny to linger by the auction ring for a bit longer until she could engage the young stockman in casual conversation. Her interest in him proved to be mutual and Jenny made an excuse to be on her way.

It was not long before the farming community was buzzing with gossip about the new romance involving a girl from England. The wedding took place in Selkirk Parish Church, followed by a traditional ceilidh at the home farm attended by more tartan-clad relatives than Constance could have imagined. Notably absent were any relatives or friends from over the border. Constance decided her memories were still too raw and she preferred a complete break from her Yorkshire past. Donald Jameson took his new wife on a two-day honeymoon to Melrose before settling her into his humble farm cottage, which enjoyed a commanding view of the western flank of the Ettrick valley.

Less than a year later, the interwoven fates of players in the Bradford clean-up saga took another decisive turn in the picturesque setting of the Yorkshire Dales. High above Buckden village in Upper Wharfedale, the grouse moor was ablaze with pink heather blossom as Major General Henry Crompton Stansfield, together with a group of tweed-clad gentlemen, headed back towards their shooting box earlier than planned after a good morning's sport. The general felt unwell and had to be supported into the building, where he collapsed. The local doctor was summoned from the village, but by the time he arrived on the scene, Henry Stansfield was beyond help. Thus ended the male line of the Crompton Stansfields of Esholt Hall, leaving only his three daughters to inherit the estate and carry on the fight.

* * *

Economic shockwaves travelled throughout Bradford's woollen industry, which had only been used to unrestrained growth and wealth creation. First came protracted and bitter industrial unrest at the mammoth Manningham Mills, resulting in four thousand workers being locked out. Families neared starvation as the stand-off continued for five months. Meanwhile, changing fashion and international protectionism led to a dramatic loss of orders for Sir Titus Salt's speciality alpaca and mohair cloth. The company was forced to call receivers in to their showpiece Saltaire mills, to the concern of other wool entrepreneurs. If Salts could go down, they reasoned, how healthy was the rest of the woollen industry? Many sensed they were witnessing the beginning of a new industrial and social order.

In contrast to this industrial upheaval, Bill Ackroyd was enjoying a rare midweek break in the tranquil setting of Guiseley cricket ground. Together with his cousin Gunther Heller and other members of Bankfoot Cricket Club, he had been invited to play in a limited-overs friendly against one of the best teams in the Wharfe valley. So they proved to be, winning by a respectable margin before lunch, leaving time for some traditional hospitality before the Bankfoot players needed to catch a train back to Bradford from the station across the road.

A couple of dozen passengers stood about the platform as the half-past-three stopping train to Bradford, via Esholt, Baildon, Shipley, Frizinghall and Manningham, steamed into view. A short stop to transfer goods and passengers was punctuated by the guard's whistle and green flag to signal clearance to depart. Bill and his team mates parked their cricket bags on the overhead racks and settled into facing seats of a compartment in the second carriage as the train slowly picked up speed on the downhill incline towards Spring Wood, passing under Leeds Road on a right-hand curve leading to Esholt junction a quarter of a mile away.

The cricketers were lost in lively conversation about the disappointing outcome of the day's play when the sound of an engine whistle penetrated their compartment. Bill glanced through the window to his left in time to see the black smoke-box of an approaching engine heading straight for them. As if in a trance, he realised the engine was on the same track and was not going to stop. Shouting a warning he dived to the floor as the awful sound of splintering wood, shattering glass and a series of screeching metallic impacts filled the air. The noise seemed to go on for a long time, ending suddenly as the carriage rocked to a standstill with the distant hiss of escaping steam and cries of trapped and injured passengers in carriages to the rear. Suffering no more than bruises, his team-mates picked themselves up and rushed to lower the window on the collision side to see what had happened. On the Leeds line, the rear carriages of the Ilkley train were stationary, the leading one apparently fused into the third carriage of the Bradford train. It was impossible to see further back towards Guiseley due to the curvature of the track, but the shouts and cries, hissing steam and broken glass and timber scattered about suggested general havoc.

Trapped on one side by the Ilkley train, the cricketers and other uninjured passengers from the first two carriages of the Bradford train clambered down on to the track and ran back to see if they could help. A scene of total devastation greeted them where the Ilkley train had smashed into their six rear carriages, reducing some almost to splinters. On the other side of the wreckage, wisps of smoke and escaping steam indicated where the Ilkley-bound engine lay on its side against an embankment.

Soon able-bodied passengers were joined by local residents who had heard the crash. They were followed a few minutes later by policemen and stretcher bearers who pulled at the wreckage to free trapped passengers and convey them four hundred yards up the track to the main road and horse-drawn ambulances. Bill and Gunther refused any help, choosing to continue helping in the rescue until everyone was accounted for. The team collected their kits from their undamaged compartment and made their way back to Leeds Road, where carriages were waiting to take stranded passengers to Bradford and Ilkley. It was only as they headed down Hollins Hill towards Shipley that Bill suddenly shivered with cold and delayed shock as he realised how close he and Gunther had come to serious injury or even death. Gone was the earlier light-hearted banter, now there was only a sober silence as each man replayed his mental picture over and over again. In due course, Bill was to read in the *Bradford Daily Telegraph* that an inquiry decided that practical and systematic signalling errors were at the root of the crash, which had cost five deaths and thirty injuries.

* * *

In spite of challenging trading conditions, a new dawn arose for Salts Mill with its purchase by four Bradford businessmen, who promised to modernise methods of production and marketing. One of the four, John Roberts, the son of a farmer and an expert in the woollen industry, proved to have the ideas and entrepreneurial skills to lift the mill out of the doldrums. Within three years he became the sole owner and had looms working to full capacity again, employing a labour force of over two thousand. Thus the gloom was lifted from the model village and an atmosphere of carnival and fun pervaded Saltaire Park across the river from the mill when what would prove to be one of Bradford's most famous outdoor attractions opened for business. Young and old queued to pay their ha'penny to ride on the quarter-mile-long Shipley Glen Tramway up the tree-lined escarpment from the park to the popular moorland picnic spot and amusement park.

One young woman, who was catching the eyes of all the young men that day, linked arms with her mother as she strolled among the boulder-strewn heather. Anna Storey knew there was no better place to find a husband for her nineteen-year-old daughter, Tilly, who envied her sister's new life in Scotland. Had she known the rigour of life for a farmer's wife, she might have envied Constance less and been content with her familiar existence among the mills and chimney-stacks of her native county. But it was Tilly's restless nature and quest for new experiences that was to take her on the adventure of her life, joining thousands of emigrants from all parts of the British Isles streaming across the Atlantic to the New World.

On the other side of town, Bill's youngest brother, James, proudly strolled through Lister Park wearing a brand-new uniform of the West Yorkshire Regiment, his latest girl on his arm. His dislike of routine had James moving from job to job after leaving elementary schooling, but without gaining any feeling of satisfaction. He spotted a recruiting poster for the county regiment, which seemed to promise everything he was looking for – travel, adventure and personal challenge – and readily accepted the Queen's shilling. To his surprise and delight, his scarlet walking-out uniform provided an unexpected bonus for the young soldier. Young women were drawn to it like moths to a candle flame, much to the envy of brother Bill and his friends. Once through his basic training at York barracks, he was expecting to be posted overseas, a prospect he anticipated with particular relish.

Tilly's eventual departure for America was a severe blow to her mother. Although Anna did nothing to thwart her daughter's wanderlust, she found it difficult to fill the void in her life caused by Tilly's absence and steadily sank into self-neglect and early dementia. With nobody willing to take care of her, she was committed to the workhouse at Little Horton, where she would remain for the rest of her life among more than five hundred aged and insane inmates.

* * *

Towards the end of the nineteenth century, the often difficult relationship between mill owner and employee became even more fractious in an increasingly hardening market for woollen products. The five-month lockout of workers at Manningham Mills was to prove the catalyst for the creation of the Independent Labour Party in Bradford. Its founders believed that a workers' party was the only way they could achieve changes in their terms of employment and working conditions.

Josh, now a grizzled and rancorous 59-year-old, was attracted by the ideology of children's champion Margaret McMillan, an ILP member, whom he heard speaking at a Fabian meeting. He joined the chorus of activists loudly denouncing what they described as the ruthless exploitation of the working classes for profit. Not surprisingly, his stance attracted the opprobrium of the mill owners, rendering him unemployable wherever their influence extended. Fortunately, his job with the council at Frizinghall was beyond the reach of those who were anxious to silence him and ongoing extensions to the plant promised him work for the foreseeable future.

Bradford's elevation to a County Borough only served to heighten the distinction between the town's growing wealth and status and its darker reputation as a source of serious pollution and worker unrest. The fouling of the River Aire was top of the agenda at the newly formed Yorkshire Rivers Board, whose members vociferously demanded action. The corporation responded with continuing extensions to Frizinghall, but to no avail. It was by now established that Bradford faced a unique problem due to it being the nation's principal wool processing centre. A totally new approach was called for, using the most up-to-date technical, chemical and biological methods to treat the mixture of sewage and wool scourings that threatened to submerge the town hall in lengthy and costly litigation.

The search for a solution eventually took an ironical turn when the corporation was ordered to find a completely new site for a treatment works capable of dealing with all Bradford's waste. The Borough Surveyor announced to a bemused council chamber that local topography dictated only one possible site for this works, a location, which happened to be the source of the most virulent imprecations rained down on council heads for thirty years. A resultant Parliamentary Bill paved the way for an approach to be made to the three daughters of the late Major General Henry Stansfield for the purchase of their entire Esholt Estate. The Misses Mary, Elizabeth and Consuello Stansfield were in no mood to sacrifice their inheritance for a sewage works, however, and the struggle for ownership of 1700 acres of prime Yorkshire country estate was underway. The corporation applied to Parliament for compulsory purchase powers, only to meet the sisters' implacable opposition at a subsequent inquiry. The town won a partial victory when they were granted a provisional order to acquire 529 acres, including Esholt Hall. This led to a long and costly fight with the sisters until a Select Committee of the House of Commons refused to confirm the order. So it was back to square one with the sisters having won the first round in the battle.

Oblivious of the momentous struggle taking place to rid the new city of Bradford of the last vestiges of medieval squalor, Bill Ackroyd's attention was distracted by the two current loves of his life. At the age of twenty-seven he had worked his way up through the corporation tramways department to achieve his long-held ambition to become a driver. No happier man stood on the front lower deck of a new open-top electric tramcar as it rattled its way from the main post office in Forster Square up Bolton Road to Wapping and Undercliffe.

Bill acknowledged the greetings of regular passengers and passers-by on his daily route, giving an especially warm wave as he passed a large grocer's shop garlanded with a row of dead rabbits hanging on hooks outside. If the gaslit interior was not too busy, he could rely on an equally warm response from one of the apron-clad shop girls. She was the girl he was planning to court, but not without stern-faced opposition from the proprietors of J and M Smith's Grocery Emporium. They entertained grander ambitions for their youngest daughter, Mary. They never tired of telling her how they started their business from nothing and were now among the better-off trading families in Bradford. They could not understand why she would want to walk out with a tram driver nearly ten years her senior when she could have her choice of the city's unattached young gentlemen, guaranteeing her a life of comfort. If she insisted on making her bed this way, they warned her, then she must lie on it and take the consequences.

Her parents' opposition only strengthened the resolve of their strong-willed, eighteen-year-old daughter to get close to the man whose eyes first looked into hers when he called at the shop to buy a pie for his supper. It was love at first bite, leading to Bill's regular shopping visits. Realising he had failed to win the approval of her parents, Mary took to meeting him close by in Lister Park where he eventually asked the girl with the open face and ready smile if she would marry him.

"Yes, I want to marry you, Bill, but they'll never give their consent."

"Then we'll get wed without it."

"But my dad knows everyone in Bradford. He'll make sure they all know he hasn't given his permission and no one will marry us," said Mary, on the verge of tears.

"Then we'll get married somewhere else. Have you heard of Gretna Green? They say you can get married there in the blacksmith's shop. You've just got to stay over the border in Scotland for a few days, that's all. Once we're wed there's nothing they can do."

"Oh, I don't know, Bill. I don't want to upset my mam, that's all. I need time to think."

"I love you, Mary, and I know you love me. I won't let you come to any harm; just trust me. We have a right to make a life for ourselves, not for our parents."

"I love you too, Bill. I'll give you my answer soon, promise."

Strollers in Lister Park that Sunday evening smiled to see two young people enjoying a passionate and lingering kiss on a secluded bench in the shade of a tall sycamore tree.

* * *

It had taken Constance Jameson some time to adjust to the seasonal rhythm of farming, but the beauty of the Ettrick valley and the friendliness of the local community won her over to life in the Borders. The early years of her marriage to Donald were particularly hard following the births of first a son and then a daughter in the confines of their basic but and ben. With her husband out in the fields all day and two babies tying her to the hillside two-room cottage, she often longed for the opportunity to join in the hustle and bustle of Selkirk on market day. But should her spirits flag at the end of a particularly trying day, they were revived by the arresting sight of Foulshiels Hill glowing salmon pink as it reflected the dying rays of the sun sliding below Deuchar Law.

Constance checked that the children were sound asleep and added more seasoning to her cooking before stepping outside into the fading palette of a particularly beautiful sunset. She loved to catch a first glimpse of Donald trudging his weary way up the steep path to the cottage in the gloamin', anticipating her first grown-up conversation since dawn. He was her link with the outside world, slaking her thirst for news and gossip. This evening there was more of a lightness to Donald's step and he half ran the final few yards, sweeping her off her feet in a swirling embrace.

"Careful, love, you'll have us both on the ground. Have you come into money or something?"

"Better than that, lassie. We're moving down the valley and we're going to have a proper farm with land, livestock, outbuildings, the lot. Uncle Angus didn't have any sons so he left The Mains to me in his will. My reward for working for him all these years, I suppose. Isn't that great?"

Constance was quick to absorb this surprising news. "You mean, we'll have our own room and the children will have theirs?"

"And rooms to spare, lass. Now, I have a terrible hunger so let's get the supper on. But we'll have a dram first to celebrate."

Aunt Katherine and Uncle Georg, both by now respected citizens of some standing in Bradford, were already waiting in the booking hall with their son Gunther when Bill and Mary arrived at Forster Square Station. Katherine, now in her sixties, still cut a sprightly figure despite her steel-grey hair. Georg sported a grey beard and generous corporation, spanned by a gold watch chain, evidence of his accomplishment and wealth. They greeted Bill and Mary warmly and handed them tickets for a compartment in the second-class carriage that was to take them on their journey to Carlisle and from there, on to Gretna Green by local train. Katherine learned about the plight of the young couple from their son Gunther, who had become a close friend of his younger cousin in the cricket team at Odsal. Decrying what they described as the snobbery of the nouveau riche, they decided to help Bill and Mary by paying for their train tickets and a boarding house in Scotland.

With final hugs and grateful thanks through the open carriage window, Bill and Mary took the last two seats in their compartment to the sound of slamming doors and the guard's shrill whistle. Bill decided to keep to himself his feelings of slight apprehension, as he was about to undertake his first train journey since the crash at Esholt junction.

"My mam and dad will go mad when they read my letter," said Mary as the station buildings began to slide past the carriage window. "Do you think they'll come looking for us?"

"Did you tell them where we're going?"

"No, but they might guess," said Mary, giving Bill an anxious glance.

"Look, we'll cross that bridge if we come to it. Just relax and enjoy the scenery. The main thing, Mary, is that we're together at last. And that's what we both want isn't it?"

"Yes, of course," Mary replied, blushing at the sudden unwanted interest of the other passengers.

The young runaways completed the first leg of their journey at Keighley, where they transferred to the Carlisle express. An hour later, Mary defied the warning notice above her head, to lean out of the open compartment window and stare in awe at the curving majesty of Batty Moss viaduct about to carry them across the wide Ribblehead valley. Her wonder at the changing landscape continued until the train steamed into the grand surroundings of Carlisle station, where they changed platforms for the last leg of their journey. It was only a short train ride to Gretna Green station, where Bill hired a waiting pony and trap to take them to their lodging house on the edge of the village. The driver, used to meeting dozens of young runaways over the years, spoke only to tell them the fare. But nothing could blunt Mary's elation at being across the border in Scotland's most romantic village with the man she loved. Her elation, moderated by only occasional twinges of anxiety, created a radiance Bill had never seen before in his young bride-to-be.

A lone piper in full Highland dress kept vigil outside the blacksmith's forge as Bill and Mary took their turn at the anvil. To the plaintive strains of the bagpipes they pledged their troth and signed their names to witness their exquisite act of defiance. They kissed on invitation to do so, and Bill paid his dues before they made way for the next couple, a middle-aged farmer by the look of his ruddy complexion and a shy young woman, probably fifteen years his junior. Not forgetting to tip the piper for good luck, Bill slipped an arm round Mary's waist as the two of them set off for their lodgings, feeling they were walking on air. They were not due to catch their train back to Carlisle until early the following day. In the meantime, they exulted in the fulfilment of their union and in anticipation of the tiny garret room with its view across flat meadowland to the muddy expanse of the Solway, a vision that would be stamped on their memories for a lifetime.

* * *

Taking over the running of the farm was easy for Donald Jameson after the years he had spent working there as a stockman. However, his pride in having fathered a son and heir was tempered by the boy's apparent reluctance to see farming as his future. Arthur liked nothing better than helping to mend or maintain the few bits of machinery scattered around the farm. However, his distaste for livestock was all too evident. His sister Fiona was showing every sign of being bookish, encouraged by her mother, who wanted her daughter to avoid becoming a reluctant farm bride if she was clever enough to carve out a career for herself in teaching. Constance was fully absorbed in the life of the farm, able to turn her hand to everything from bookkeeping to helping to deliver a lamb when the need arose. With her half-sister in America, she could no longer see any reason to visit her Yorkshire origins and every reason to blend into her new community where she felt she truly belonged.

"He's a bonny baby, right enough. Didn't I tell you we'd make fine babies," said Donald, proudly cradling his newborn son. "He's come as a bit of a surprise after his brother and sister, but he's no less welcome for that. And see, he's even got red hair, the mark of a true Scot."

"He's half English," Constance reminded him.

"But we'll give him a Scottish name."

"I've already thought of that; how about Gordon? That's a name that straddles the border."

"Can we settle for Donald Gordon then? I think that covers everything."

"So long as he's known as Gordon," she insisted.

"That's just fine with me, lassie," said Donald as the baby stirred in his arms. "He's got a good pair of lungs on him; they'll be good for calling in the beasts."

"What makes you think he'll be a farmer? He might be clever and want to go to university. We'll just have to see."

"Well, we'll just need to make more sons then to work on the farm."

"That's enough of that. We have enough mouths to feed as it is," Constance scolded him. "Anyway, I'm going to feed him now, so you can go about your business."

As was often the case in the fast-changing society at the end of the nineteenth and beginning of the twentieth centuries, the joy of new life was overshadowed by loss and grief. In 1901, the whole nation mourned the death, on the Isle of Wight, of its longest-serving monarch. Aged eighty-one, Victoria had been on the throne for sixty-three years, so long that there were very few who could remember much about life before her long reign began in 1837. The outpouring of grief was as much about the passing of an era of unprecedented growth and stability as fear of what the future without her reassuring presence might bring. Her son and heir to the throne, Edward VII, did not find favour with all of his countrymen because of his indulgent lifestyle. The new kingdom held its breath as it contemplated its journey into the unknown.

* * *

The coach, still bearing the initials WRCS in large italics on its deeply lacquered doors and pulled by two greys, turned off Harrogate Road just beyond Apperley Bridge railway station, passing a small stone lodge as it joined a wide driveway. Two hundred yards further on, the drive bent to the right, affording the horses an easy trot down a gentle incline and along a straight tree-lined avenue framing the distant outline of Esholt Hall. From her leather-upholstered seat inside, Elizabeth Crompton Stansfield glanced from side to side at the verdant Aire Valley where she had spent the whole of her thirty-eight years. Although it would be a dreadful loss to have to give up this idyllic landscape, especially for such an unwholesome development as a sewage treatment works, she intuited that the increasing pace of change in the new century was unstoppable. A unique era had passed with the death of Queen Victoria the previous year although, of the sisters, she was the only one hard-headed and pragmatic enough to recognise it. She considered Mary and Consuelo to be in a state of denial, clinging to the belief that they could hold off mounting demands for them to sell their birthright.

Bradford Corporation, itself under considerable pressure to find an effective treatment for its continuing waste problem, tried once more to obtain the permission of Parliament to acquire a parcel of land, which would include most of the Esholt estate. The House of Lords threw it out, but the Commons replied with an Act of Parliament requiring the city to create a sewage treatment works, as directed, by the end of the current year. This prompted the urgent meeting at Bradford Town Hall from which Elizabeth was returning with the latest news for her sisters, who had appointed her their representative.

Hearing the approach of the horses, they were waiting for her on the front steps of the hall as Elizabeth stepped from the coach. Ignoring their anxious enquiries, she shepherded them towards the conservatory overlooking their high-walled kitchen garden. Elizabeth gave her sisters a detailed account of the meeting, reporting how the city's representatives had explained their extreme predicament. They insisted there was no suitable, alternative site for the development due to the unique topography of Bradford. The narrow valley running down to Shipley provided inadequate acreage to build a works of sufficient size to treat the increasing flow of waste.

"But how on earth do they think they're going to get over Idle Moor?" asked Mary, clearly upset at the pressure being applied by the city council.

"They have all that worked out; they say they'll go under it," Elizabeth replied. "They plan to build a tunnel through to Dawson Wood."

"A tunnel! So what's wrong with Frizinghall? They've already got a works there and that's not affecting anybody, is it?" asked Consuelo, who seemed unable or unwilling to understand what her older sister was telling them.

"Well, as I said, there isn't enough space at Frizinghall to build the size of treatment plant they are going to need to deal with the wool grease. They also need somewhere that is not close to houses; the corporation is getting more and more complaints from people living in Bolton about the smell from the works."

"I don't see any of it as our problem," said Mary, petulantly. "Stansfields have lived here for generations, causing no trouble. Uncle William even gave up part of the estate for Titus Salt. Now we're being persecuted and driven off our land; I won't have it."

"They're trying to get back at us because Uncle William created a fuss about the river," added Consuelo. "It isn't fair."

"They are offering us a good price for the estate," said Elizabeth, finding her sisters still implacably opposed to the sale. "And if my judgement is right, I think history will be on their side. We're living through huge change and we have to be careful we are not just swept aside. With the money for the estate, we could all rebuild our lives elsewhere. I think we should all consider their offer carefully before turning it down."

"Well, I've already considered it and I say no," said Mary.

"I feel the same," said Consuelo. "They think they can ride roughshod over us. Well, I say we should stick together and oppose this takeover."

"So be it," said Elizabeth. "But I think they will keep up the pressure on us until we agree. Anyway, I'll write to our agent and convey your feelings."

Faced with yet another setback, the corporation applied for and obtained an extension of the Bradford Corporation Act to 1904. In the council chamber the sisters were portrayed variously as over-privileged landed gentry out of touch with the modern world, as Luddites standing in the way of progress and as parasites who were not prepared to make any contribution towards the wellbeing of the ordinary citizens of Bradford.

* * *

Georg Heller emulated his expatriate colleagues in their highly successful business ventures, fuelling Bradford's ascendancy in wealth and status during the latter part of Victoria's reign. After many years rising through the echelons of the Delius group of companies, he accepted a directorship with a smaller, rival concern, which needed his experience and business contacts in a very competitive trading environment. Georg was a man of substance in the city, a prominent member of the Chamber of Commerce and an active patron of the arts, actively promoting Bradford's growing musical reputation based at St. George's Hall. His one regret had been his inability to father a child with Katherine, whom he maintained in luxury and comfort at their opulent home near Ilkley.

Their lack of success in conceiving a child had gradually led to their emotional estrangement, while avoiding mutual alienation. They were seen as a devoted couple by all who were unaware of their private disappointment. But Georg also had a dark secret he had been able to keep from Katherine only because she lived so far out of the city. Seeking to fill the sexual void in his life, he had succumbed over the years to the charms of several women of varying status and was now paying the price. The signs of his deteriorating health were unmistakable and his overriding fear was the speed at which the syphilis would develop and at what point he would have to face up to the inevitable social stigma. Whatever happened, he vowed he would never put his wife in harm's way and would ensure she was comfortably off in the event of his death.

He had even managed to keep his deteriorating state of health a secret from Josh, who had been living with them for several months since being declared unfit for work due to cancer of the bowel, for which the prognosis was bleak. Gunther and Jack had long since left the family home, Gunther heading back to his childhood town of Aachen, while Jack was pursuing a musical career in London, having been inspired by fellow Bradfordian and friend of the family, Fritz Delius, now living in France and composing to international acclaim.

Katherine was one of the first residents of Ilkley to have a telephone. It sat on the hall table and on the few occasions the bell rang, it tended to startle her. Usually it would be Georg telephoning her from his office in Bradford and sometimes Jack, asking for more money to pay for his expensive lifestyle in London. When the bell summoned her from the garden on this particular day she put the listening part to her ear, as usual fearing bad news.

"I'm going to have to go away for a little while," Georg informed her. "It's important business in Germany and I can't send anyone else. You'll have Josh there to keep you company."

She let the terse message sink in for a moment before replying, "Josh is quite ill; he might have to go into hospital if he gets any worse."

"Well, you'll have enough money; I've seen to that. So don't worry about hospital bills. I want Josh to be well looked after."

"You sound as if you're going to be away a long time."

"I don't know how long, yet. It depends on how well the talks go. Can you put together a travelling case for me and send it down on the train. I have to leave before first light to catch a ferry."

"You won't be coming home first, then?"

"I'll write as soon as possible," he reassured her, side-stepping her question. "I'll try to call you on the telephone, if possible. Don't worry and remember, I love you."

"I love you too," were the last words Katherine spoke before hearing a click, as the connection was broken. A surge of anxiety filled her heart. Although she had been aware of a *froideur* between them for some time, she could not put her finger on the reason for it. For all Georg professed his love for her, he had been behaving strangely and keeping his distance. Tears filled her eyes as she made her way upstairs to fill his case, not wanting to believe her intuition that Georg might be walking away from their life altogether.

Within two days he was crossing the Swiss frontier and heading for Berne where, he had been informed, a clinic claimed to use a revolutionary new treatment to fight the disease. The stigma of owning up to syphilis meant he might have left it too late to seek effective treatment. He saw the Swiss clinic as his last and possibly only resort, since there was no other known cure at that time. As far as his business colleagues and social contacts were aware, he had gone to Switzerland for the pure mountain air to cure his bronchial problems, as was the custom of citizens escaping smoke-polluted Bradford.

As days turned into weeks Katherine preoccupied herself by nursing her ailing brother. Bill and Mary made regular visits to the house at first, but failed to raise the spirits of their father, who complained bitterly and frequently about the hand fate had dealt him. In the end they relied on Katherine to keep them informed about Josh's condition, sadly failing to make it to his bedside when eventually he breathed his last.

A respectful turnout of Labour Party members escorted the coffin through Undercliffe Cemetery to the grave he was to share with Lily. Conspicuous by their absence were any representatives of the mill owners or their managers, who viewed Josh as seditious and a threat to their businesses during the latter part of his life. They underestimated the part played by Josh in helping to create a new political force that was to act as a counterbalance to the previous monopoly of power enjoyed by the main beneficiaries of Bradford's growing fortune.

Bill and Mary comforted their aunt as the mourners walked slowly back between the glistening new monuments to Bradford's industrial aristocracy. Georg had finally admitted, in a letter to Katherine, the severity of his illness and his poor chance of recovery. So she could not help wondering if this was only the first of two visits she would be making to a cemetery. Having turned her first widowhood into a life envied by most of her family, it was now turning into a life less enviable. It was only a matter of weeks until she received the telegraphed message she had been dreading. It came from the Swiss clinic informing her that Georg had died and left instructions for his body to be taken to Germany for burial in the family grave in Westphalia. Katherine set out at once to join relatives and a representative group of people from Bradford to pay their last respects to a man who was judged to have played a significant role in his adopted city.

* * *

Mary's parents were becoming less antagonistic and more emollient as they faced the fact that their daughter had taken matters into her own hands and defiantly run away with her tram driver. It would take a lot for them to accept him as a son-in-law, but they wanted to make contact with her to know she was safe and well. They told her they would welcome her back into the family home if things did not work out for her. They were really haunted by the fear of their daughter having a baby with no father in sight, bringing withering shame on the entire family in the self-righteous, middle-class stratum of society they now inhabited.

For a few weeks after their marriage, Bill and Mary stayed with their grieving aunt in Ilkley to comfort her, following the loss of her brother and husband in quick succession. Travelling to Bradford every day soon became an onerous and expensive chore, so, with the financial support of Katherine, they rented a modest cottage in the expanding suburb of Undercliffe, just a stone's throw from Mary's childhood home. Her parents, true to form, were quick to find fault when she disclosed the identity of their benefactor.

"Why, was our money not good enough?" demanded Mrs. Smith, failing to see the irony of her complaint.

"Bill is very proud and didn't want to ask you and dad while he wasn't being made to feel welcome in our family. I love him and if you can't find it in your hearts to love him as well, we'll just have to go our own way."

"Now then, Mary love, it was a shock you running off to Gretna, that's all. Maybe we just need to get to know him better," said Mr. Smith, not wanting to fall out with his daughter.

"Well, we'll be living just down the road and I'm going to need help with the baby when it arrives," she announced, slyly revealing her pregnancy for the first time in the hope of softening her mother's heart.

"Fancy, our Mary's going to have a baby," thrilled Mrs. Smith, beaming a smile at her bemused husband. "You can have it with us, love, if your cottage isn't gradely."

"It's a bit early for that," Mary replied. "It might be just a humble cottage, but Bill says he can make it homely. He's good with his hands."

She decided it would be sensible not to reveal their choice of name for the newborn – Jack or Fanny after Bill's grandparents – to avoid antagonising her parents again.

The safe arrival of Jack Ackroyd in the last year of the nineteenth century proved to be the unifying event Mary had prayed for. Her mother fussed around her at the birth and Bill, much to his irritation, found himself vying with his in-laws to hold his new son.

"Anybody would think they were moving in with us," complained Bill to his wife. "I hardly get a look in."

"Don't worry, love. It'll settle down. It's just good to be one happy family at long last."

"As long as I'm still captain of my own ship."

Three miles away at Esholt Hall, the last salvos were being fired in a desperate attempt to prevent the tide of twentieth century expansion consigning to history an heirless branch of the ubiquitous Stansfield family. An air of acrimony pervaded the stately home as the sisters argued the pros and cons of accepting Bradford Corporation's offer to buy the whole estate. Elizabeth, forever the realist, took the view that the corporation would win by slow attrition eventually.

"The pressure to clean up the Aire is such that Parliament will come round to Bradford's way of thinking," she told Mary and Consuelo, seated in the library for a crisis meeting. "We might not get such a good offer again if we hold out. With the money, we'll each be able to live in comfort wherever we choose."

The others remained unconvinced. "They can't just chase us out of our legitimate home," protested Mary. "There *must* be other places they can build their disgusting sewage works. It's just not right."

"Uncle William will be spinning in his grave," said Consuelo. "It seems his campaign to clean up the river could cost us our birthright. He would be fighting this tooth and nail if he was alive. I think we should keep fighting as well."

"Things have changed a lot since Uncle William's day," said Elizabeth. "People were more respectful towards the landed gentry in those days. I gather local gossip portrays us as three spoiled spinsters standing in the way of progress."

"That's just these so-called socialists; they would destroy all that's best about society if they have the chance," said Mary. "I say we tell the hoi-polloi to leave us alone and mind their own business."

"I agree," said Consuelo, "So are you with us Elizabeth?"

"I would hate to give all this up," said Elizabeth with a sweep of her arms embracing the book-lined room and sunlit gardens viewed through tall deep-set windows. "But I do not want to emulate Canute, either. I think we have to be pragmatic."

"Well, if being pragmatic means giving in to those who would drive us out of our home, I'm damned if I will," shouted Consuelo.

"Me neither," added Mary as the two of them shot their sister a despairing look, gathered up their skirts and swept out of the room, red-faced and angry.

Elizabeth absently watched men at work in the high-walled kitchen garden as she meditated on the seismic events that could soon bring about irreversible change to their lives of preordained privilege. She had already given much thought to her life after Esholt, but she needed the co-operation of her sisters to achieve her objective. After the fractious discussion it was not going to be easy to convert them to her way of thinking. Perhaps money would win them over in the end, so it was essential for their agent to continue negotiating for the best possible price for the house and estate.

At Frizinghall, urgent experiments to find a solution to Bradford's hitherto untreatable blend of sewage and wool grease eventually led to a breakthrough. It was discovered that adding sulphuric acid to the raw material separated out the solids, leaving the liquid effluent to be filtered and discharged into the beck. This unfortunately created another problem. Faced with increasing quantities of precipitated solids, the management resorted to dumping this 'cake', as it was called, on to the limited amount of spare land available. During warm weather this led to complaints from nearby residents about the dreadful smell pervading the area.

In a northerly wind, the smell was carried as far as Valley Parade, where rugby followers had been holding their noses on the terraces for the past few games. Falling gates and an acrimonious meeting, however, led to the abandonment of rugby for the increasingly popular game of football. Bill Ackroyd was among the near-capacity crowd of Bradford City supporters who saw the Lord Mayor kick off the first home match against Gainsborough Trinity. Although the visitors won by three goals to one, nothing could dent the enthusiasm of the newest city to field a team in the Football League. Bill felt a particular sense of pride having spent many winter hours, on Saturday afternoons, indulging in his latest passion on playing fields in and around the city. He had been a regular attender at meetings in the Market Tavern to establish a professional football side and was among the first to celebrate City's rapid acceptance into the League.

Mary indulged her husband's passion, knowing that she would have to learn the basic language of soccer and cricket to share Bill's involvement throughout the sporting calendar. She was swept along by the enthusiasm for Bradford's new football club among stallholders at the indoor market in Darley Street where she worked selling greengroceries. Each Monday during the season started with assessments of that weekend's performance, comparing the merits of individual players with predictions for future games. These inevitably led to noisy but friendly disagreements as football fever began to take over the city.

* * *

The denouement for the Stansfield sisters came about as Elizabeth predicted. Early in 1904 they assembled in the library at the invitation of their agent to hear the newest offer from Bradford Corporation for their entire estate, a figure not far short of a quarter of a million pounds. "In my opinion it is a very good offer," the agent told them, "and I strongly recommend you to accept."

Mary put a comforting arm round Consuelo's shoulders as her sister began to sob quietly. Elizabeth took the lead again, asking how soon they would have to move out of the hall if they accepted the offer.

"There will be plenty of time for you to make alternative arrangements," the agent told them. "I expect two years at least."

"What will become of us?" sobbed Consuelo. "This is our home, our life, our birthright. We love it here."

"We wouldn't necessarily want to spend the rest of our lives here together," reasoned Elizabeth. "If we marry, for instance. But I think the bigger consideration is that Bradford Corporation will have their way, eventually, one way or another, and I think we should acknowledge that fact, painful as it may seem now."

"It feels like the end of an era," said Mary, still comforting her distressed sister. "I will hate to go, but it seems we're destined to be dispossessed like so many of our class, by this levelling tide from the slums of Bradford."

"Or you could say we are really victims of Bradford's success," said Elizabeth. "The city is getting bigger and wealthier and we're paying the price. I just want to live as far away from it all as possible; this money will help us all to do that. Do we agree to accept this offer?"

Elizabeth took Mary's single nod and Consuelo's tear-stained silence as offering no objection. She instructed the agent to convey their acceptance to the corporation. Through the library windows, hidden by the expansive sweep of lawns, the River Aire continued to flow in fetid silence between strands of willow, weeping for times past and times still to come.

* * *

A frisson of excitement rippled through the expectant farmers and townsfolk as the oncoming sound of galloping horses echoed around the marketplace. Gordon Jameson, now a robust seven-year-old, tugged excitedly at Constance's sleeve as the leading tartan-clad common riders clattered into the square, rearing to a halt beneath a breeze-taut Saltire. It was the first time Constance had journeyed into Selkirk with Gordon and his older brother and sister to see the ancient summer tradition that always drew a large and fiercely patriotic crowd. The watchers raised a loud cheer when the leading rider held aloft the flag captured at the Battle of Flodden in 1513, and which was flourished every year in this ancient ceremony.

For all her English blood, Constance now considered herself a naturalised Scot, having lived in the Borders for almost twenty years. She was always ready to lend a hand to her neighbours at lambing or harvest time and regularly took part in local ceilidhs, having mastered the intricacies of Scottish dancing. A simple country life shaped by the rhythm of the seasons and dictates of the weather proved no great challenge for her. She was less comfortable within the strict constraints of Presbyterianism, which ruled the rural border communities, preferring to worship at the small Episcopal Church in the town, her only tenuous link with her background.

Several years had passed since she paid a visit to the workhouse at Great Horton where she found her mother reduced to a childlike state, unable to recognise her own daughter. Constance could see no reason to visit the feared institution again, finally severing the already fragile mother and daughter relationship. From occasional letters that found their way to the farm from America, she learned that Tilly was enjoying her new life in Baltimore, where she had married a successful bar owner and local worthy. Tilly wrote that she hoped her half-sister would cross the Atlantic one day to see the wonders of the New World. But Constance knew she would never persuade Donald to leave his farm for such an adventure and could never imagine making the crossing on her own, even if she could find the fare in the first place. For all the farm paid its way, there was rarely any spare money once all the bills had been settled. A farmer's wife could only dream of shrugging off the omnipresent yoke that was her lot in life. Constance told herself she had no regrets, but found it hard to stifle a deep itch within her for something she could not even explain. How she came to scratch her itch surprised even Constance and would cause a scandal that reverberated within the strait-laced community.

* * *

Bill Ackroyd spun the brake wheel and shifted the power regulator to start his tram up the steep incline at surprising speed. The new electric tramcars had good acceleration, even on streets radiating out of the city centre. If the wheels lost traction on horse dung or ice, sand released directly on to the track usually got them gripping again. But even the skill of the driver could not always prevent the trolley pole springing off the overhead power line, bringing the tram to a premature halt to the annoyance of other road users. A long hooked pole was employed to capture the trolley pole and relocate it back on the line. This operation was usually accompanied by ribald comments from passengers if they were enduring the chill of the open deck.

On this particular day not even a sprung trolley pole could dent Bill's good humour, knowing he was the father of a second son born only two hours before his shift. Thomas Ackroyd's healthy arrival at four in the morning ended weeks of worry, mitigating their intense disappointment at the loss at birth of a baby girl two years previously. Jibes turned to sincere congratulations from regular top-deck passengers as Bill dispensed the good news to all and sundry before carefully stepping back down the steep twisting stairs to his driving platform. He had left Mary and his new son in the capable hands of Aunt Katherine, who would be staying with them for a few days until Mary felt fit enough to resume her chores.

Bill finished his shift in Forster Square, where he boarded a tram to Undercliffe and home. His uniform invariably attracted the attention of fellow passengers, who were always keen to pass the time of day with the holder of a much-respected office in the town. A short walk from the tram stop brought him to his front door and the sound of a lusty pair of infant lungs. Bill greeted Mary with a kiss before striding to the crib and proudly picking up the crying bundle with a swift admonishment from Katherine to take care. The baby stopped crying as Bill rocked him in his arms.

"You see, we haven't lost our touch," he comforted Mary, who had never fully got over the stillbirth of their baby daughter. "We'll have this one playing for City if I've anything to do with it."

"He's got a name, Bill," said Mary. "We decided to call him Thomas, remember?"

"That's his Sunday name, lass. Tommy'll be good enough for the rest of the week and Tommy's good enough for me."

"He'll probably get Tom as well. Our Jack's ever so good with him, not at all jealous. I hope they'll be good pals as there's only four years between them."

"Give him here, you'll spoil him," interrupted Katherine, taking the baby and laying him gently back in the crib. "No doubt you'll be ready for your dinner."

A knock at the door was answered by Bill, who found a telegram boy on the doorstep. He took the buff-coloured envelope and extracted a single sheet advising him that his younger brother James was in hospital in Portsmouth. It gave the location and ward with a number to ring. The last Bill had heard from his brother was a brief letter written in South Africa telling him he was well and would be home soon. It had been written several weeks earlier, while James was serving with the West Yorkshire Regiment in the Boer War.

"It's our lad; he's in hospital down south. It doesn't say if he's badly hurt. I'll have to get down to see him – see, I've got a number to ring."

He passed the telegram to Mary, who was quick to observe, "If he was hurt over there, at least they've got him home where he'll get proper nursing."

"The poor lamb," said Katherine. "In hospital and all that way from home."

"I'll ring after I've supped," said Bill. "Where can I get a train to Portsmouth? I'll need to call in at the tram shed after dinner to get time off, but I don't think they'll mind as it's my brother."

* * *

The thirty-two-mile journey to Buckden over spine-jarring roads took its toll of the Stansfield sisters' demeanour in the confined interior of their coach, in spite of stops at Addingham and Threshfield for refreshment and to rest the horses. As they swung into the gates of Buckden Manor, Elizabeth voiced again her conviction that the new horseless carriages would one day take over the roads of her native county and cut their five-hour journey by half. Her sisters were less convinced, citing the proven reliability of horses against the unreliable and horribly smelly automobiles appearing outside the grand houses of their friends and acquaintances.

"Just smell that fresh air," said Mary as she climbed down from the coach, stretching and yawning. Her sisters followed, their eyes scanning the steep shrub-covered sides of the green flat-bottomed valley bisected by the meandering River Wharfe. Random white clouds projected moving shadows across the pastoral landscape dotted with sheep and cows, the whole scene defined by dry stone walls and solid stone barns.

"I love this place," confessed Elizabeth, "as we know our father did. I feel such a sense of peace and freedom out here compared to Esholt."Mary and Consuelo looked around them again before stepping through the front door of the manor without offering a comment.

Later, sat round a blazing log fire following their evening meal, the sisters got down to the real reason for their combined visit to their country retreat. "We will each receive somewhere in the region of £75,000 from the sale of the estate," Elizabeth began. "That should be more than enough to provide for us during our lifetimes, whatever we propose to do. For my part, as I said before, I would be perfectly content to live here in this village. Now that the estate is going, I shall not miss life at Esholt. Everything there is changing, while here I can put down new roots in a real community."

"As lady of the manor," suggested Consuelo. "You mean to be a big fish in a small pool, Elizabeth."

"Well yes, I suppose, if you wish to put it that way. I have already been made to feel welcome here and it seems like a natural move. What say you Mary?"

"It would not suit me living all this way out of society. Fine for a holiday, but to live here all year round, no, thank you."

"So do I have agreement of you both that I make Buckden Manor my home and will you assign your shares of this estate to me? You know you will always be welcome to come to stay here when you feel like a weekend in the country."

"Consuelo and I have already discussed it and we think it would be a good idea to have you living here and looking after the property," said Mary. "Neither of us wishes to live here permanently, so we are happy to surrender our shares to you and live our lives elsewhere. We already have plans, as you know. I will be dividing my time between Broxholme and Hampshire; Consuelo will be at Kirkby Overblow with her Scottish Clergyman. By the way, are we going to have to buy new hats this year, Consuelo?"

The youngest sister blushed and promised they would be the first to hear about any wedding plans. "Meanwhile, let us enjoy this, probably our last occasion to be together in just each other's company."

* * *

Bill Ackroyd was relieved to find the public telephone free when he pushed open the door of their local sub post office. Nervously, he lifted the earpiece and gave the operator the number on the telegram.

"Just a moment, I'll put you through."

After a short wait, punctuated by a series of clicks, a female voice announced, "Military hospital".

"I'm enquiring about James Ackroyd of the West Yorkshire Regiment. I'm his brother."

"Please hold the line."

He was left hanging on for a good minute before a clipped military voice asked him to confirm his name and kin to James Ackroyd.

"It is my painful duty to have to tell you that your brother passed away this morning from infected wounds received in action. I am very sorry."

Bill was so shocked by this unexpected bad news that he was only aware of the voice in the earpiece, but not what it was saying.

"I'm sorry, could you repeat that?" he asked.

"Yes, I realise this will have been a nasty shock for you. I was saying that arrangements will be made to have your brother's body sent back to Yorkshire for burial and you will receive a letter from his company commander."

In a daze he ended the call and made his way from the sub post office to his home where Mary immediately guessed the bad news from his expression. "It was what he wanted to do," she comforted her husband. "He lived life to the full and made us so proud of him."

Where There's Muck

While Bradford was engaged in a struggle to prevent increasing volumes of human and industrial waste reaching the beck and the river, some far-sighted councillors saw significant financial relief for the rates in this morbid material. The city's pre-eminent position in the wool business delivered to Frizinghall every working day a turgid cocktail that initially defied all attempts to treat it. Human waste was mixed with a high proportion of grease and fats washed from thousands of fleeces. This changed the nature of the effluent, thwarting attempts to reclaim the wool grease and separate out the liquid content for purification and return to the river. Since 1873, private companies using a variety of materials had failed to solve the problem at Frizinghall. The corporation was forced to take over and made some progress using lime filtration. But it was the introduction of sulphuric acid to the process that was to prove to be the solution they had been seeking.

In spite of their progress, the corporation was no nearer satisfying the river authority about the quality of Frizinghall's discharge into the beck. They remained under considerable pressure to push forward plans for a much larger capacity sewage treatment works on the newly acquired green acres, which were until recently the home of the Stansfield sisters. In the Town Hall there was general agreement that, in order to silence their critics once and for all, the new Esholt treatment works would incorporate the very latest scientific and engineering techniques from around the world, showing once again that Bradford was a city of innovation and progress.

In 1899 Joseph Garfield was appointed Sewage Works Engineer with responsibility for achieving this aim. He faced the formidable challenge of transporting the sewage from Frizinghall to Esholt through a three-mile-long tunnel under the 650-foot bulk of Idle Moor. It would then cross the Aire valley on a half-mile aqueduct to an elevated location on the north side, to be treated with acid in a series of huge sunken precipitation tanks. His unique design then harnessed the force of gravity alone to channel the separated liquid effluent into acres of filter beds and ultimately through them into the river. Using techniques developed at Frizinghall, the separated solid matter would be pressed to release the valuable grease for sale to make the whole process pay for itself. At the end of 1907 the detailed plans were submitted to the council with an estimated cost of just less than one million pounds. Approval was given the following spring for a sewage treatment works that was expected to receive world recognition for its unique features and cost-efficiency.

Bill read about the city's ambitious plans in the *Bradford Daily Telegraph*. What caught his eye was not the clever design of the works, but that to cover such a huge acreage it would have to be served by more than twenty-two miles of internal railway lines. "That would be right up my street," he told Mary after reading the newspaper article to her.

"But you like your job on the trams," she protested, "and you yourself said it was steady. Why would you want to change now?"

"Because I know every cobblestone of every route I drive; I need something new. I wonder if they'd give a tram driver a job on the railway; I'd love to change to steam. After all, I'd still be working for the corporation. Our Jack and Tommy would just love to ride on a steam engine."

"You've no experience of steam engines. It takes years to become a steam engine driver."

"That's on the main lines; this would be driving on a works railway and can't be all that different from what I've been used to. I think I'll ask about it next time I'm at the Town Hall." Gathering up five-year-old Tommy and sitting him on his knee, Bill called to his nine-year-old brother, "Jack, how would you like your dad to be a steam engine driver?"

"Yes!" the boys shouted in unison. "Will you let us have a ride on your engine, Dad?"

"Your dad's not got the job yet," chuckled Mary, "and it may be some time before they start taking on engine drivers. So just hold your horses and kiss your dad goodnight, Tommy; it's past your bedtime." Jack resumed his seat by the fire and continued to carve away at a piece of wood he was shaping into a dagger.

"There's no harm in asking, love," said Bill, putting an arm round his wife. "You know what they say: nothing ventured, nothing won."

"Every boy's dream is to drive a steam engine. You're just a big boy at heart yourself."

* * *

Doors were already being opened as the Bradford train slowed to a halt in Ilkley station. Bill and his sister Hannah stepped on to the platform and headed for the exit, where a coach was waiting to take them to the convalescent home on the edge of the moor. A short journey up a steep street brought them to a rhododendron-lined driveway leading to a large stone mansion that once belonged to a mill owner. From the grand entrance hall, they were led up a curving flight of stairs to a room off a short landing. Inside, propped against pillows on a narrow bed, lay their aunt Katherine, untidy grey wisps of hair framing her sallow face. Her face was so drawn that her cheek-bones projected in sharp relief under translucent skin. Sunken eyes, no longer radiating the vitality of old, gave evidence of her battle against the cancer that would soon take her life. Bill could not help contrasting the sunlit open moorland he could see through the latticed window, with this overheated, airless room witnessing the ultimate fragility of life.

Katherine acknowledged her nephew and niece with a wan smile and struggled to speak through painfully drawn breaths. "I have already told Gunther and Jack, but I want to tell you. Make sure they carry out my wishes," she whispered.

"Carry what out, auntie?" asked Bill while Katherine fought for breath.

"To take me to Germany when I die so I can be with Georg. Do you promise?"

"Yes, of course," they said in unison.

Katherine sank back on to her pillows as her nephew and niece brought her up to date with family news. She listened to them with her eyes closed, but they soon realised she had slipped into a shallow sleep and it was time to leave.

"How long?" Hannah asked the nurse outside the room.

"Only a matter of days, we think," she told them and added, "It will be a relief for her. We will call you immediately, of course."

The train journey back to Bradford was attended by memories of times past and punctuated by long silences as they gazed through the carriage windows, lost in private thoughts.

"She comes from a distant time and a distant place that has gone forever," said Hannah.

"You could add, a distant land too," said Bill, "to which she intends to return. She was so much in love with Georg right up to his death, for all his unfaithfulness."

In due course, Katherine's wishes were carried out to the letter, as she was laid to rest next to her beloved Georg in a wintry Westphalia. Neither Bill nor Hannah could make the journey, but Gunther and Jack were well supported by the elite of Bradford's woollen community, including several first and second generation Germans eager to pay their respects to the wife of one of their expatriate countrymen.

* * *

The Stansfield sisters drove a hard bargain through their agent during negotiations to sell their estate. Led by the formidable Elizabeth, they were determined that many of the fine fixtures and fittings in the hall should not be left behind to grace the offices of a sewage works. Under considerable pressure to acquire the estate, Bradford readily agreed to their demands in order to reach a settlement as quickly as possible. In the weeks following the sale, a succession of carters were summoned to the hall to load up treasured items and transport them to the sisters' new demesnes. The biggest prize went to Consuelo, who stripped out the fine oak staircase and oak panelling to install them in her newly acquired manor near Kirby Overblow. A number of carved figures were removed from the landscaped gardens to the altogether sweeter air of the North Riding.

In the first century-and-a-half of its existence on the site of the former nunnery, Esholt Hall's resident families experienced an unusually high incidence of descendancy by the female line. Followers of local folklore claimed this substantiated the curse rumoured to have been placed on anyone possessing properties of the dissolved monasteries. The departure of the Stansfield sisters without a male heir caused even sceptic villagers to observe that there might be something in the legend after all.

* * *

It was her husband's accident that led to Constance's undoing. Donald Jameson was transferring stooks of hay from a cart into the barn when the horse suddenly reared up in fear between the shafts. The cart slammed back into the barn, trapping Donald and breaking his lower spine. Confined to a wheelchair, he was forced to hire a young helper to carry out the heavier tasks that he and his wife were incapable of doing. Increasingly frustrated by the subsequent lack of any physical element in her marriage, Constance was attracted to this likeable and good-humoured young man, twenty years her junior. Jamie Robson gradually became aware of her interest and, while doing nothing overtly to encourage it, enjoyed working in close proximity to his employer's wife. Donald's restricted movement in his wheelchair gave the pair ample opportunity to work together without raising suspicion and Constance, meanwhile, took every opportunity to use Jamie's height or strength to augment hers.

He never took advantage of their situation until fate intervened. Stacking bales of hay in the barn one day he lost his balance and fell backwards, instinctively grabbing at Constance and causing her to fall on top of him. They laughed as they lay in an untidy heap among the hay. When he tried to get up, she pinned him to the floor and kissed him firmly on the mouth. To her relief and considerable pleasure, he returned the kiss with equal passion, rolling her beneath him and starting to unbutton her blouse.

Carried away by this late-flowering fulfilment of her physical needs, Constance grew careless, encouraging trysts in a variety of places until the day she and Jamie were caught in flagrante delicto in an upper meadow by a town busybody who could hardly believe her luck. Concluding that Jamie was the innocent party lured into the affair by an older woman, he was spared the opprobrium meted out to Constance. She was forced to confine herself to the farm, where she suffered the silent contempt of a downcast Donald. Jamie was swiftly replaced by another farmhand and promptly left the district to find his fortune elsewhere.

In the year following her disgrace, Constance continued to receive the support and friendship of one or two of the less judgemental townsfolk, gradually returning to the community, which had once embraced her. But she never completely overcame her stigma, nor regained the full respect and acceptance of the hard core of devoted churchgoers.

* * *

Bill Ackroyd crossed Market Street, his usual buoyancy ebbing away as he approached the soaring Gothic façade ahead. Once inside the Town Hall, he was directed to a waiting area on the first floor and told to take a seat. Twenty minutes elapsed before he was shown into a spacious room bisected by a large oak table ringed by leather-backed chairs bearing the city's coat of arms. At a smaller table, two men in suits sat facing an empty chair on which Bill was invited to sit. In response to a request from one of the men, he gave his name and details of his schooling, family background and work experience.

"So you already work for the corporation. Why do you want to give up tram driving?"

"I love my job, but it's time to move on. I'd like to do something similar, so to speak. When I heard about the new Esholt railway, I thought that's just the sort of thing I'm looking for."

"What makes you think you could drive a steam engine?"

"Well, I've already got rail sense, if you see what I mean. All I need do is learn the steam controls, which can't be that hard. The rest is common sense and I reckon I've got plenty of that."

"Have you ever had an accident on the trams or been reprimanded for speeding?"

"The only collision I had was with a bull. It escaped from a slaughter-house and was right mad. Just ran at my tram and bashed in the side with its head. But I've never been told off for speeding."

"What happened to the bull?"

"It was a bit dazed and they caught it. Happen it ended up in my in-laws' shop hanging from a hook," he replied, to suppressed chuckles from the other side of the table.

One of his interrogators pointed out that the footplate of a steam locomotive was a lot dirtier than the front deck of a tramcar. "There will be plenty of muck and bad smells at Esholt and some heavy lifting as well. Do you think you're up to it?"

"I'm not fazed by hard work. In fact, I'd relish it given half a chance."

"Alright, that's all from us for now. We'll let you know in due course."

Bill thanked them and left the room preoccupied with thoughts of what he might have said to improve his chances. He flipped between optimism and pessimism as he took a tram to his depot to begin his shift for the day. Either way, he had made his bid and it was now in the lap of the councillors.

Once permission was given for work to begin, the former Esholt estate quickly became a hive of activity. Huge excavators began removing the bulk of Strangford

Hill before construction could proceed elsewhere. Sludge presses were transferred from Frizinghall to a new press house near the canal. Sewage was then transferred through a compressed-air pipeline, finally putting an end to the pollution of Bradford Beck.

The tunnel from Frizinghall to Esholt was to have a difficult gestation. A private contractor began work on it in 1913, but soon went out of business. Before inviting further tenders, the corporation sank two shafts along the line of the tunnel to investigate geological conditions. A second contractor began tunnelling only to abandon the work when it proved difficult to obtain materials and men, which were being sucked into the war in Europe. The sewage works committee were keen to press on with the project, but the insatiable demands of war brought work to a halt.

Bill collected the letter from his front door, noting the Bradford coat of arms on the envelope. He tore it open, unfolded the single sheet and read with a feeling of disappointment that, although he was considered suitable for driving a steam engine at Esholt, no appointments were being made until after the war when work at the sewage works site was expected to resume. He was assured that his name would be retained for contacting at the earliest opportunity.

"Looks like I'll be driving trams a bit longer, lass," he told Mary. "Unless, of course, I'm called up. But at forty-three I reckon they'll only want me if things are going badly over there. Our Hannah's lads are raring to go and she's dead against it. Joe and Bert have both signed up with the Pals. They reckon it'll all be all over by Christmas."

"I do hope they're right because they say they're going to lock up Germans living in this country until the war's over. That'll be bad for a lot of people in Bradford."

"They have to look out for fifth columnists, love. Anyroad, have you heard our Hannah's joined the Suffragettes? She says if women had the vote there wouldn't be any wars. God knows what she'll get up to now; maybe she'll chain herself to the railings outside the Town Hall. You mark my word, she'll end up in the clink."

"Well, I think she's got a lot of guts," said Mary, "and I think it's right what she's fighting for. Why shouldn't we have the vote? It's *our* sons have to go to war after we've brought them into this world and cared for them. It's not men as have the babies."

"Men would rather go to war," said Bill. "Anyroad, they had no trouble recruiting for the Pals, who can't wait to get the Hun on the run. I'm only sorry I can't go with them."

"Why would you want to put yourself in harm's way if you don't have to?" protested Mary. "I don't think it's going to be a picnic over there. Lots of men are going to get killed before it's over."

"We've got the best soldiers in the world, love. Just you wait, they'll give the Hun a right good hiding and the lads will soon be on their way home. We're going to need them here to cheer on Park Avenue now they've got promotion to Division One."

It wouldn't be long before Bill's two expressed aspirations in life were to be realised. He often shared with his mates at the tram depot his ambition to become a steam engine driver and voiced his regret at not being part of the war effort. Arriving for his shift one day, a fellow driver asked if he had seen the previous day's *Telegraph*. He produced his own folded copy and handed it to Bill.

"Page five, I think it is, the page with news about the war. Seems the army's looking to train engine drivers. But they don't want young men vital to the war effort. Sounds just what you're looking for."

"Thanks," said Bill, turning to the relevant page and finding a short report near the bottom stating that previous rail or tramway experience was essential. Applicants should be no more than forty-five years of age.

Notwithstanding Mary's alarm at this unexpected turn of events, Bill soon found himself facing yet another interview, this time with a Royal Engineers recruiting team in Leeds. If selected, he was told, he would be based at the Army's Longmoor Camp in Hampshire for training on the Woolmer Instructional Military Railway. Afterwards he could be posted wherever there was a need for an engine driver at home or abroad. His service would last for three years or as long as was necessary for a successful prosecution of the war.

It did not take Bill long to conclude that it was an opportunity he could not afford to miss. Apart from playing his part in the war effort, he would leave the Army with all the skills and experience needed to be an engine driver at Esholt. His biggest challenge lay in persuading Mary that it was the right decision; that he was unlikely to be near any front line action and would emerge from the war with a new career ahead of him. When he gave her the news, she remained unconvinced and fearful, but realised he had made up his mind. She would just have to get along in his absence like many thousands of war widows, who bore the worry and stress without any of the purging adrenaline.

Over The Top

Two thousand young men from every part of Bradford cheerfully swapped their working clothes for khaki uniforms and headed off to war. Even the unlikely possibility that it might not be a short-lived conflict failed to quench the spirit of the Pals, joined in their camaraderie by familiar names and a common accent. Their visceral marching songs and bawdy northern humour provided a vital antidote to the cold reality of industrial warfare as they deployed to the front line at the Somme on 1 July 1916. Soon after dawn, a series of whistle blasts along the line of trenches gave the signal to go over the top. Bayonets fixed, each man set off at walking pace across no man's land with the object of taking the French village of Serre. Just one hour later, 1770 of these incredibly brave young men lay dead or wounded due to the ferocity of German machine gun fire. In spite of the huge loss of life, the most disastrous single day suffered by the British Army, no ground was gained. But in just sixty minutes, Bradford had lost irreplaceable brain and sinew that should have been the determinant for its future.

True to his word, Bill Ackroyd was never sent into the front line after training at Longmoor. He spent his war driving trains, crammed with soldiers and materiel, between the Channel ports and forward depots, where light, narrow-gauge railways took over. He loved his job in the Army, but hated the war with a passion, which he expressed to Mary on his rare visits home on leave.

Bill's descriptions of the common soldier's lot in France inflamed his sister to the point where she painted an 'End the War' slogan across the front of the General Post Office in Forster Square, resulting in her arrest. Given a three-month prison sentence, Hannah immediately started a hunger strike and had to be force-fed. Within a week of her release, she was back on the streets handing out Suffragette leaflets to all who would take one. This brought her several more cautions and a further custodial sentence for causing a breach of the peace. It was while she was in prison for the second time that news came through that both her sons, Joe and Bert, were casualties of the war. Joe was missing and Bert badly wounded.

Many believed it was this news that caused their father Joseph to suffer a stroke, which left him partially paralysed. Until Hannah's release from prison, he was looked after by their nineteen-year-old daughter Carrie whose husband, Robert White, was dodging German submarines in the Atlantic. A petty criminal and con man, White had only escaped going to prison, for committing serial acts of burglary, by volunteering for the Merchant Marine. He had charmed Carrie into marrying him and given her a daughter before going to sea with the promise he would return a reformed man. He managed to give her a second daughter on his one shore leave at home before getting up to his old tricks and seeking sanctuary on his ship.

At this time work on the tunnel from Frizinghall to Esholt was suspended due to the lack of construction materials. A chronic shortage of labour followed the introduction of conscription, following heavy losses on the Western Front. The corporation paid off the contractor, selling off the plant and construction materials. Meanwhile, sewage continued to be piped to Esholt for treatment, but the process fell far short of the capacity needed and threatened to reverse gains in the quality of effluent released into the river.

* * *

Donald and Constance Jameson's eldest son Arthur was already working in Glasgow when war broke out. To his father's disappointment he had showed no interest in farming, preferring to take an apprenticeship in the Clyde shipyards, building desperately needed warships. This earned him the status of a reserved occupation, avoiding conscription into the forces. On the farm Gordon replaced the hired labour when he finished his schooling. He was also exempted from the call-up because of his father's incapacity, to the clear relief of Constance and his older sister Fiona, who was teaching in nearby Galashiels.

Gordon showed an early flair for agriculture, bringing a number of new ideas to improve the land and achieve a better price for their cows and sheep at market. His outgoing personality made him a prominent figure in Selkirk, where he was regarded as the life and soul of any local event. He was never short of a dance partner at a ceilidh and could give a good account of Scotland's Bard each January 25th. Many a person deceived by his rustic demeanour was caught out by the sharpness of his mind, which he put to good use at various auctions around the Borders.

Recognising his son's ability to run the farm profitably, Donald gradually handed over increasing amounts of responsibility, while retaining an advisory role as to the direction of their business. Constance, meanwhile, had a full time job running the household, keeping the books and caring for Donald, who had mostly forgiven her for her transgressions. Even in the inward-looking Selkirk farming community it was only the inveterate curtain-twitchers who continued to give her a wide berth. She gradually eased herself back into church and community life, eventually gaining a good reputation for organising a range of social events aimed at generating parcels of food and warm clothing for "our boys in France", as she described them. By so doing, Constance was also assuaging her feeling of guilt for not having any sons in uniform when so many of the local families were grieving for lost fathers, sons and brothers.

* * *

Mary Ackroyd wept when she read about the losses at the Somme and was even more distraught when Hannah told her about her sons. Joe was still listed as 'missing in action' while Bert was in a field hospital behind the lines awaiting transfer to Britain once he was well enough to travel.

"Bill is safe, but I'm scared something may have happened to Jack. I've not had a letter from him in weeks," Mary told her sister-in-law. "How long do you think this hellish war is going to go on? Please God, it'll be over before our Tommy is old enough to go. I just couldn't bear it."

"Trouble is, wars are easy to start, but not so easy to stop," said Hannah. "That's what we've been saying all along. It won't change anything in the end, except that we'll lose our best young men over there. Let us pray this will put an end to all wars."

If any good could be said to have come out of the war for Mary, it was full reconciliation with her ageing parents. Rather than see her struggle to bring up Tommy on her own, they welcomed her back to work in the shop and made sure she always had enough provisions. Mary was determined that her parents' new-found charity would extend to Bill after the war, but decided to let sleeping dogs lie for the time being. She disagreed with Hannah's assertion that the war would not change anything. She was certain that afterwards there would have to be a new beginning for everyone. It would be a case of trying to piece together lives torn apart in what was being described as 'the war to end all wars'.

As it dragged bloodily on into a fourth year, more and more women in Bradford were drafted into jobs normally undertaken by men, who were increasingly being shipped to France. Through this forced realignment of gender roles, women began to move more rapidly towards the emancipation for which Suffragettes had fought and even died. Hannah reaffirmed her commitment to the movement following the deaths of her husband and son; Joseph from the effects of his stroke and Bert from complications after having a leg amputated in a field hospital behind the lines. Feeling that at last the political tide was flowing in the direction of votes for women, she attended meetings and rallies throughout the city. These attracted many prominent speakers who rallied audiences to keep up the pressure for change now that women were playing an equal part to men on the home front. At last, Parliament began to pay heed to the demands of the militants and the first moves were made to introduce voting rights for a limited stratum of women in society. Throughout the land, demands for universal suffrage continued unabated.

* * *

Mary was about to leave her cottage when there was a sharp knock at the front door. On the doorstep, a youth, barely out of school, reached into a satchel and handed her a buff-coloured envelope. She managed to stagger back into the parlour and collapse heavily on to a chair before extracting the single sheet that confirmed her worst fear. Jack had been killed in action. Paralysed with grief, she was still sitting in the parlour when her mother called in an hour later to find out where she had got to. The telegram was quickly followed by a letter from Jack's commanding officer, praising his heroism under fire. He was being recommended for a posthumous award for single-handedly neutralising a German machine gun, saving the lives of several of his colleagues. But no medal could compensate Mary who was inconsolable at the loss of her eldest son and she retired to her bed for three days, leaving her mother to look after Tommy.

At the armistice, Bill Ackroyd was forced to admit he'd had a good war doing what he most wanted to do, well behind the front lines. His contribution to victory was nonetheless vital, considering the thousands of men and huge quantities of materiel his trains had ferried to and from the Channel ports. Demobilised and back in Bradford, he was surprised and delighted to be given a warm welcome by Mary's parents, prompting him to whisper in his wife's ear, "I feel like the Prodigal Son."

With thousands of men returning from the war, Bill worried he might be beaten to a job at Esholt where work was about to get under way once more. He approached the Sewage Works Committee again and was granted a further interview at which he explained what he had been doing in France, emphasising his training and considerable experience of driving several types of steam locomotive. As before, he was told he would receive their decision by post in the next few days.

Each day seemed like an eternity as he rushed to meet the postman. But, at last, he was handed a white envelope bearing the Bradford coat of arms. With Mary at his elbow, he tore it open and read that he had been taken on as an engine driver at Esholt Sewage Works and was to report to Esholt Hall the following Monday for instructions. This good news, the first she had experienced for as long as she could remember, reduced Mary to tears of relief. Bill held her in his arms saying, "I've done it, love, better late than never. We'll be able to move, maybe to Thackley or Esholt Village, so I'm close to the job. What do you say to that?"

"I think we'll go to church to give thanks and pray for our Jack who's joined our little lass in Heaven. It's been a horrible war, Bill. Every street in Bradford is mourning someone. I doubt many will ever get over it."

"Well, we beat them in the end, so none of our lads died in vain. But we've got to look forward now, lass, for our

Tommy's sake. Just pray there'll be no more wars like that one."

Heavy machinery was already being operated at the sewage works site when Bill reported for work. The first half-mile of railway had been laid to link up with the main Midland Railway line near the eastern end of Thackley tunnel. He was told he would be driving the first saddle tank engine, hauling construction materials from the main line to new buildings under construction next to the Leeds-Liverpool canal. Work had restarted at both ends of the Frizinghall to Esholt tunnel using direct labour employed by the corporation. Among them was Bill's son Tommy, who had found work as a gofer. Each evening he would keep Bill and Mary enthralled with stories about the alien world of tunnelling deep beneath Idle Moor, where the navvies were encountering seams of coal and old mine workings as they progressed.

"You're following in your grandad Joshua's footsteps," Bill told his son. "He helped to build the first main sewer from Bradford to Frizinghall over fifty years ago. He'd be proud to see you working on this tunnel today."

Tommy was always anxious to please his father but felt uncomfortable in the claustrophobic gloom endured by men carving out rock from the Esholt end. Many who had seen service in the war were old beyond their years. Like any curious teenager, Tommy wanted to know what it had been like for them in France, eavesdropping mealtime conversations in the hope of hearing tales from the trenches. To his disappointment, for all it was only a year since they were demobbed, the veterans seemed to have locked away their war experiences. To his direct enquiry, "What was it like?", the usual response was, "Hell on earth, lad," followed by a thoughtful silence. This vested these taciturn former warriors with a near-mythical quality in the mind of their young workmate.

Across the broad valley, surveyors and engineers marked out sites for a series of huge sunken receiving tanks, precipitation tanks, a sulphuric acid plant and acres of filter beds with their ancillary buildings, all served by miles of standard gauge railway. They were confident this mammoth undertaking, the biggest single public project in the history of Bradford, would at last cope with the enormous outflow of sewage from the city once the tunnel was completed.

Due to the war, the cost of the planned aqueduct connecting the Esholt end of the tunnel to the north side of the valley had increased and was no longer affordable. After much debate, engineers came up with the novel and cheaper solution of a half-mile-long, three-pipeline inverted syphon, to be tunnelled under the canal and bridged over the river. This proved to be an effective alternative, although not without its hazards for the tunnellers when the unstable canal floor caved in. The free flow of sewage through the siphon was to be achieved by passing huge wooden balls through each of the pipes at regular intervals. Once through the acid precipitation process on the north side of the valley, gravity would complete the journey of the separated liquid through coal-filled filter beds and into the river. On its way it would flow over water wheels at a row of machine houses, powering pairs of distributors up and down the filter beds, requiring no additional power. On the south side of the valley, rows of huge presses would receive the precipitated solid matter to provide Bradford with valuable revenue from the extracted wool grease, leaving the remaining pressed 'cake' to be sold as fertiliser. The works was so revolutionary and on such a huge scale that it soon attracted attention from far and wide. Delegations of dignitaries, engineers and chemists from home and overseas became a regular sight as it began to take shape. Bradford, once cited as the filthiest town in England, was rapidly gaining accolades for having the largest and most progressive sewage treatment works in Europe.

In Bradford few mourned the permanent closing of the canal, brought about by competition from the railway and loss of traffic during the war. Soon infilling would reduce much of its route to nothing more than a memory in the minds of older citizens.

Long hours and heavy lifting was taking its toll of Mary's ageing parents at their grocery emporium in Bolton Road. Now in their sixties, they relied more and more on their daughter as the shop continued to flourish. Bill regularly lent a hand when he could, but it became increasingly obvious that a decision would have to be made about its future.

"We would be happy to let you run it, love," Mary's father told her one evening. "But it takes more than one and your Bill says he wants to stay at Esholt."

"Yes, Bill loves his job and says he'd feel suffocated working in a shop. Our Tommy says it's not exciting enough for him either."

"What about Bill's sister, do you think she'd be interested?"

"No. Hannah's a wild card. She's too bound up with the Suffragettes. I couldn't imagine her settling to a job in a shop. But there's her lass, Carrie. Her husband's in the Merchant Navy and she's not working at the moment. She's a bright lass and gets on with people, so she might be just the job, if she's interested. I'll have a word with her."

When Mary put the offer to her, Carrie looked astonished and could only manage, "Are you sure? I hope you're not joking with me; that would be unkind."

"Not at all, I'm perfectly serious. I'd love to have you working with me in the shop, Carrie. It's a good business, as you know, and with hard work, I think we can grow it even more."

"Well then, yes, I'd love to," stuttered Carrie, flattered to be asked. "When do you want me to start?"

"There's a lot to learn, so come in on Monday and we'll take it from there. My mam and dad will be relieved to know they can step back. They'll still be on hand, of course, to offer advice if and when it's needed."

"Shopkeepers, eh? That's a turn-up for the books," said Bill when Mary gave him the news. "I expect that means we'll be staying at Undercliffe for the time being. Anyroad, our Carrie's got a good head on her shoulders; she'll be good for the business."

From the open-fronted upper deck, father and son enjoyed their daily overview of the Aire valley as the tram rattled and swayed across Five Lane Ends and began the descent of Bradford Road towards Idle. Excited by reports of Bradford's nascent car industry, Tommy craned to view progress at the new Jowett production plant taking shape at Springfield.

"Now, that's where I'd like to work," he told Bill. "They say they're going to make motor cars by the hundreds there. I hope I'll be able to own one some day."

"Nay, you're dreaming lad; they're for the rich. The likes of us will never be able to afford one. Anyroad, they'll be a danger on the roads, I reckon."

"I think they're terrific. Just think, we'd be able to go anywhere we like in a motor car; up to Skipton and even up into the Dales for a picnic on a Sunday. I know you got me the job at Esholt, Dad, but I just can't stand working in that tunnel. I'm going to try my luck with Jowett's, even if I just end up working on the new buildings."

Father and son completed the rest of their journey to Thackley in contemplative silence. It was Bill who spoke first as they made their way beneath the fresh green canopy of Dawson Wood down to the tunnel outflow.

"I don't suppose it matters where you work as long as you're happy in the job. If you can't stand tunnelling, you're just as well out of it. We'll both go to Jowett's after work and see what's doing."

"Thanks, Dad," said Tommy, giving his father's arm an affectionate squeeze as they parted company to begin their respective shifts.

* * *

Constance felt a mixture of excitement and apprehension as the train slowed to a halt in Galashiels station. The first passengers to alight were already heading for the exit before she spotted Tilly emerging through a cloud of steam. The half-sister she had last seen as a little girl back in her native Yorkshire morphed before her eyes into a tall middle-aged woman with elegantly coiffured grey hair surrounding a healthy, tanned face. She wore a finely tailored costume, complemented by expensive jewellery and a tiny handbag.

That first glimpse of her sophisticated sibling threw Constance into near panic when she considered her own country wife's attire. But Tilly's obvious joy at meeting her half- sister again, expressed in a warm kiss and full body hug, restored her confidence as she returned the affection with the greeting, "Welcome to Scotland. I've been so looking forward to this moment. You're looking just great."

"So do you, Sis," returned Tilly with evident sincerity. "It's been too long. George would love to have been here too, but he couldn't leave the business right now with his expansion plans and all. He says to tell you 'Hello'."

"You're so American," laughed Constance. "You've got the accent and everything."

"And you're so Scottish. I'm surprised you're not wearing plaid."

"Wait 'til you see your nephew in Highland dress. He really looks the part," said Constance, beckoning a porter to follow them with Tilly's enormous sea trunk on a trolley.

The journey by horse and trap to the farm drew gasps of admiration and delight from Tilly as they made their way between the wooded green slopes of the Ettrick Valley. Constance listened in awe as her younger half-sister spoke about her life in Baltimore; her marriage to George Schultz, now the owner of a chain of bar restaurants throughout Maryland and Delaware; and their two grown sons, working for their father. By contrast, Constance felt she had led a constrained life on the farm, as she described the rural rhythm of the quiet Borders community. She explained about Donald's invalidity and Gordon's passion for agriculture that was beginning to rank them among the better-off farms in the area. Tilly changed the conversation by asking, "Do you ever go back to Yorkshire?"

"Not since our mother died. She didn't recognise anyone in the end, so it seemed pointless to make that long journey for her not to know who I was or anything."

"Did you know the hall's been sold? You know, Esholt Hall, where mother used to work. A friend told me about it in a letter. It seems the Stansfields have moved out and Bradford Corporation have taken over the big estate. Seems such a shame really, after all those years."

"Well, I suppose the sisters couldn't see any future for the estate without a male heir. Anyway, mother never forgave the Stansfields for the way she said she was treated," replied Constance.

"Did she ever talk about it, I mean, what really happened?"

"Not really. She said she was a chambermaid there. She had to leave when rumours were spread about because she was having me. I don't think she'd be shedding any tears for the Stansfields if she was alive now."

"Scotland is really beautiful," said Tilly, again changing the subject to the relief of Constance, who did not want to share with Tilly her private suspicions about her own origins in case they met with incomprehension or ridicule.

"Yes it is, but it gets a bit wild in winter. Anyway, this is where we turn off. Before we get to the farm, I just want to warn you that Donald has not been too well lately. As I said, he's confined to a wheelchair and it makes him a bit grizzly. He means well, so don't be upset if he appears a bit rude at first. He'll be fine once he gets to know you."

"Thanks for the warning, Sis. I'll be all charm."

Constance's caution was unnecessary in the event as Donald Jameson greeted his sister-in-law cordially, welcoming her to their home. Gordon soon arrived in the doorway, filling it with his six-foot frame as he advanced on his aunt with a broad grin, a kiss on the cheek and a bear hug.

"My oh my, my sister was right about you. What a handsome young man. Are all the others as good looking as him?" she asked Constance, to Gordon's mild embarrassment. "I can see I'm going to enjoy my stay in Scotland."

"Then let's have a dram to celebrate. You do enjoy a wee whisky, don't you?" asked Donald.

"Why, sure, on the rocks, sour, on its own, whichever way it comes."

With glasses raised, it was Donald who proposed the toast, "Slàinte Mhath, that's the Gaelic to wish you good health."

"I'll drink to that," said Tilly.

* * *

In a tunnel nearly three miles long, even a slight miscalculation could lead to a serious misalignment. After four years of navvies continuously chipping away with pneumatic drills, this thought was uppermost in the mind of the project leader as he rode the last hundred yards to the head of the southern section. At a pre-arranged time, men set to work with drills at the heads of both sections, attacking the solid rock with deafening vigour. Suddenly, a faint glimmer of yellow light became a gleam as friable material fell away exposing a hole big enough for hands from each direction to be clasped, raising a hoarse cheer from all witnessing the breakthrough. As the hole widened, it became clear that the tunnels had met exactly as planned, a fact quickly relayed to assorted dignitaries gathered at Frizinghall.

Within days, contractors moved in to begin lining the tunnel with bricks, a task that was to take a further year and which culminated in a drive-through by three Jowett Seven Tourers hot off the Springfield production line. One of the proudest people that day was twenty-one-year-old Tommy Ackroyd, newly promoted to the Jowett factory maintenance team, having served his five-year apprenticeship at Five Lane Ends. Because his father was one of the first Esholt workers, Tommy was given special permission to join the welcoming party when the three cars emerged from the tunnel into daylight.

This publicity stunt was a welcome shot in the arm for Jowett sales at a time when the economy was already showing signs of stress. Within two years, the country was reduced to chaos as unions rallied to a call for a nationwide general strike in support of miners who were suffering a cut in their wages. In spite of the disruption, work continued on the construction of the sewage works, allowing it to be brought into partial use. An ever-increasing outflow from the new tunnel resulted in huge sales of grease, helping to reduce the rates burden on Bradford homes and businesses.

Even with its newfound income from extracted wool grease, Bradford was still having to find ways to alleviate pernicious child poverty. The city was the first in the country to introduce free school meals for underprivileged children, following pioneering work by the Bradford Cinderella Club since 1890. The General Strike proved to be the club's greatest challenge to provide essential welfare in the form of food and clothing to complement the work of the overstretched corporation. The club even gave landlocked Bradford children a taste of the sea at a holiday home at Hest Bank near Morecambe. This required the help of dedicated volunteers such as seventeen-year-old Betty Grimshaw, who accompanied the children on the charabanc journey across Lancashire. A pretty, confident brunette, she had caught the attention of Tommy Ackroyd in the Jowett canteen where she worked as a server. He made every effort to engage her in conversation at lunchtimes, annoying people behind him in the queue when spending too long choosing his meal. Despite all his efforts, she steadfastly refused his blandishments until the day he learned about her work with the charity. Collecting a plateful of fish and chips, Tommy asked her if they needed more volunteers at the club.

"We always need volunteers," Betty replied, showing new interest in this persistent young man who always made a point of choosing to be served by her. "We're busier than ever because of the strike. We could do with more pairs of hands."

"How do I join then?" he asked, feeling this was his best chance to get close to the girl.

"Well, we're giving out clothes outside the Cathedral on Saturday if you want to come along. Twelve o'clock sharp, mind."

He was reminded where he was by a sharp prod in the ribs. "Ay up, lad, you're blocking the queue. Some of us want to eat so do your courting elsewhere."

"We're not courting, you cheeky blighter," said Betty, blushing, "and if you want to get a decent portion in future you'd better keep that kind of talk to yourself."

"Oh, come on, lass, only joking. He's far too ugly for you anyhow."

Tommy just smiled at the banter, gave Betty an affirmative nod and took his tray to an empty table. If food was the way to a man's heart, he mused, perhaps charity was the way to a girl's.

* * *

Carrie stared through the compartment window at the seemingly endless, flat landscape of the East Riding. Her entire life had been spent within the close embrace of the Pennines and these wide open spaces only added to her growing unease about the forthcoming meeting. Soon the leaden-grey waters of the River Humber signalled the approach of her destination, affording a fleeting glimpse of huddled smoke-shrouded trawlers before the train steamed to a halt in Hull's cavernous Paragon Station. After receiving directions at a newspaper kiosk, a short walk through busy streets brought her to the red brick Mission to Seamen situated close to Princes Dock. She considered the sixty-mile journey was little enough to try to save her eleven-year-old marriage to Robert, whom she had not seen for over a year while he was at sea.

Inside the mission she was shown into a large room where a number of men, many of them foreigners, were standing or seated in small groups engrossed in conversation. Several heads turned in her direction as she searched the suntanned faces until she recognised the florid features of her husband who was half-lying on an ornately woven antimacassar. With only the slightest attempt at a greeting, he slowly uncoiled his large frame from the low furniture and beckoned her to follow him into an anteroom.

"How are you, Bob? You look well," she began nervously. "I got your letter; that's why I'm here, of course. Dorothy and Sally are both well. They've missed their father and..."

"I've brought presents for them," he interrupted. "I sail again in the morning, so I won't be able to see them this time. But I'll send them a card when we hit shore."

Intimidated by her husband's physical presence and unwelcoming demeanour, Carrie strove to open up the conversation she had been dreading since leaving Bradford. "Will nothing change your mind, Bob? We all love you and miss you. Can't we just talk this over? The shop's doing really well and I have a good wage from it..."

Again she was cut short. "It's no use, Carrie. As I said in the letter, I want a divorce, and I'm willing to be the guilty party to get it. I'm leaving the sea when we get to Australia and starting a new life where there's room to breathe."

"So you *have* met somebody else," reproached Carrie bitterly, studying her husband's face for his reaction.

"Well, maybe I have and maybe I haven't," he replied. "It makes no difference. I'll give you all the evidence you need for the court."

"But what about the girls? What am I going to say to them?"

"I'll write to them and send them presents when I get to Australia. Look, I have to get back to my ship; I'm on watch in an hour."

He began to ease past her and made to leave the room, pausing to say he would send an address where he could be contacted. Carrie, unwilling to let her husband walk out of her life so easily, placed herself between him and the door, clutching at his seaman's jacket in desperation.

"What did I do wrong? If I have been a disappointing wife, let me try and start over again. Just think of the girls growing up without a father."

"I'm not saying you've done anything wrong. It's just that the war changed everything. I need to be free and that's all there is to it. I would be no good to you or the girls if I stayed. You'll all manage just fine without me."

"Bob, please, give it time," she pleaded. "I'll give you all the space you want, but let's not break up, for the girls' sake."

"Look, I've got to get back to my ship," he said, pushing past her. "As I said, I'll write as soon as I can, but I've got to go." In one movement he opened the door and walked out of the room, leaving Carrie stunned and in tears.

Unaware of the drama that had just taken place, a young naval chaplain entered the room to find Carrie sobbing bitterly. He managed to extract only the briefest explanation before calming her with a cup of hot sweet tea and emollient words. Life at sea could change some men, he told her, especially if they were caught up in the war. Usually, they just needed time to sort themselves out. With her faith in God and the power of prayer, he was sure things would turn out right for her in the end.

As the train carried her back towards the life and people she loved and trusted, Carrie reflected on the chaplain's words, but resolved to take firm control of her destiny from now on. She would emulate her mother's courage and independence to bring up her own daughters with sufficient confidence to prevent them ever having to face a similar situation to herself.

"What a complete bastard," was Mary's reaction when Carrie told her in the shop about the meeting at the Seaman's Mission. "You're better off without him. Anyway, I think I can help you to put all that behind you. Now my parents have left me to run the emporium, I need someone to share the day-to-day responsibility; would like you to be my partner? It's doing really well, so you won't have any money worries. What do you say, Carrie?"

Surprised by the generous offer, Carrie took some moments to respond, "I…I'm flattered and highly honoured, Mary. But, if you're absolutely sure, well, yes, I would love to be part of the business. Thank you for being so kind," she said tearfully, giving Mary a tight hug for her trouble.

"You've been a real asset to the shop and guess what, we've been doing so well we've bought a motor car. Well, Bill thought it was time we offered a delivery service and with our Tommy working up at Five Lane Ends he was able to get us a good deal. I'm going to ask one of the assistants to learn to drive so he can do our deliveries. But I'm looking forward to going for runs on Sundays – we'll all go and take a picnic basket. Anyway, we'd better crack on, now, as there's a queue building up."

Mary's confidence in her bolstered Carrie's hope that her life would soon regain an even keel surrounded by the love of family and friends. She managed to deflect her daughters' questions about their absentee father by giving them opaque answers about life at sea. But she realised there would come a time when the girls would demand to know more, and Carrie determined that only his 'disappearance' would bring closure for them all. She felt fully justified intercepting any attempts he might make to contact the girls. As far as she was concerned, he had squandered that right and no longer existed.

* * *

The economic woes of the West Riding continued even though most of the strikers returned to work within a month. It was a further six months before the miners went back, having suffered tremendous hardship in spite of charitable handouts. In Bradford, the Cinderella Club continued to support families of jobless textile workers, giving Tommy Ackroyd the ideal opportunity to stay close to Betty Grimshaw. Weekends found him sorting clothes or handing out gifts of food to families in the poorer districts, earning the tacit approval of his would-be girlfriend and the disdain of his father, who wanted his son beside him on the terraces at Valley Parade. As summer approached, Betty let it be known she would be joining a charabanc full of Bradford youngsters being taken for a two-week holiday at Hest Bank holiday home on Morecambe Bay. The children, drawn from the steep cobbled streets of terraced back-to-back houses, would rarely, if ever before in their lifetimes, have been into the country and never seen the sea.

Much of her enjoyment, she told Tommy in the canteen one day, was from seeing the wonderment on the faces of the youngsters as they passed through the majesty of the Dales and caught their first glimpse of Morecambe Bay. For some it was all too much, calling on Betty's maternal instincts to mitigate feelings of homesickness and estrangement in the unfamiliar surroundings. For others, liberated briefly from grinding poverty, it was an excuse to release pent-up mischief and self-expression, requiring a firm fatherly hand. This was where Tommy's opportunity presented itself when a male helper was incapacitated due to an accident at work. On a warm June day Tommy found himself sharing a bench seat with three boisterous children at the rear of an open-top charabanc heading up the Ribble Valley towards Settle, all singing 'ten green bottles' in full voice. Three rows in front, her dark hair blowing in the wind, Betty Grimshaw turned mid-song to give him a broad smile. No further evidence was needed, Tommy told himself. She liked him and he was going to use this holiday to make her his, by hook or by crook.

* * *

In spite of the difficult economic times for businesses across the West Riding, construction of the huge treatment works continued unabated at Esholt. Enormous sunken settlement tanks and filters beds, half a mile wide, stretched for more than a mile across the former estate. Processes were already in operation, separating out valuable wool grease, stockpiling the residual 'cake' manure and purifying the remaining effluent by passing it through deep beds of graded coal. Bill was joined by more drivers as new steam locos were acquired to haul trucks carrying pressed 'cake', drums of grease and construction materials to far-flung parts of the site. His favourite run was from the mainline siding at Thackley, between the main works buildings, across the river and up the northern escarpment to the acid plant, passing Esholt Hall on the way: a mile and a half of uneven, sometimes steep, track affording the best views of the thickly-wooded Aire valley. It was on one such run that his army experience came to the fore after another driver took a particularly tight curve on an adverse camber too quickly, jumping clear before his locomotive settled on its side on a cushioning mound of 'cake'. When the works steam crane was brought to the scene, Bill directed operations to lift the derailed engine back on to the track, an operation he had overseen several times in France.

From her vantage point on the newly constructed, concrete-covered culvert leading from Esholt village towards the acid plant, Elizabeth Stansfield viewed the continuing transformation of her once tranquil estate with distaste. Returning home after representing the Stansfield family at a service in St. Paul's Church, formerly the estate chapel, she was using the occasion to pay her first visit to the estate since she and her sisters left ten years earlier. The unfolding panorama viewed through the windows of her Austin Seven Saloon shocked and saddened Elizabeth, and it was with a sense of relief that she rejoined the main road for the journey back to her small Dales fiefdom.

* * *

Tommy's first days at Hest Bank passed in a blur as he and Betty separately found themselves committed to the constant demands of excited children from daybreak to dusk. He used every opportunity to test Betty's feelings for him by engaging her in conversation, however fleeting. Her relaxed manner and warm smile went some way to reassure him, but he longed for the opportunity to get her on her own away from the children. That opportunity presented itself on the third day, when the supervisor told them to take the afternoon off.

"Would you like to go into Morecambe?" Tommy asked Betty, half fearing she might have plans of her own.

"Love to," Betty replied, before adding coquettishly, "Are you coming too?"

Tommy laughed with relief and delight at the teasing familiarity of her response, allowing himself the risky rejoinder, "Only if I'm asked."

She took his hand in hers and to his surprise leaned forward to plant a light kiss on his cheek saying, "You're asked."

Sunlight reflected from the wide high-and-dry expanse of Morecambe Bay under a clear blue sky as the bus followed the coast road south through Bare to 'Bradford by the sea', so-called due to the large number of holidaying millworkers who made the journey across the Pennines each summer. Tommy and Betty got off outside the Winter Gardens and, deep in conversation, strolled along the busy promenade past the old Midland Hotel, each aiming to learn as much about the other as possible.

"Let's go on the beach; I want to paddle," said Betty.

"You'll have a long walk, love. The tide's out," laughed Tommy, pointing to the exposed acres of brown mud stretching almost as far as the eye could see.

"I'll find a pool, then," said Betty, running across the ribbed mud in bare feet.

After much laughter and splashing, they retreated to a quiet part of the beach to sit on a grassy bank looking out to sea. Tommy turned his head to find her studying him, a slight smile playing about her lips.

"A penny for them."

"I was just thinking about you getting into trouble for holding up the dinner queue at Jowett's when I was being a bit offhand."

"A bit!" exclaimed Tommy, earning a cuff on his ear for his pains. "Anyroad, just goes to prove that persistence pays in the end because here we are, you, me and the sea.""Silly beggar," said Betty in his left ear. A quick turn of his head found her lips engaging his, a position he was in no hurry to change.

With his father's blessing, Gordon Jameson bought two small adjacent farms to double their acreage and create one of the largest holdings in the Ettrick Valley. Unfortunately, Donald did not live long enough to savour the benefits of their new prosperity. A farm worker found him slumped in his wheelchair in the hay barn having succumbed to a brain haemorrhage. After a crowded funeral service in the parish church, Constance, nearing her sixtieth birthday, gently hinted to her son that it might be time for him to find himself a wife to share the increasing burden of the farms. Gordon, now approaching thirty, told her, "All in good time, mother. I'll know when the right lass comes along."

He met the future Mrs Jameson on a visit to Hawick market where he was selling the first lambs of the season. Crossing the yard to the main auction ring, his ankles were attacked by two frisky border collies. As he tried to fend them off, a loud whistle from behind brought them to order. He turned to see a young woman he later described as 'an angel in gumboots.' Gordon fell head over heels for the whistler, a raven-haired lass with cornflower blue eyes, dressed in a striking Fair Isle jumper and brown corduroy trousers. In return, Elspeth Graham, the twenty-two-year-old eldest daughter of a modest Teviot hill farmer, showed unequivocal interest in this handsome, and by all appearances, successful young man. Their subsequent brief but intense courtship drew the approval of family and friends alike and they were married in lowland tradition in the old parish church in Hawick, followed by a feast and Scottish dancing until midnight in the parish hall. Much fuss was made that night of special guests of honour, Tilly and her larger-than-life, Stetson-wearing husband George, who joined in the celebration with typical American gusto.

Elspeth was made very welcome on the farm by Constance and soon proved to have a head for bookkeeping and financial management in spite of her limited education. She was a natural with the stock and baulked at no job that came within her physical capabilities. Within a year the first son and heir was born to Gordon and Elspeth on Constance's sixtieth birthday, to her delight and relief that the farm would be passed on to a new generation of Jamesons. A good proportion of Selkirk farming folk crammed into the old parish church for the Christening of baby Angus, followed by the traditional 'head-wetting' in the parish hall, employing ample quantities of Tweeddale whisky, a favoured dram blended in the nearby town of Coldstream.

* * *

After the statutory time had elapsed, Carrie obtained a divorce from her estranged husband on the grounds of his desertion. She heard from an acquaintance living in Freemantle that Robert told everybody he had no intention of returning to England. He was believed to be involved in a relationship with a sailor he met on the high seas. Carrie was profoundly shocked by the news, realising at last why he had been so cold towards her at their last disastrous meeting. He had clearly decided that Australia would provide a less hostile environment for his unorthodox and possibly illegal lifestyle. She told the girls their father had been lost at sea, ensuring that she intercepted any attempts he made to communicate with them. Carrie felt justified in maintaining this fabrication to allow her daughters to grow up without the hurt of knowing he had deserted them so he could be with another man. She was sure she would manage now the shop was providing them all with a good living and with the loving support of her cousins Bill and Mary Ackroyd.

Hannah, now in her mid sixties, rejoiced in the knowledge that all her personal sacrifices over the years had played a small part in persuading Parliament to give women the vote at long last. Now her mission, as she saw it, was to persuade women that they could influence the course of history by exercising their new right at election time. Her radical passion undimmed, she threw all her energy into meetings and doorstep canvassing to get women into the polling booths. She found an unexpected ally in her nephew's fiancée, Betty Grimshaw, whose political interest had been stimulated through her work with the Cinderella Club in the poorest parts of Bradford. Betty saw at first hand the creeping blight of poverty, hunger and hopelessness that achieved remission only through acts of charity, unacknowledged in wealthier, more complacent parts of the city. Soon the gathering speed of economic recession would reach into the homes of all social classes, replacing hubris with a nervous realisation that years of prosperity and growth might be coming to an end.

As construction of the remaining filter beds at Esholt neared completion, the Sewage Works Committee were faced with the sobering news that the entire project was likely to cost more than double the estimate a quarter of a century earlier, mainly due to the war. This was partly offset by revenue of more than one hundred thousand pounds from the sale of pressed 'cake' for manure and well over one million pounds for wool grease extracted from the city's sewage, once considered untreatable. However, sales of this valuable by-product from the state-of-the-art treatment process were slowing in the economic downturn, and committee members expressed concern about the loss of income support for the rates. When they wondered if there were other uses for the mounting stockpile of unsold grease, they were told it was being used to fuel the works' boilers. This brought unanimous support for the establishment of a research laboratory at Esholt to look into ways of incorporating wool grease into a new range of marketable products.

In the threatening economic gloom, Bill Ackroyd acknowledged his good fortune to be working for the corporation in a job he loved. Mary was bringing home a good income from the flourishing emporium that she and Carrie were expanding into new departments. Their lifestyle was in stark contrast to many of the men employed casually on construction work at Esholt, who were uncertain how long their employment would continue or where their next job would come from. Bill and Mary enthusiastically supported the work of Hannah and Betty, giving generously to the Cinderella Fund and distributing parcels of food at weekends in their Jowett Seven. They were regular attenders at the local chapel where they never neglected to give thanks to God for their agreeable lifestyle. One of their immediate concerns was for Tommy, who was among a number of men paid off by the Jowett Company to cut costs. Bill managed to secure some casual work for his son on the filter beds in the hope that Tommy would have sufficient skills to be employed at Esholt on a permanent basis. He enrolled his son in evening classes, which Bill and Mary paid for, to gain additional qualifications in building maintenance. Tommy repaid his parents' support by gaining a certificate for his studies, transferring to the Esholt maintenance department as a probationary worker. This gave him the opportunity to hitch a lift on the footplate of his father's locomotive from time to time when he needed to move around the extensive site. Realising it was his best chance to gain a secure job in desperately difficult times, Tommy applied himself conscientiously to his work, being the first to volunteer for any out-of-hours emergency call-outs. This eventually earned him a permanent position in the maintenance team and a workers' cottage in Esholt village to follow his marriage to Betty.

The ceremony took place in Greengates Church near her family home in Apperley Bridge. Defying the sober mood of the times, she was radiant in a full veil and white organdie wedding dress as she walked down the aisle on the arm of her proud father, joining the nervous groom who felt slightly ill at ease in unfamiliar morning dress. After the signing in the crowded vestry, bride and groom posed for their wedding album before being driven in the ribbon-bedecked Jowett Seven the short distance to their reception in Carr Bottom Road.

"Our Jack would have just loved this day," said Mary, brushing away a tear later as she and Bill joined the bride and groom in the wedding waltz.

"It's worse for our Hannah," said Bill. "She's had more than her share of sorrow, but she doesn't let it get her down. The likes of her are the salt of the earth. She deserves a medal."

The reception was still in full swing when Tommy and Betty slipped away and found the Jowett Seven where Bill said it would be parked for their quiet getaway. They were just congratulating themselves on their stealthy exit when a clattering noise from the rear caused Tommy to pull into the kerb to investigate. As well as the strings of empty tin cans tied to the rear bumper, scrawled across the back of the car in large white letters were the words 'Just married'.

"That's my dad," said Tommy. "He's always the practical joker. I'll have these cans off right now."

Within an hour, the car's headlights were picking out tall hawthorn hedgerows each side of the narrow, winding lane above Gargrave as they drove towards the source of the River Aire and their honeymoon destination in the tucked-away Dales village of Malham. Soon a large wooden sign proclaimed 'The Buck Inn', prompting Betty to lean across and kiss Tommy on his cheek as he drew to a halt outside the front entrance. "It's so romantic. I've never stayed in a proper hotel before," she confessed.

"It was a wonderful wedding, but now it's just the two of us. Let's go and find out where we'll be sleeping tonight, Mrs Ackroyd," he teased his blushing bride.

* * *

Farm duties weighed heavily on Constance's shoulders after the sudden death of Donald, leaving little time for a social life. Elspeth provided both the companionship she craved and the considerable help she needed with the increasing complexity of farm business. Gordon used his newfound prosperity to upgrade the two-hundred-year-old steading, adding an extension for his mother while he and Elspeth took over the Mains. The additional room was soon required for their second son, Eric, whose arrival provided another excuse, if one was needed, for the farming community to let its hair down once again.

Gordon recognised that the most efficient farms were continuing to prosper in spite of the encroaching economic depression. Although he had been forced to hire additional hands to cope with his increasing absences on business, he subscribed to the mechanical revolution taking place in farming, which promised reduced labour costs and increased profitability. He invested heavily in technology, including one of the first Fordson tractors in the Borders, gaining the envy and respect of his neighbours in equal measure. His status as one of the leading burghers now assured, he cut a striking figure at the annual Common Riding, which he first attended at his mother's knee a quarter of a century before. Elspeth, meanwhile, continued to justify his early confidence, playing an increasing role in farm business and proving to be a valuable source of ideas and inspiration in addition to attending to the needs of two boisterous sons who constantly took advantage of their devoted grandmother. For her part, Constance declared that in spite of failing health, she had never known greater happiness.

* * *

A succession of large black limousines converged on Apperley Bridge railway station from the north and south before turning off Harrogate Road past a gatekeeper's lodge and processing along the tree-lined drive leading to Esholt Hall. Where, less than thirty years before, the Stansfield sisters would have gazed upon an unspoilt verdant landscape, this modern motorcade enjoyed a view across acres of coal-filled filter beds straddled by pairs of slow-moving skeletal distributors on rails. Each pair was hauled by cables attached to machinery driven by a pair of liquid-effluent powered water wheels in a series of squat stone buildings.

The cars drew to a halt beside one of the filter beds, disgorging gentlemen and ladies dressed for the cool September weather in top coats and fur stoles, men of rank distinguished by their black bowler hats. Next to one of the bunting-fringed machinery houses, the assembled guests gathered round to watch Arthur Greenwood, Minister of Health in the Ramsay MacDonald Government, open a valve to direct liquid effluent on to the water wheels, setting in motion two distributors drawing the same liquid from cast-iron troughs and spraying it on to the surface of the coal at the start of the purifying process on its way to the River Aire. The ceremony, in the presence of Lord Mayor Alderman Alfred Pickles, marked the completion of the fifty three acres of bacterial filter beds by Bradford Corporation, drawing praise from The Minister for the city's bold and imaginative solution to its unique sewage disposal problem, which had plagued the city and polluted the river for much of the past century. Esholt sewage works enjoyed international recognition for turning once untreatable waste into profitable products, which had earned the corporation well over a million pounds, mostly through the sale of recovered wool grease.

"But we are not resting on our laurels," works engineer Howard Wontner-Smith assured the assembled dignitaries. "We aim to maintain and hopefully increase sales of our mounting grease stockpile by finding new outlets in a difficult market. To this end, we shall be opening a new research section of our laboratory in the near future to identify profitable new by-products." Then, preceded by The Minister, The Lord Mayor and Lady Mayoress, clutching a large bouquet, the party made a quick tour of inspection before driving in convoy to the hall for refreshments.

The last of the limousines was pulling away from the kerb as Tommy Ackroyd steered his lorry to a halt close to where the opening ceremony had taken place. His job was to take down the bunting and clear away any rubbish left behind by the guests. As he stepped down from the cab, his attention was drawn by the sound of an aero engine high above. Rooted to the spot, he watched in fascination as a bi-plane dived from behind a light cloud and completed a slow barrel roll before heading off in a northerly direction.

"I'd give my right arm to be in one of those," he confessed to his less than overawed workmate.

"You'd have a job flying it if you only had one arm," came the jokey reply.

"It'll be from Yeadon. I read in the T&A that Yorkshire Aeroplane Club are about to start flying from a new aerodrome there."

"I don't think your missus will be too pleased, you talking about flying; not in her present state at any rate."

"I'm going to find out if I can join anyway. I'll just tell her afterwards. Fancy a pint at The Commercial when we've finished here?"

The two men had just ordered their beer in the village pub when a woman neighbour burst in to announce, "She's started. You need to come quick." Tommy followed the neighbour at a trot to find Betty already being attended to by the family doctor, who had been visiting a patient nearby.

"She's all right, lad; all's well," calmed the doctor. "Just get me some warm water and towels and leave it to me."

The wait downstairs seemed interminable as Tommy paced the room. "Here, you'll need this," said his mate, pushing open the front door with a foot while brandishing two full pint glasses of beer. "Good Health!" Tommy only managed one swallow before a shrill cry announced the arrival of his first child. He was summoned up to the bedroom where Betty, her face scarlet and damp with perspiration, cradled a tiny bundle in a white shawl.

"Come and see our Peter," she invited Tommy. "He's got the Ackroyd nose, all right."

"Well done, lass," he told her, kissing her damp forehead. "Let me have a good look at my son and heir."

The following Sunday, three generations of Ackroyds were joined by most of the village in St. Paul's Church to welcome baby Peter into the church and the community. The service was held early by arrangement with Tommy, who said mysteriously that he had to keep an important appointment that afternoon. So as not to alarm Betty, he failed to add that the appointment was with Yorkshire Aeroplane Club at Yeadon, where he would discover if at the age of twenty-eight it was still possible for him to achieve his dream of learning to fly.

"We have people from all backgrounds here," he was told in the large shed that served as their first clubhouse. "Everyone from bankers and solicitors to tradesmen and farmers. It's mostly about aptitude and then the ability to pay for lessons, of course."

"If I'm accepted, I'll find the money," said Tommy.

"Well now, let's see how you get on with a test flight. Are you ready to have a go?"

"Never more so."

Once in the air, Tommy took control of the Gypsy Moth and was guided through various basic manoeuvres as they flew over Harry Ramsden's opulent fish and chip palace at Menston before circling over an unsuspecting Betty and son at Esholt. He felt a sense of elation he had never experienced in his life before, and knew he had found his true destiny in this wood and fabric biplane. Back on the ground he waited until they taxied to a halt and the engine was switched off before asking how he had done.

"You did fine; you're a natural. We would be very happy to have you as a member. All you need to do is arrange to pay for the lessons."

Back in the village, Tommy let himself into his cottage long after the last guest had left. He greeted Betty with a kiss and peeked into the cradle at his sleeping son.

"Where have you been?" she enquired irritably. "We missed you. Everyone came back here from the church afterwards and wondered where you'd gone."

"Did you see that aeroplane flying over the village about an hour ago?"

"Yes, I wondered why it kept flying in circles."

"Well, that was me, love," he told his astonished wife. "They say I'm a natural flyer, and I'm going to have lessons. What do you think of that?"

"Well I'll be damned! You sneaky beggar, Tommy, not telling me what you're up to. I'm not keen on you flying and, besides, where do you think we're going to find that kind of money? We're not rich, you know."

"I know, love, but it's something I've always wanted to try my hand at and this new aerodrome at Yeadon's right on our doorstep. It feels like I'm born to fly, so I'll find the money somehow."

"What's this I hear about you being up in an aeroplane?" asked his father the following morning when Tommy climbed up to the footplate of Nellie outside the grease house.

"Oh, you've heard then. That's what I was coming to talk to you about; it was the best time of my life up there. There's nothing like it, Dad, and they'll teach me how to fly, the Yorkshire Aeroplane Club that is, if I can pay for the lessons."

"And how do you think you'll manage that?" challenged Bill Ackroyd, testing his son's commitment. "This club sounds a bit grand to me. Do they welcome the likes of us?"

"They've already told me I'd be welcome if I can find the brass. They've got all types there, and I just can't wait to get started. Anyway, I wondered if you and mam could help me out. I'll pay you back."

"I'll have to talk to your mother as she holds the purse strings. Although, whether she'll be happy about you flying, the Lord only knows. I expect we might have a bit to spare with the shop doing well."

Tommy returned to his lorry, elated by the thought that his dream might be about to come true. If it meant working longer hours or taking on other work, it would be worth it to become a pilot. But his workmate remained unimpressed. "I'm keeping my feet firmly on the ground, me. If God had meant us to fly he would have given us wings."

Tommy just smiled and slipped the lorry into first gear.

Campbell's Soap

A passenger on a late-night tram raised the alarm when he saw smoke coming from a cellar grating outside Mary Ackroyd's emporium in Bolton Road. By the time he got to a public telephone box to call the fire brigade, flames could be seen through the plate-glass windows fronting the street. A small crowd of men and women from nearby houses was starting to gather as a shrill ringing sound heralded the arrival of two fire engines.

"They're still in there," shouted one of the bystanders as firemen began to roll out canvas hoses. Another fireman attacked the double front doors of the shop with an axe.

"How many?" asked the officer in charge.

"Mrs Ackroyd and her sister-in-law. They usually work late," shouted the bystander.

Black smoke curled upwards from the breached entrance as a fireman directed a jet of water towards the seat of the flames just inside the shop. Suddenly, through the smoke emerged the crouching, stumbling figure of Mary, a towel clutched to her face. A fireman ran forward in time to catch her as she collapsed into his arms, coughing and spluttering.

"Our Carrie's in there. Hurry, she's in the back. It's the smoke; she can't see."

A murmur went through the growing crowd of onlookers as two firemen wearing breathing masks disappeared into the smoke-filled interior. After an agonizing wait, a cheer greeted their re-emergence as they carried the limp body of Carrie between them.

"Oh my God," screamed Mary. "How is she?"

"She's breathed in a lot of smoke, love, but she should be right. We've sent for an ambulance to get you both off to the infirmary. They'll take care of her."

"Someone needs to tell my husband and her daughters. They'll worry when we don't arrive home."

"We'll look after that, love," volunteered a police constable, newly arrived on the scene. "Where do you live?"

Mary was giving her address as an ambulance arrived. She was helped into the back of the vehicle to join an inert Carrie, who was being given oxygen to help her laboured breathing. An acrid smell hung in the air as the ambulance doors closed on a dramatic scene; smoke still curling past the smashed shop doors and a bloated hose snaking into the interior of the smouldering emporium.

Mary reached across the narrow vehicle to clutch one of Carrie's hands as she wakened with a series of racking coughs.

"Where am I?" she asked as their eyes met.

"You're safe, thank God. You had a narrow escape, but you're going to be all right. The Good Lord is looking after us."

A visibly shocked Bill hugged his wife at her bedside later that night before escorting her from the infirmary after she was found to have suffered nothing more than slight smoke inhalation. Carrie was kept in under observation.

"I got a hell of a scare when the policeman called," Bill told Mary on their way home. "I just pray our Carrie's going to be all right."

It was late the following day before Mary felt able to make the journey down Bolton Road to see for herself the effect of the fire on her emporium. The worst of the damage was confined to the floor of the main shop immediately behind the front entrance, which led the fire brigade and police to conclude that it could have been started deliberately.

"Who would want to do this to us?" she wondered as she picked her way between water-saturated goods. "At least our Carrie's going to be okay," she told Bill that evening. "I'll get the store up and running again with help from you and Tommy. But I'm still racking my brains trying to think who might have enough of a grudge to make them do such a dreadful thing. The police are looking into it, but we'll have to be on our guard from now on."

* * *

An invigorating autumn chill greeted the confident young chemist as he stepped from the Huddersfield train under the two glazed arches of Bradford Exchange Station. A short walk brought him to the carbon-black frontage of the Gothic town hall as its carillon announced the hour with a faithful rendering of a well-loved Yorkshire hymn tune. Directed to a first floor committee room through exotically tiled corridors, the smart-suited thirty-four-year-old was invited to take a seat facing an interview panel, chaired by Esholt's works engineer. The two men had met before when Howard Wontner-Smith was on the lookout for an innovative research chemist to find new by-products to reduce Esholt's growing stockpile of wool grease and so help mitigate the rising cost of treating Bradford's sewage. He had been impressed by Sidney Campbell's research, at a Slaithwaite company, into potential uses for Esholt grease and invited him to join the other applicants for the new position.

Wontner-Smith got his man, who three months later moved into Nunwood House on a wooded hillside overlooking the filter beds. The property once belonged to Victorian architect Henry Francis Lockwood of Lockwood and Mawson fame, the company that designed Saltaire, Bradford Town Hall, St George's Hall and the Wool Exchange. Nunwood House afforded its new resident a mile-long walk to and from the works through fields and beside filter beds, in complete contrast to the steeply urban landscape of the Colne Valley.

An immediate challenge for the Chief Research Chemist was to convince sceptical Esholt colleagues that a young Londoner could turn mounting stocks of unsold wool grease into profitable by-products during the worst economic recession in living memory. Their disbelief was compounded when they learned that initial experiments were looking into ways of making soap. Scorn at the presumption of being able to sell soap made from sewage led to all further research being carried out in secret until a final viable product was ready to be unveiled. The grease laboratory was also under constant pressure to justify the corporation's spending on pure research in such straitened times. But Wontner-Smith's faith in his fledgling department was to bear fruit under the gathering clouds of war.

* * *

"I've got my little girl at last," was all Elspeth could find the energy to say, half- laughing with pleasure and half-sobbing from exertion at the difficult birth. It was twelve hours since Gordon collected the midwife at the first positive sign the baby was on its way. Now he sat by her bedside beaming with pleasure as she cuddled little Helen.

"She was more trouble than wee Donald; trust a lass to make an entrance," he joked. "Anyway, we have our three boys to run the farm, so we can afford a wee lassie now."

"Gordon Graham, don't be so rude about our new daughter. She'll pull her weight just as much as the others, you'll see."

"You get some sleep now," the midwife told Elspeth, lifting the baby gently away from her. "I'll clean her up and she'll be ready for a feed when you wake up."

"She's a lucky girl," the midwife told Gordon as she bathed Helen in the farm kitchen, warmed by a blazing log fire. "With three older brothers, she'll never be short of boyfriends, that's for sure."

"Aye, and three brothers are all she'll have; that's our family complete, right enough."

A commotion at the door signalled the arrival of seven-year-old Angus, his five-year-old brother Eric and Donald, aged just two. "Come and see your baby sister, boys," shouted Gordon as the three grubby children tumbled into the kitchen and took up positions round the midwife cradling the sleeping baby girl, swaddled in the traditional family shawl.

"Where's Gran?" asked Angus, puzzled by Constance's absence at what was clearly an important family occasion.

"She's having a wee nap as she was up with your mother most of the night," Gordon told him. "Let's go and see if she's awake, so we can show her wee Helen. She'll be happy it's a girl; that's what she's been telling us all along."

"I'm just up," Constance greeted Gordon sleepily as he pushed open her door with an elbow, still holding Helen in his arms. "I was right wasn't I? It's a girl."

"Here, take your new granddaughter," he replied, transferring Helen across to a now beaming Constance.

"I told you so. Isn't she just beautiful?"

* * *

In Bradford the police let it be known they were on the lookout for a middle-aged man who, they believed, could help them with their enquiries into the fire at the Bolton Road emporium. A local resident had seen the suspect loitering in the vicinity of the shop before the incident. The informant told the police he had not linked the man to the fire until he read a report in the *Telegraph and Argus*. Detectives were working on the possibility it was the same man reportedly seen putting petrol in a can at a nearby filling station. The descriptions tallied, especially the fact that both men were reported to have a distinctive scar on the left cheek.

Convalescing at home after her ordeal by smoke, Carrie picked up a two-day old copy of the newspaper and read an account of the police investigation for the first time. Suddenly she felt a stab of fear. It might be no more than a coincidence, but she felt she could be in real danger. Her telephone call to the police station quickly brought a plain-clothes detective and a constable to her door. She explained her fear, having read a newspaper description of the suspect, and insisted she needed protection for herself and her daughters.

"What makes you think you're in special danger?" asked the detective.

"Because if it is Robert, back from Australia, he'll be out to get revenge because I cut him off from the girls. I'm frightened; you don't know what he's like."

"Well now, don't get yourself in a state, love. Constable Smith here will stay with you for the time being. With your detailed description, if it is your former husband, I'm sure we'll soon pick him up."

Carrie was on tenterhooks until Dorothy and Sally arrived home from the Technical College. She would have to warn them of her suspicions for their safety and knew she was going to have a difficult time explaining why she lied to them about their father.

"Sit down, I've got something to tell you," she instructed her daughters as they walked through the doorway, immediately sensing they were about to hear bad news. The girls heard her out without interruption, and then sat silently trying to make sense of what they had just learned. It was unbelievable that their father might be alive after all, and may even be trying to harm their mother in some insane bid for revenge.

"I'm truly sorry it has come to this; I just wanted to protect you," sobbed Carrie. "You are the last people on earth I would want to hurt. Please try to forgive me."

After a few more moments of confused silence, the girls rose and together put their arms round their distressed mother, reassuring her that nothing would ever change their love for her. They just needed time to absorb these surprising and shocking revelations. In the meantime, it was important they all look out for one another until the matter was resolved, one way or another. Two weeks later, on a tip-off from a neighbour, the police raided a house in Girlington and arrested a man fitting the description of the wanted person. He gave his name as John Brown and vigorously protested his innocence, claiming to have been nowhere near Bolton Road on the night of the fire. His defence collapsed when the police confronted him with Carrie at the central police station.

"I'll do for you yet, you bitch," he spat, as she pointed him out in an identity parade as her former husband. Robert White remained in custody until his trial at Leeds Assizes, where he was found guilty of committing arson with intent to cause harm. He was sentenced to five years in Armley Gaol.

"He's horrible, and we're glad he's in prison," Dorothy told her relieved mother. "But what shall we do when he gets out?"

"We'll just have to cross that bridge when we come to it. You both had a terrible shock and I'm sorry for putting your love to the test like that. So thank you for standing by me. We will get through this together."

"Have you seen the T&A?" asked Betty when Tommy Ackroyd arrived home from work. "The Bishop's having a right old go at the King for some reason. For all they say about him, I like Edward because he's a man of the people."

"No, love, I've not seen it," said Tommy, dismissively keen to impart some news of his own. "The RAF's moved into Yeadon. I had a word with one of the officers and I think they'll let me have a go in one of their new Tiger Moth trainers. They've got all sorts up there now."

"I just don't know what you see in it, Tommy. I'm frightened to death every time you go up in one of those flimsy things. I just worry about something happening to you, that's all."

"It's what I've always wanted to do, Betty love. It's what I was put here for. It's the second love of my life…after you, of course."

"I wonder," was her terse response.

In public bars and cafes, on the trams and trolley buses and in the workplace there was only one subject on the lips of Bradfordians as they went about their daily lives. Bishop Alfred Blunt had unwittingly provided the catalyst in an address to his diocesan conference, a copy of which he traditionally forwarded to the *Telegraph and Argus*. His intended criticism of King Edward's casual attitude to religion was interpreted by the Press as a condemnation of the King's clandestine affair with an American divorcee. Suddenly this ill-kept secret was on all the front pages, forcing the King to abdicate only eight days later. Six months on, the crown was placed on the head of his ill-prepared younger brother Albert, affectionately remembered in the city for his visit a decade earlier when, as Duke of York and accompanied by his wife of five years, the former Elizabeth Bowes Lyon, he laid the foundation stone for the new infirmary on Duckworth Lane.

* * *

Carrie was warned that her damaged lungs would be a recurring health problem for the rest of her life. A few minutes more in the smoke-filled shop would have sealed her fate; she was lucky to be alive. What no one, not even Mary, realised, was Carrie's continuing anxiety about the proximity of her revengeful ex-husband incarcerated at Armley. Remembering her mother's recent concern, she could not free her mind of thoughts of him seeking her out following his release, perhaps after just two-and-a-half years. Several weeks went by before she revealed to Bill and Mary her recurring nightmare.

"I can't help it. I just keep imagining him threatening me and the girls. He'll be even madder when he gets out. We'll just have to go somewhere he can't find us."

"No you will not," said Bill firmly, putting an arm round his distraught niece to comfort her. "I'm retiring from the corporation soon, so I'll be around all day to keep an eye on you. Anyroad, Mary can do with some extra help in the shop."

"That's right," said Mary. "We'll make sure he doesn't get

anywhere near you and the girls, so don't worry. Everything's going to turn out all right, you'll see."

In Esholt village two regulars stood in the middle of Main Street watching the landlord of the Commercial hang a string of red, white and blue bunting across the stone frontage of the public house.

"Expecting a royal visitor are you? You'll have to stop watering your beer then," barracked one of the men.

"Cheeky sod. Here, make yourselves useful and hold this ladder. And as you've asked, it's for Bill Ackroyd's retirement night. Everyone's invited, even you two if you give no more lip."

"You'll need more parking for the Baildon and Guiseley lot now they've shut the station. Pity enough people didn't use it after the Stansfields left."

Hours later, the crowded pub reverberated to the clatter of flat Yorkshire vowels at increasing volume as the revellers took advantage of free pints of Tetley's best bitter, accompanied by pies and mushy peas, courtesy of Bill's workmates, the works management and villagers. Thanking everyone present for their generous contribution to the evening and for all the kind sentiments expressed on his behalf, Bill told a now hushed pub, "I've had the best job in the world with the best mates a man can hope for. But it's time to chuck in my oily rag and give the young 'uns a chance. And talking about young 'uns," turning to look at Tommy, "I'll not have to worry any more about him checking on me from up there while I'm stopped having my bait." He broke through the laughter to tell them, "I'm retiring, but I'm not going to be idle. Just drop into Mary's emporium in Bolton Road anytime if you like to discuss old times, and I'll make sure you don't leave empty handed."

More laughter echoed through the darkened Esholt lanes, bouncing off the shadowed cottage where little Peter Ackroyd was having a restless dream about Grandad's steam engine racing through a long dark tunnel, pursued by an immense wooden ball.

* * *

'We never closed', defiantly proclaimed the banner strung across the front of Mary's emporium as Bill alighted from a trolley bus and made to cross Bolton Road.

"That's a bit rum," he observed, pointing to the banner as he stepped into the renovated interior where the air still held a faint hint of smoke despite the extensive application of fresh paint.

"Okay, so we had to have a stall on the pavement for a bit," said Mary in response to her husband questioning the veracity of the banner. "But we never stopped selling groceries. People round here were marvellous; so loyal when they heard what had happened. We were back inside the shop within a month. It nearly broke my heart having to chuck out so much smoke-damaged stuff, though."

"Thank goodness your mam and dad took out insurance," said Bill. "We could have been ruined. Anyroad, I'm looking forward to working here with you and Carrie. Don't worry; I won't get in your way. I'll stick to hardware, which I want to expand. There are so many new household gadgets around these days."

"We could do with you about the place. Carrie's still not right and only comes in mornings at the moment. She just doesn't seem to have the energy these days. When I think of that monster..."

A bell alerted them to a tumble of children from the nearby school piling into the shop. "Keep an eye on them, they're a light-fingered lot," warned Mary.

"Right boys, come on now, what do you want?" Bill demanded in his most authoritarian voice, relishing this new challenge at his time of life.

* * *

In spite of Neville Chamberlain's assurances to the nation that there would be 'Peace for our time,' more sceptical politicians, like Winston Churchill, read Germany's intentions differently and actively sought a state of readiness to meet any onset of hostilities. One proposal that met with a positive response in Whitehall was the establishment of a largely civilian organisation to ferry military aircraft between factory production lines and RAF aerodromes.

After gaining his pilot's licence at Yeadon, Tommy Ackroyd longed for something more challenging than "pootling about the sky over the West Riding", as he put it. It was while he was idly turning the pages of a *Yorkshire Post* in The Commercial that he came across a short item about the air ferry, which was planning to use qualified civilian pilots. He might be too old to follow his passion in the Royal Air Force, he mused, but this organisation seemed to offer the opportunity he had been looking for. He tore out the news item and resolved to find out what he could about the organisation, without alarming Betty, of course. She still worried every time he took to the air and he had yet to persuade her to let him take their seven-year-old son for a flight.

Peter was proving to be a bright boy at his primary school and he too was aeroplane mad, nagging his father constantly to take him up. Tommy decided he would wait until Betty was away visiting her aunt in Morecambe before giving his son a treat. His opportunity came a few weeks later when Betty was summoned hastily to the bedside of her ailing aunt, taking James and Sheila with her and leaving Peter in the care of his father.

"Now, Peter lad, what do you reckon to a flip in a Gypsy Moth tomorrow, if it stays fine? All right, all right, I can see you're keen," said Tommy as Peter flung his arms round his father's neck. "We'll keep it a secret between us and tell your mam after she gets back. Okay?"

Warmly wrapped in an over-sized flying jacket and wearing a brown leather helmet and a large pair of goggles, Peter was helped into the front cockpit of a Gypsy Moth parked outside the club hanger at Yeadon Aerodrome. He was strapped into the seat and turned his head to get a reassuring thumbs up from his father as they began taxiing across the short grass. A final alignment and they were speeding across the aerodrome, slowly lifting off the ground into a blue sky dotted with small white clouds. A bank to the left and soon Tommy was shouting to his son to look down as they flew over their village. Another bank left and a short while later they were circling Undercliffe, Tommy pointing to the emporium below. Soon Pudsey and Horsforth slid beneath them before he lined up with the aerodrome, flanked to the north by a huge construction site, and made a smooth landing, taxiing the final hundred yards to the club hangar.

"Well, son, what did you make of that?" Tommy asked Peter rather needlessly given that the excited youngster was grinning from ear to ear as he was lifted out of the cockpit and set down on the grass.

"That was wizard, Dad. When can we do it again?"

"Depends on your Mother, Son. Remember, it's our little secret until I find the right time to tell her."

Betty arrived home to find a meal waiting for her and a vase of freshly picked flowers on the table. Her suspicions, which had been aroused by this uncharacteristic display of domesticity by her husband, were answered during a cosy fireside chat when all the children were in bed. As her storm of indignant protest about the clandestine flight abated, Tommy considered the concomitant withdrawal of his conjugal rights a small price to pay for the unalloyed pleasure of having seen the sheer joy on the face of his eldest son.

There was a sombre air in their living room as Tommy and Betty joined Bill and Mary around the family wireless set to hear a special announcement by the Prime Minister. Sensing something important was about to happen, Peter hovered in the background while his brother and sister played outside. When Chamberlain began speaking, everyone in the room was stunned to hear that Britain was at war with Germany once again. All the warning signs had been there for some time but the chilling reality of the announcement rendered everyone silent in their own thoughts when the set was switched off. Bill was the first to break the silence, "I lost a son and two nephews in the last war. God help us that it should come to this again."

"All war is stupid and unnecessary," said Betty. "Wars never solve anything. People just get killed for nothing."

"Well, not always for nothing, love," said Tommy. "Sometimes we have to fight to stop people like Hitler walking all over Europe. Anyroad, we'll soon have him licked."

"They said that the last time and it lasted four long years with millions dead," said Betty.

In Selkirk, Gordon plugged the farm wireless into a power socket next to the bed where Constance now spent much of her time. Elspeth and the four children joined them to hear the announcement that was to affect all their lives.

"I'm just glad Donald isn't alive to hear this," said Constance. "He hated war. He said it robbed Scotland of its brightest and best sons, all for no benefit. Now here we go again."

"Our family were lucky," said Gordon. "We lost no one in the war, but there are plenty of local lads named on the memorial in Ettrick Terrace. Unfortunately, they had no choice. We all have to do our bit."

On his way home from work, Tommy stepped inside a telephone kiosk and asked the operator to put him through to the number on the torn-out piece of newspaper in his hand. A voice confirmed he was through to the RAF recruiting centre in Leeds and, in response to his enquiry, transferred him to a different section where he was invited to come for an interview the following week. Betty's not going to like this, he thought as he made his way into the new City Station for his train back to Apperley Bridge. Still, I'm sure she'll come to realise we all have to make sacrifices now. There's a war on, after all.

* * *

"I never realised finnan haddie was such a vital target for the Germans," quipped a haberdashery stallholder as Kirkgate Market stirred back to life after the dramatic events of the night.

"They reckon Jerry just offloaded a couple of bombs on his way home from Liverpool," her hardware neighbour replied, "and the fish market copped it."

"Well, it certainly gives a new meaning to battered fish," laughed the haberdasher. "Anyroad, it'll take more than that to shut us down here."

Such was the defiant spirit of Bradfordians as they prepared to face the storm of conflict after the calm of the phoney war. Many of those judged too old for conscription into the armed services were still eager to get involved. Tommy Ackroyd had already cleared the first hurdle towards his ambition by being referred to the RAF's Central Flying School in Wiltshire for assessment of his flying skills. He had blunted Betty's hostility to his plans by pointing out that as a pilot in the Air Transport Auxiliary, he would be able to spend some time at home and would not be flying in combat like so many of his fellow countrymen.

"You've still got the Cinderella Club," he told her. "Now all the youngsters are in school, you'll be able to do your bit as well. There's lots of families needing help with their men being away at the war."

"They're already packing children off to Hest Bank in case of air raids. Maybe I can help out there; I want to do something useful."

"Well, so do I, love, don't you see? It's just the same really. We both want to do our share. Anyroad, I thought we'd treat ourselves, so I've got these."

"George Formby at the Alhambra! In the front stalls as well. You must have come into money."

"They were hard to get because it's a sell out. But I thought we could all do with a bit of cheering up."

An upgrading of his pilot's certificate at Upavon to twin-engined aircraft qualified Tommy to fly Ansons from the Avro factory at Yeadon to active service airfields throughout the country. Proudly displaying the winged badge of the ATA on his uniform, there was no happier man or woman in the skies over Britain. Now he had only to log the required number of flying hours in the Anson to qualify for his next ambition: flying the mighty, four-engined Lancaster bombers rolling out of the Yeadon factory. However, he thought it might be wise to keep these thoughts to himself for the time being.

In the new research laboratory at Esholt, efforts to identify profitable by-products from wool grease switched to military applications as the management recognised the financial potential of War Office procurement. Huge quantities of paint were required to camouflage the vast Avro factory to blend in with surrounding countryside.

The Esholt researchers found that specific brown and green pigments added to wool grease provided a suitably weatherproof coating that would help to fool German raiders into dropping their bombs elsewhere. A basic axle lubricant for railway wagons was also developed to release scarce petroleum-based grease for the war effort. Soldiers were able to waterproof their all-important footwear using Esholt's wool grease dubbin, which also protected feet from mustard gas. At last, the worrying piles of grease-filled drums began to diminish as the war provided the treatment works with a much-needed financial bounty.

* * *

The rhythm of farming life changed little for the folk of the Ettrick valley in the first months of the war. Young men who could be spared from the farm were called up into the three services, with girls often taking their place. The citizens of Selkirk quickly got used to blackout curtains and dimmed lighting to avoid giving German bomber crews a navigational aid on their way to the Clyde. To five-year-old Helen Jameson it was all just a scary game being played outside her world, a world in which granny Constance played a big part. Helen would sit close to her grandmother in front of the inglenook fireplace in the kitchen, listening to tales of long ago when her grandmother was a little girl and there was a big mansion with ladies in fine clothes riding in fairy-tale coaches.

One night the magic spell was broken by a deep thrumming sound that seemed to go on and on. Gordon and Elspeth rushed to the door and stood in their yard staring upwards into the darkness towards the arrhythmic throb of multiple dark shapes intent on delivering death and destruction from the sky. In less than twenty minutes, incendiary bombs and high explosives would be raining down on Clydeside on the first night of the blitz that was eventually to claim more than five hundred lives. War censorship prevented the full horror of the raid being reported and it was a couple of days later that Gordon answered a knock on the door to be greeted by the grim-faced local policeman, Calum Armstrong.

"Can we talk inside, Gordon?" asked the constable, stepping into the kitchen. "I'm afraid I've got some bad news. It's about your brother, Arthur – he was caught up in the Clydeside blitz. It seems he was making his way home when the bombs fell. His body was identified at the casualty clearing station. I'm sorry to have to give you this bad news, Gordon, but there are many, many more in the same predicament. As he lived alone, I assume you will want to make the necessary arrangements."

"Yes, of course," replied Gordon, stunned that the war that had seemed so far away should have come so close to his family. The kitchen door opened and Elspeth appeared, who, seeing the policeman, immediately intuited the bad news. "It's Arthur, isn't it?"

"Calum's just told me he was a casualty of the raids the other night. They've only just identified him."

"Oh my God," exclaimed Elspeth. "Another hellish war..." she sobbed, bursting into tears as Gordon placed a comforting arm round her shoulders.

"I'll be on my way," said the constable. "I've got another family to call on. It's not a pleasant job, but it has to be done.

I might have more information to pass on if you drop into the police station tomorrow."

Gordon volunteered to break the news to his mother, who was still in her bed next door. "Be gentle with her," cautioned Elspeth. "She's very frail and this kind of shock could kill her." Constance kept to her bed for a week as she grieved for her eldest son. For the children, the news that their uncle had been killed by the same planes that had disturbed their sleep only a few nights ago brought a new recognition that war was no game; people really did get hurt.

Peter Ackroyd knew all the types of allied and enemy fighters and bombers from a book given to him by Carrie for his birthday. Like any ten-year-old, he was excited by the war in the air, but not unaware of the seriousness of the situation. His initial thrill that one of our night fighters, and perhaps an ack-ack unit at Rawdon, had between them downed a Junkers 88 was tempered by the subsequent news that four people died when it crashed on to cottages in Idle. He hoped that one day he might learn to fly like his father and get to sit in the cockpit of what he considered to be the most beautiful aeroplane ever made, the Supermarine Spitfires of 609 (West Riding) Squadron he had seen on his last visit to Yeadon.

Betty prayed the war would be over before either Peter or James would be needed to go and fight for their country. She continually reminded them that they had to pass exams if they were to make anything of themselves after the war, when there would be huge competition for jobs. Peter repaid her persistence by gaining a scholarship to Bradford Grammar School and was duly rewarded with a second-hand bicycle bought from a dealer in Saltaire. On this he spent some of the happiest days of his childhood, riding the byways and exploring the countryside of lower Airedale as the tide of the war turned in the Allies' favour.

* * *

The affair began innocuously enough. Tommy Ackroyd's promotion to second officer and his assignment to Lancasters found him spending more nights on airfields in Lincolnshire and East Anglia, where entertainment was mostly confined to the officers' mess and camp cinema. Male and female ferry pilots spent their evenings relaxing over a drink and sharing experiences before retiring separately to accommodation specially provided for them.

On two previous occasions he had found himself enjoying the company of a spirited and loquacious female pilot in her late thirties who kept him amused with a series of tales about her ferrying exploits. She particularly enjoyed relating the occasion she delivered her first Anson to its active aerodrome. As she walked around the aircraft to meet the welcoming party in a Jeep, she was asked if the pilot was still on board. Only a search inside the aircraft convinced them that she had indeed flown the Anson single-handed from Woodford Aerodrome in Cheshire. The third time their assignments coincided, he borrowed a camp vehicle so the two of them could visit a village pub away from the base. Celia told him her husband was serving with the RAF in the Far East and she had chosen to become a ferry pilot to relieve the boredom of being at home all day. She thanked Tommy for enlivening her evenings, rewarding him with a kiss on the cheek and a squeeze of his hand.

"It's a bit too public in here; why don't we go and find somewhere more private to talk?" he suggested. On the road back to the airfield she suggested they turn up a wooded cul-de-sac, where they sat talking in the dark for several minutes before Celia leaned across and kissed him firmly on the lips. Her hand found his spontaneous reaction, as he returned her passion and wordlessly they relocated to the back seat. "Are you sure you…?" he began, failing to finish as she pressed two fingers to his lips. "Shhhh…haven't you heard, there's a war on? Carpe diem," she whispered.

Over the following weeks, Tommy looked forward to his ferrying flights with a mixture of excitement and guilt. He was disappointed when his flight did not coincide with Celia's at the same aerodrome. But they made up for these disappointments with passion whenever they were given the opportunity. He did not want to hurt Betty but did not want to give up Celia either. If his wife detected any change in him, he reasoned, she would surely put it down to the stresses of war. Then, after several weeks during which Celia failed to appear, he began to ask discreetly around the RAF stations if anyone had any information about her. All he could discover was that she had left the ATA and was working for the War Office somewhere in the south. Although Tommy's passion for flying and his ferrying missions remained undimmed, he missed the added excitement of his illicit trysts with Celia in the free-for-all hedonism that prevailed during the war.

* * *

Mary was concerned about Carrie's continuing ill health and persuaded her to come into the emporium for only two or three hours a day. Carrie spent the time sitting in the tiny office at the back of the store, keeping the books and organising the hundreds of ration coupons that passed across the grocery counters every day. Out front, Mary had to use all her charm to avoid offending regular customers who tried to use their long association with the shop to get around the strict rationing. As she explained, if she gave an extra ounce of butter to one, she would have to give it to everybody. But, it was hard to turn down a rare pair of coveted nylon stockings or a bottle of almost unobtainable Scotch whisky in return for off-ration meat or cheese. She suspected less scrupulous shopkeepers were open to such blandishments, judging by the number of sharp-suited spivs who somehow managed to find enough petrol to roam the city in their pursuance of the black market.

By this time the emporium had become a truly family business, with Bill attending the wholesale markets at the crack of dawn and Carrie's daughters, Dorothy and Sally, sometimes helping out in the evenings and at weekends. From her office vantage point, Carrie routinely scrutinised the faces of all males who came into the store, still fearing she might be attacked by her ex-husband. The girls, concerned about their mother's continuing anxiety, wrote to their father in prison, leaving him in no doubt they wanted nothing more to do with him. There was no reply and it was three years later that the girls heard their father had gone back to sea after leaving jail. Further enquiries revealed his intention of returning to Australia where he hoped to be able to settle.

* * *

For the first eleven years of his life, Peter Ackroyd revelled in his free-as-air rural lifestyle. Now, for all his pride in the reflected image in the hall mirror, the smart new uniform felt stiff and alien on this first day of his first term at secondary school. Pulling on his cap, he set off through the village up Station Road to Hollins Hill. It was unfortunate the village railway station that would have provided him with a train into Forster Square station, only a stone's throw from the grammar school in Manor Row, had closed a couple of years earlier. Instead, he made for a bus stop to wait for the red West Yorkshire low-decker from Ilkley, which would become his daily transport. He climbed to the top deck where the long bench seats gave him the best views of Baildon Bottom and Shipley. The top deck was inevitably shrouded in pungent exhalations of Woodbine and Capstan full-strength cigarette smoke, which had turned the roof of the bus a rich ochre. In winter, passengers braving the top deck fug suffered the additional discomfort of dripping condensation if passengers nearest the windows insisted on keeping them tightly shut. However, none of this proved off-putting to Peter, who was pre-occupied with thoughts about his day ahead. He was relieved when another first-day pupil joined him a few stops further on. For the rest of the journey they engaged in anxious speculation about the terrors that might await them. After a short walk from their stop in the city, the boys approached with apprehension the smoke-blackened two-storey stone school building with its formidable Gothic tower. Each had been well briefed by older pupils about the feared room behind the bay window where the headmaster meted out appropriate punishment for a variety of clearly defined transgressions. Within a few weeks, however, the culture and rigour of the curriculum absorbed Peter's full attention, pushing even the war into the background.

Constance never recovered from the news of her eldest son's death in the Clydeside blitz. She withdrew from life on the farm to such an extent that meals had to be taken to her room where she spent most of her day. Only Helen could lift her grandmother's spirits by shining a ray of sunshine into her stygian gloom. It was Helen who ran back into the farmhouse one day saying she could not get any response at gran's door. They found Constance in her bed, apparently having passed away peacefully during the night. Some said she had died of a broken heart. She was in her seventy-fifth year. A notable absence from her well-attended funeral in the parish church was half-sister Tilly, who could not make the Atlantic crossing in wartime, but arranged for a huge bouquet of lilies to be placed on her coffin. Helen, her three brothers and their mother and father stood in solemn vigil as the coffin was lowered to its final resting place in the heart of the Ettrick Valley where Constance had made her home.

* * *

Bradford joined in the general mood of rejoicing at the end of the war in Europe with a series of spontaneous street parties throughout the city. Bill and Mary were joined in Undercliffe by Tommy and Betty and the children, who were dazzled by the unfamiliar array of pies, sandwiches and cakes weighing down linen-covered trestle tables, thanks to the wartime resourcefulness of mothers, wives and sweethearts. Their street excelled in part due to the creative input of Mary's more relaxed interpretation of Ministry of Food rationing. Bottles of sherry and whisky, sequestered until the end of the war, again saw the light of day to enliven the festive mood. Cinema newsreels reported the national air of euphoria that marked VE day but reminded audiences that a grim war was still being fought in the Far East. While it continued, Tommy remained in uniform, ferrying aircraft to the south of England in preparation for their shipment to the Pacific war zone.

With Atlantic convoys no longer under threat from German U-boats, American liberty ships were converted to send tons of food from Uncle Sam to ease food rationing in Britain. These urgently needed supplies were quickly distributed to depots across the nation, from where they were assigned to High Street shops. It was while he was loading boxes of tinned goods into his car at a depot in Kings Road that Bill collapsed, suffering from a heart attack. He was unconscious when he was stretchered into an ambulance and rushed to the infirmary where all attempts to resuscitate him failed. He had already left instructions, in the event of his death, for his funeral service to be held at St.Paul's church in Esholt Village, which was almost filled by his family and a large turnout of his former colleagues. On top of his coffin was a floral tribute specially made in the shape of Nellie, his favourite locomotive at the treatment works, where his ashes were subsequently scattered on the day an atomic bomb laid waste the Japanese city of Hiroshima.

Without Bill at her side, Mary found the emporium a struggle. Carrie's health continued to deteriorate and neither Dorothy nor Sally showed any real enthusiasm for joining the business. Before she could contemplate retirement she would have to find someone to take over from her.

"I'm willing to give it a try," Tommy told her, when she revealed her concerns to him and Betty during a stroll in Peel Park. "They're disbanding the ATA and I don't really fancy going back to maintenance work at Esholt."

"Well, son, I never thought of you being interested in shop work," said Mary. "But I suppose if I stay on for a while to show you the ropes..."

"James and Sheila are old enough not to need me all the time," said Betty, "so I could work in the shop as well, if you like."

"Do you think you can manage the books? Carrie's not really up to it now."

"It's just like running a house, only bigger. Yes, I'd like that."

"After all the work your dad and I put in, it would be nice if it stays in the family," said Mary.

* * *

During the severest winter in living memory, Carrie's poor state of health continued to deteriorate until she was diagnosed as suffering from pleurisy. She obstinately refused to go to the infirmary, relying on her aunt and cousin to take it in turns to deliver shopping to her outlying cottage and generally keep an eye on her. It was Betty who found her lying on the floor next to her kitchen sink, where she had apparently been about to fill a kettle. Her ill health and death at the early age of thirty-nine was attributed directly to the criminal act of her husband setting fire to the emporium. On the day of her funeral, deep snow prevented the hearse reaching her cottage door, requiring four bearers to struggle with Carrie's coffin two hundred yards to the main road. Only Mary, Tommy and Betty and the children were able to join Dorothy and Sally in the crematorium chapel, where each service was on a strict time limit to cope with the increasing number of funerals in the prolonged big freeze.

Arctic conditions exacerbated post-war austerity by creating a fuel shortage that led to frequent power cuts. When woollen mills in Bradford began to run out of coal, the corporation decided, largely out of self-interest, to sell its huge stockpile filling Esholt's filter beds. The treatment works needed the wool-scouring process to continue producing the grease that made such a valuable contribution to its coffers. Soon lorries were queuing to receive their share of the sixty thousand tons of 'black gold' dug out of the deep beds, to be replaced by crushed stone.

In the grease research laboratory, newly relocated to the rear of Esholt Hall, the focus returned to developing peacetime bi-products, such as paint, for expanding estates of council houses. Some of the houses took on pastel shades as various types of weatherproofing colour wash were applied to external brickwork. Wool scourers welcomed the use of Esholt's grease-based sheep-marking fluid, which could be washed out of fleeces completely, improving the value of the wool. Dales farmers joked about their sheep getting their own back. Esholt wives became guinea pigs for soap products, while their children played with wool grease-based crayons and modelling clay. Esholt grease also found its way into wax polish and carbon copying papers, glazing putty and leather dressing. By the late forties, Esholt achieved the distinction of being the only sewage treatment works in the country paying its way from its own processes. But even as the hall prepared to hold a jubilee bi-products exhibition, there were ominous signs that Bradford's golden era might be coming to an end.

* * *

Gordon Graham was never busier or wealthier than during the immediate post-war years when farmers intensified their methods to meet the insatiable demand for food to fill the nation's depleted larders. His oldest sons, Angus and Eric, were already playing an important part on the family farm, while young Donald was completing his studies at Selkirk High School with the intention of going on to the Agricultural Centre at nearby Newtown St. Boswells. Helen, meanwhile, made it known that life on the farm was not for her. Her independent spirit longed for the excitement of the city in contrast to the slow rhythm of life in the Ettrick valley. She excelled at junior school, showing a particular aptitude for maths and music. At home her brothers frequently complained about her parsimony and thrift on family excursions.

Gordon, who rarely failed to accede to his daughter's wishes, recognised her restless quest for the greater educational challenge she believed was offered by private schools. After listening to friends who boarded there, Helen cited St. George's School for Girls in Edinburgh as her ideal and persuaded her parents to let her apply. Elspeth was unhappy that she would lose the close companionship of her daughter who would also have to become a boarder. But, when Helen was accepted, she decided not to stand in the way of her daughter's happiness, saying she looked forward to joining her for shopping trips to Princes Street. When the day came to leave the farm, Helen gave her mother a farewell hug and a kiss, threw her case into the back of the Land Rover and climbed into the passenger seat with a feeling of excitement tinged with apprehension. At Galashiels station, Gordon helped his daughter on to the Edinburgh train, waiting and waving until her carriage was out of sight before returning to his vehicle. "She'll do just fine," he told himself as he set off back to the farm, his mind already engaged on tasks for the day.

* * *

Bradford played host to many hundreds of European refugees fleeing the westwards march of Communism after the war. Many were to become permanent settlers, establishing their own communities and cultural centres and finding work in the mills and factories. They were followed by a steady flow of immigrants from the Indian subcontinent, encouraged to take advantage of the British Nationality Act to stay and work the anti-social night shifts that the indigenous workforce was reluctant to take on. With them they brought their own religions and a culinary tradition that was to revolutionise the habits of many hitherto conservative diners in Bradford. While nothing could convince Tommy or Betty of the merits of garlic or the delights of Asian cuisine, Peter, like many of his generation, would go to great lengths to track down the city's first curry houses.

Although he was well up to the academic challenges of the grammar school, Peter disliked the dull austerity of the gloomy soot-blackened Victorian building in Manor Row. Staff and pupils were united in their desire to transfer into the modern sandstone building at Frizinghall, completed just before the outbreak of war, during which it had been used for the war effort. He was in his sixth and final year before making the move along Manningham Lane to Keighley Road, where he achieved two GCE 'A' levels to go with the six 'O's gained previously. They were enough to gain him admission to any redbrick university of his choice, and Peter chose King's College, Newcastle, on the recommendation of a friend who was already studying there. He looked forward to the freedom of living away from home for the first time in his life, provided he could obtain deferment from National Service for three years.

Cheering schoolchildren waving paper union flags lined Harrogate Road as the royal limousine carrying the Duke of Edinburgh swept through Greengates on his way to formally open the grammar school, ten years after the last stone was laid. The wide clean frontage of the building, set in extensive grounds opposite Lister Park, was in stark contrast to the smoke-blackened Victorian city centre, which did not satisfy the mood for modernity that swept through so many municipal authorities after the war. As the last trams rattled their way into Forster Square, city fathers and planners were already considering ways to replace the Victorian architecture with state of the art concrete and glass to bring Bradford firmly into the second half of the twentieth century.

Peter loved his new life in the north-east of England: the down-to-earth friendliness of the people and easy access to the coast. He shared a flat with two other students in West Jesmond, a mile from the college. They would often stroll in nearby Jesmond Dene or take an electric train from the adjacent station to Whitley Bay for weekend shenanigans at Spanish City. When a notice went up in the college inviting students to share a coach trip to London to visit the Festival of Britain, he was one of the first to add his name to the list. Peter would have admitted he was thinking more about a weekend of untrammelled fun than the austerity-defying exhibition on the South Bank.

One crate of brown ale was sufficient to spark the male students, occupying seats at the rear of the coach, into gutsy renderings of rugby songs as they made their way down the A1 through County Durham. At Scotch Corner a toilet stop was demanded by the songsters, who jostled their way to the front of the coach without waiting for the front seats to clear. Unfortunately for Peter (or fortunately, as he later admitted) he happened to be passing a female student as she emerged from her seat, causing her to remonstrate loudly when he trod on her foot. Her withering look, in spite of his abject apology, stirred his interest for the first time, but she ignored his presence throughout the remainder of the long journey. This made him all the more determined to get to know her. After all, stepping on someone's foot was as good as an introduction; he would just wait for the opportune moment.

The sheer brio of the national post-war exhibition, from the amazing suspended skylon to the contemporary concrete structures, was in sheer contrast to the drab post-war world of the North. Peter loved every minute of his time at the festival, extolling its virtues in a hurried postcard home. On the tube back to their Bayswater hotel, he chose a seat next to the trodden-on female student, marvelling at the underground railway system as a way of breaking the conversational ice.

"I'm sorry about your foot. Is it okay?"

"I'll live."

"What did you think of the exhibition?"

"Too many people, but it was interesting."

"My name's Peter."

"Yes, I know. They kept shouting your name out on the coach – drunken lot."

"Well, you know what it's like with students," he said, sensing that the ice was thawing. "Do you fancy having a drink after dinner tonight? We could find a bar round the corner."

"I'll let you know. I don't know if my friend has plans."

"See you at dinner then…er…"

"Jess, it's short for Jessica," she told him as they left the tube and joined the rest of the group for the short walk back to their hotel.

Later that evening after their meal, Peter managed to extricate himself from a group of male students to seek out Jessica, who agreed to let him take her for a drink. They settled for the lounge bar of a nearby public house where, over a brace of beers, they talked about the festival, compared London with Newcastle and discussed life at university before getting on to their personal backgrounds. She told Peter her family name was Brownridge and her parents lived in a town called Consett, about ten miles from Newcastle.

"My dad works in the steel works. So does my brother, James. He's quite a bit older than me, which, I suppose, makes me an accident. I'm the first one to go to university. It's still a bit unusual in Consett."

"What are you reading?" asked Peter.

"Biology. I'm finding it a bit of a struggle. You?"

"Applied maths. I'd like to go into banking or something in finance. But I haven't made my mind up yet. Anyway, there's plenty of time for that. I'll have to do National Service first."

The two undergraduates gradually warmed to each other in the smoky fug of the lounge, surprised by how much they had to tell the other about themselves and their ambitions for the future. Both were startled by the bell for last orders, neither aware how much time they had spent engrossed in conversation.

"I'll keep in touch then?" asked Peter as they walked back to the hotel.

"Yes, I'd like that," said Jessica. "But watch where you're putting your feet, okay?"

"I promise," he laughed, as much in relief as newfound happiness.

Royal Accession

During her first days in the city, the sheer majesty of Edinburgh produced a mixture of excitement and awe in the girl from the country. But within the ambience of the inclusive school buildings and the fellowship of the other girls, Helen soon grew to love life at St. George's. The emphasis on academic rigour and self-discovery chimed with her need for achievement and independence, which was to take her a long way from the farm to a future at the cutting edge of female emancipation. While not excelling at sport, she enjoyed warm summer days on the tennis courts, taking advantage of every opportunity to visit the steep, winding streets and closes of Edinburgh's historical heart. Holidays back on the farm provided a brief contrast when she immersed herself in a late haymaking and early oats harvest when the weather allowed. But she was soon restless for her very different life in the city, which exerted an irresistible pull.

* * *

"Have you heard the news?" asked sixteen-year-old Sheila Ackroyd as she met her friend at the girls' entrance to the formidable Victorian bulk of Hanson Grammar School in Barkerend Road. "The King's dead. It was on the wireless this morning."

"Oh? Do we need to turn our badges upside down then? Who's going to be King now?"

"No, we're going to have another Queen — Queen Elizabeth II. I think it's great having a woman on the throne again."

"I don't really care who's on the throne. But when's all this happening?"

"It's happened already; she's on holiday in Africa right now with Prince Philip, but she's the Queen — its automatic. There'll have to be a coronation, of course."

"Maybe she'll come to Bradford. Anyway, we'd better get a move on or we'll be late for assembly."

On the winding cobbled streets of the West Riding, the ubiquitous Bradford van and its stable-mate the Javelin saloon, were being joined by the first production models of Jowett's most ambitious venture, their Jupiter sports car. Ahead of its time, the streamlined body of the Jupiter turned heads wherever it went. It was regularly sighted during routine test runs along Harrogate Road, trailing a smell of burnt paint from the hot exhaust pipe.

For Tommy Ackroyd it was love at first sight. He was among the first to join the queue to purchase what he described to Betty as his 'dream machine'. The Five Lane Ends production line struggled to meet demand from all parts of the country, managing to make fewer than a thousand Jupiters before financial pressures forced Jowett to cease all further production. Tommy was among the last of the few lucky people to acquire one of the finest products to leave a Bradford factory. He loved nothing better than driving Betty into the Dales on a sunny Sunday in summer, visiting popular weekend venues such as Grassington and Kettlewell.

On her one and only outing in the dark green, open-top Jupiter, his mother wore several layers of outer garments, plus a hat and woollen scarf, to accompany her son on a trip to Morecambe. She braved a cool breeze from the bay to stroll along the promenade, recalling earlier visits to the popular resort with Bill in their younger days. Betty thought Mary might have caught a chill on the outing that led to a bad cold. But Mary would have none of it, maintaining that she had thoroughly enjoyed her day out, even if the journey was a bit long. For a week she swallowed a series of over-the-counter remedies for her cold and racking cough, refusing to bother the doctor. When she collapsed at home and was confined to bed, her doctor immediately diagnosed pneumonia. An ambulance transferred her to the infirmary where she drifted in and out of consciousness for a day and a night before losing her fight for life at the age of seventy-three.

St. Augustine's Church was filled to the doors, with people standing in the aisle, as most of Undercliffe wished to pay their respects to Mary, who had served their community for more than half a century. At the cemetery and in the church hall afterwards, mourners spoke of her many acts of kindness to less fortunate customers using her emporium, helping them to survive the darkest days of two world wars and the great depression.

"They don't make many like your mother," one of the shop regulars told Tommy. "Not in Yorkshire, anyroad. Should be a statue to her in Peel Park. Today it's all about money, not service."

"We'll all be serving ourselves if these Yankee supermarkets catch on," added another mourner. "I don't get it myself. People like to be served by people."

Tommy said he was not so sure considering the pace of change since the end of the war, to which Bradford seemed fully signed up. He thought it was just a matter of time.

With National Service just over the horizon, Peter thought it would be wise to prepare for this dramatic change of direction after his studies. In his second year at Newcastle he joined the University Officer Training Corps to learn as much as he could about life in uniform. To his surprise, he enjoyed his involvement in military matters, especially the camaraderie during summer training camp. His relationship with Jessica had blossomed into a mutual love affair, which seemed to offer the prospect of life together beyond university. As evidence of this, she accompanied him to celebrate Christmas at Esholt, where she met with the immediate approval of his family.

Under the same roof Peter took advantage of his younger brother James's demob leave to quiz him about his National Service with the Royal Army Service Corps, where he drove huge tank transporters between training grounds in Germany.

"Take it as you find it and you'll enjoy it," James told him. "Spend your time moaning like some and you'll hate it. I've had good fun in the army and made some good mates. The rule is: keep your nose clean and never volunteer."

Amused by his brother's mildly cynical take on army life, Peter asked him if he had thought of signing on if he enjoyed it so much.

"No, I'm looking forward to being back in civvy street. I've already got a job lined up with British Road Services in Leeds. And I've a lass waiting for me, so I've got no regrets about leaving."

* * *

Every available seat was placed in tiered semi-circles in Tommy and Betty's living room facing the family's newest possession, a brand new television set with the latest twelve-inch viewing screen. Invited friends and neighbours took their seats with mounting anticipation as they waited for the promised moving pictures of events about to unfold two hundred miles away in London. For most in the room, it was their first encounter with this 'modern-day magic lantern' everyone was talking about. Some had driven past the incredibly tall television transmission mast at Holme Moss, reputedly balanced on a large steel ball bearing. But it took a huge leap of imagination to believe that moving pictures could be sent from there through thin air to living rooms across Yorkshire.

The first flickering black and white image of the BBC logo drew gasps of surprise followed by amazed "ee bah gums" from the darkened room as it was replaced by a picture of Buckingham Palace. Soon mutterings of "it's magic" and "can you believe it?" were stilled as the coronation of

Elizabeth II got under way in Westminster Abbey for all the world to see, a welcome antidote to the cheerless austerity still gripping the nation after the second world war.

* * *

On graduation day Peter and Jessica, resplendent in gowns and mortar-boards, collected their second-class degree certificates at different points during the long ceremony, before meeting up for a celebratory drink at their favourite pub in Newcastle city centre. Their conversation turned from the happy outcome of their three years at university to their sadness at the prospect of being apart during Peter's deferred national service. Then, to the surprise of other drinkers and astonishment of Jessica, Peter suddenly got down on one knee and asked her if she would marry him. "Why...er...yes. But please get up," she stuttered, seriously embarrassed, but inwardly flattered that he should have gone to such lengths to win her acceptance. People at nearby tables clapped and added their congratulations as Peter resumed his seat next to his deeply blushing fiancée.

"You really are one for surprises," Jessica told him as he produced a diamond ring and slipped it on her finger to her obvious delight. "It's absolutely beautiful, thank you," she said, giving him what she thought was a discreet kiss but which drew another round of applause from fellow drinkers.

"I don't know where I'll end up in the army, so I wanted us to get engaged now," he told her.

"Don't worry, darling, I won't run away. And when you get out of uniform, I want a big white church wedding."

"Wouldn't have it any other way, as long as your parents agree. It won't be cheap."

"I just hope the army don't send you abroad so we can still see each other from time to time."

"That's in the lap of the gods. For now, we must go up to Consett so I can formally ask your dad for his daughter's hand in marriage."

"Knowing my dad's sense of humour, he'll probably tell you to take all of me," she laughed.

* * *

By his own admission, Tommy Ackroyd was not a regular newspaper reader. He relied on the wireless to keep him up to date with events during the day and tried to catch the television news each evening. It was Betty who insisted they get the *Telegraph and Argus* "for the hatches, matches and despatches", as she put it. The shop had started to sell all the daily and Sunday papers, which Tommy usually collected from the wholesalers and sorted for delivery by a team of boys and girls.

It was while he was enjoying an early morning mug of tea and flicking through the *News Chronicle* that a headline caught his eye. A feature article under the headline 'Heroines of the SOE' reported that newly released files told of the daring exploits of women smuggled into France during the war to help the Resistance. A reporter had tracked down one of these women, now living an unremarkable life with her husband and children in a quiet West Sussex village. Her current anonymity belied the extraordinary story of Celia Burdon's war, from flying Ansons in the Air Transport Auxiliary, to acting as a courier and vital link between London and the Maquis under the very noses of the Germans. She modestly refused to accept her role in France as heroic, asserting that flying all types of aircraft, from fighters to bombers in all weathers, demanded real courage from her female colleagues in the ATA, whose story was largely untold.

Tommy felt his heart racing as he read of Celia's betrayal and near capture by the Gestapo, after which she had to keep on the move until her part of France was liberated by the Allies in 1944. "It's her; it's got to be her," he told himself, feeling a heady mixture of elation and nostalgia at this possible explanation for his lover's sudden disappearance in 1942. But the lack of a photograph to accompany the article frustrated his need for proof.

Thinking that Celia's story might be taken up by the more sensational Sunday papers, he went to the shop earlier than usual that weekend to start flicking through the most likely ones first. And there, staring out of an inside page of *The People*, were the eyes he had gazed into so long ago. The face, though older, was unmistakably his Celia, with the same quizzical half-smile. He folded the paper, paid for it and stuffed it into his coat pocket to read later in the privacy of his car. At that moment he could not think clearly enough through a tumult of emotions. Recalling the wartime maxim to 'keep calm and carry on', he decided this was sensible advice to follow in his present situation.

* * *

Unlike his brother, Peter never had the opportunity to see foreign parts during his national service. Instead, he spent most of his time in the Intelligence Corps attached to the War Office in London. That suited Jessica, who loved travelling by train to be with him for the occasional romantic weekend, spiced with visits to the theatre, art galleries and restaurants. His less frequent leave trips to the North East were interspersed with visits to his family at Esholt, where Jessica joined him in support of his duties as Best Man at the wedding of James to Shipley girl Elsie Hanson in Saltaire Methodist Church.

"This is as good as a dry run for ours," Jessica told Peter at the reception later. "Only I'll want masses more flowers and a vintage Rolls Royce on my day," she teased.

"Right, and I was thinking of borrowing my dad's Jowett Jupiter for our honeymoon. What do you think?"

"Then let's hope it doesn't rain," smiled Jessica.

* * *

"What a shame. It's coming down in stair rods," commented a guest as Jessica's white Rolls Royce drew to a halt outside St. John's Church in Shotley Bridge. Umbrellas were quickly deployed to protect the bride, resplendent in a calf-length silk brocade wedding dress with half veil, as she made her way into the church. Inside, the groom waited nervously in top hat and tails, accompanied by his brother, in a reversal of their previous wedding roles.

"You didn't plan the weather very well, James," said Peter, partly to ease the tension of the moment.

"You'll be all right. I've ordered two wet suits for the Jupiter."

Jessica arrived at Peter's side on the arm of her proud father, drawing an involuntary gasp of admiration from her husband-to-be and an appreciative wink from James. Following the service and signing in the vestry, the wedding party and guests were assured the rain had stopped as they were ushered outside for photographs. By the time they were making their way into the reception hall, blue gaps were beginning to appear between the leaden clouds.

Six hours later, Peter and Jessica were given a rousing send off in the Jupiter, followed by a small convoy of vehicles, horns blaring as they drove past astonished late-night pedestrians on the streets of Consett. "We'll give them the slip," said Peter, putting his foot down to the floor. The last of their tail was soon left behind at traffic lights as Peter deftly doubled back through side streets to begin heading out towards Edmondbyers along the high southern flank of the Derwent Valley to their destination for the night. In a few more miles their headlights picked out a roadside sign announcing Blanchland, before highlighting an arched stone portal leading into a medieval village square and the welcoming glow of The Lord Crewe Arms.

"Well done, darling," said Jessica, rewarding his driving with a peck on his cheek. "You showed them a clean set of wheels. But I must admit I was a bit frightened on those narrow roads in the dark."

"Mr and Mrs Ackroyd?" asked the receptionist as they carried their bags into the warm entrance hall, smelling invitingly of wood smoke and lavender polish. "Welcome to the Lord Crewe Arms. The bar is still open if you'd care for a drink."

Jessica shot Peter a quick glance. "We're a bit exhausted after our long day," he replied. "I think we'll just go straight up once we've registered, if you don't mind. Perhaps we could take a couple of drinks up to our room, if that's all right."

"Perfectly, sir. I'll have them sent up," said the receptionist with what might have been the faintest trace of a smile on her lips. "Just sign in here, and I'll show you to your room. Breakfast is between eight and nine thirty. You've got a smashing view from your bedroom window, provided it doesn't rain again of course."

"I just can't wait for daylight to see that smashing view," Peter joked in their room as they sipped their nightcaps while preparing for bed.

"Daft beggar," said Jessica, slipping between crisp white sheets and reaching to switch off her bedside light. "Don't forget we've got an early start if we're going to make Stirling by tomorrow evening."

* * *

Office workers and shoppers in Hall Ings stopped in their tracks to stare at the dramatic destruction of their familiar Victorian cityscape as demolition gangs got to work on Market Street, Bridge Street and Broadway. Extensive publication of architects' drawings of the modern concrete and glass shopping centre divided opinion about the merits of the corporation's bold new vision for Bradford. Older citizens, who had grown up with smoke-blackened elevations, mourned the loss of their traditional city centre. Young people, on the other hand, cheered on the fashionable drive for modernisation, aimed at securing Bradford's place in Britain's post-war urban regeneration. Victorian railway pioneers may have denied the city the major rail hub enjoyed by its bigger neighbour Leeds, but the bold new development would attest to the true status and wealth of Britain's wool capital, tucked into an eastern fold of the Pennines.

* * *

Helen arrived at the bottom of the Waverley Steps in time to see Elspeth alight from the Carlisle train and nervously search the platform ahead of her. Mother and daughter met, embraced warmly and made their way back up to Princes Street where Helen steered them towards her favourite coffee shop. Once seated, each drew on their close mother and daughter bond to confirm their mutual wellbeing and exchange immediate news from their vastly different worlds.

Reaching into her handbag, Elspeth drew out a brown envelope and, without further explanation, handed it to Helen. "It's for you; look inside," she instructed her daughter. Helen withdrew a handful of twenty-dollar notes and asked incredulously, "What's this?"

"It's from your Gran's half-sister, Tilly, in America. She was eighty-seven when she died and left you and your brothers two hundred and fifty dollars each. Wasn't that kind of her? I thought I'd keep it as a surprise until I met you here."

Helen studied the windfall in amazement. "I never met her. What was she like?"

"Well, she was very lively, the life and soul, you might say. Your gran always kept her informed about the family. Tilly loved Scotland, you see, ever since her visit over thirty years ago. What will you do with the money?"

"I'm still getting over the shock, but it'll come in very handy when I go up to Glasgow University in the autumn. Provided I pass my Highers, that is. But as we're sitting in the best shopping street in Edinburgh, I think I can be allowed a little indulgence with my newfound wealth."

"I've been looking forward to it," said Elspeth.

* * *

If fate had not intervened, the connection would probably never have been made. After reading and re-reading the newspaper article, Tommy endured days of agonising indecision, pulled one way by his powerful desire to reignite an old passion and the other by a constricting feeling of guilt. He buried the article at the bottom of a bedroom drawer and told himself that what was past was best forgotten. That was, until the fateful letter dropped on to his doormat, inviting him to a reunion for former ATA pilots to be held in a Brighton hotel later that year. He felt his heart miss a beat as the significance of the invitation sank in. Had fate provided him with the perfect excuse to re-live a dream? He would make Betty the offer of a weekend break on the south coast, fully expecting she would say she could not leave the shop, urging him to go on his own.

Which is why he found himself checking into a Brighton hotel weeks later with the newspaper article tucked inside his case. Once established in his room, he made his way back down to the ground floor and nervously pushed through double doors into the crowded hotel lounge, where he scanned animated groups of grey-haired men and women for a familiar face. Heads turned towards him in greeting but none of the faces wore the features he hoped to see. Suppressing his disappointment, he joined the melee, soon becoming immersed in the bonhomie born of nostalgia for a unique time and place in history.

In response to his discreet enquiries, he learned that Celia Burdon lived in the small South Downs village of Fulking near Devils Dyke. She had sent word that she would be unable to attend due to an earlier commitment but wished to be remembered to all who knew her from her ATA days. As soon as he was able, Tommy slipped away on the pretence of looking for the men's toilet and borrowed a telephone directory from reception. Noting that there was only one Burdon in Fulking, he quickly wrote down the number and address and rejoined the gathering as they took their seats for dinner. Exchanging anecdotes with his immediate neighbours about their experiences during the war, Tommy's mind continually drifted to formulating a plan of action for the following day.

Shafts of sunlight illuminated the cosy parlour of the neat stone cottage with spectacular views of chalk downs, as Celia Burdon picked up the telephone receiver. A male voice answered her greeting, "I'm sorry to trouble you, but I am trying to contact Celia Burdon."

"Yes, that's me. How can I help you?"

"Celia, it's Tommy Ackroyd. I am at the ATA reunion in Brighton and they told me you lived nearby. So I thought I would give you a ring for old time's sake."

"How do I know you?"

"We were in the ATA together during the war, both flying aircraft into Lincolnshire, if you remember. I lost touch and later learned you were at the War Office, although I have since learned it was a bit more exciting than that."

Celia's mind raced as she searched her memories of those heightened times, the thrill of living day by day and the Yorkshire pilot she knew only by his first name. It was the same voice, only with a deeper intonation. But that was wartime when so-called normal life was suspended. It belonged to a very different world, a world to which there could be no return.

"Oh, yes, how are you? I am afraid I couldn't make the reunion as it was our anniversary this weekend."

They politely exchanged updates on their lives since the war and hoped they might meet at a future reunion. She thanked him for his call and wished him good luck for the future.

"Who was that, dear?" asked her husband from the kitchen.

"Oh, just someone I used to know in the ATA who's been at the reunion. We were just re-living some old memories."

In his hotel room, Tommy replaced the receiver with a sigh. He retrieved the newspaper article from the bottom of his case and read it once more before slowly crumpling it and tossing it into the wastepaper basket. He recalled the opening line of his current bedside reading: 'The past is a foreign country: they do things differently there.'

* * *

After the grandeur of the so-called 'Athens of the North', Helen had to adapt to the grittier, no-nonsense charm of Glasgow, which made up in true Scots ethnicity what it lacked in genteel sophistication. She erred towards the wilder side of student life, enjoying the ongoing emancipation of women by playing a leading part in debunking stereotypical attitudes wherever she encountered them. In spite of attracting the hostility of some traditionally minded male members of staff, she graduated with a creditable first-class degree in business studies, earning her a number of offers from firms in the city.

She chose a well-known brokerage with its head office in the City of London, in the belief that she would have to move south of the border, eventually, if she wished to advance her career. Helen loved the pressured dealing and quickly earned respect for her ability to convert risk into profit for her employer. But she hated the testosterone-charged atmosphere in the company, drawing enmity for making it all too clear she did not suffer male chauvinist colleagues gladly.

For the same reason, she flitted in and out of a series of romantic attachments with remarkable insouciance but to the disappointment of her parents, who were troubled by her restlessness. They eventually gained satisfaction from Helen's revelation that she may at last have found Mr

Right. Ten years her senior, Greg Young was the first suitor to respect her views without condescension, while able to challenge her more extreme opinions without fear or favour. They became engaged on a weekend trip 'doon the watter' to Dunoon, to Elspeth's obvious delight and Gordon's promise of a wedding for Selkirk to remember.

While Peter secured a position at the National Provincial Bank in Newcastle, Jessica was recruited by ICI in Billingham nearly forty miles to the south. They compromised by buying a house on the outskirts of Durham City, Peter using the train to get to work, while Jessica travelled by car. Most Saturdays were spent sharing their newly acquired love of sport, Peter on a golf course, while Jessica honed her tennis skills on courts near their home.

One of their favourite weekend getaways was to walk among the high tussocky sand dunes at Druridge Bay in Northumberland, sheltering from cool North Sea breezes in a deep hollow where their intimate embraces were hidden from prying eyes. Both were convinced that their first child, whose arrival was welcome, if unexpected, was conceived in those very dunes. It was their private joke to name her Sandra, to be known more informally as Sandy among family and friends.

Family responsibilities forced Jessica to give up her job with ICI after only a year, so they decided to try for a second child without delay, resulting in a brother, Paul, for Sandra.

"You've got a handful now, darling," Peter told his wife, who was worrying about the loss of her income if she stayed at home looking after the children. "Our family is the most important thing. Anyway, my salary is perfectly capable of keeping the wolf from the door and I'm in line for promotion. So stop worrying."

"Well, I must admit I miss going to the lab. But I expect I'll find work again when the children go to school. ICI might take me back."

"We'll cross that bridge when we come to it," said Peter, unaware that his impending promotion would lead to a dramatic change in their lifestyle. His surefooted dealings on behalf of the bank had attracted the attention of the London office, which summoned him to Bishopsgate for a meeting with senior managers. He was told there was a job for him if he was prepared to move his family south. All moving expenses would be met.

Within weeks, the apprehensive but excited couple were driving south down the new M1 motorway with their two young children to begin their new life in Harrow.

"I doubt I'll be able to buy stottie cakes down here," Jessica quipped.

* * *

"There's a man been asking for you. Says it's important and he'll call back," the young shop assistant told Tommy and Betty when they arrived back at the emporium with a vanload of provisions.

"What did he look like?" asked Betty.

"Quite posh, in a suit and everything."

"Did he say what he wanted?" asked Tommy

"No. Just said he wanted to talk to you both. He asked when you'd be back and said he'd call round again this afternoon."

"Well, I can't imagine what it's all about," said Betty. "It usually means bad news, that's what I'm worried about."

They had just managed a late sandwich in the back room when the assistant knocked on the door and announced, "He's here again, asking for you."

"Tell him we'll be out in a minute," said Tommy.

In the main store, a well-presented young man with a clipped moustache and wearing a suit and tie, introduced himself and asked if they could talk in private. He was ushered through to the back office where he immediately took a seat and unfastened a well-worn leather briefcase.

"You've probably heard about the new self-service store in Girlington," he began.

"The so-called supermarket?" interrupted Tommy. "We went and had a look. I'll be surprised if Ken Morrison gets paid for the stuff people take off his shelves. He'll need eyes in the back of his head."

"Yes, well, all the experts agree it's the way the grocery business is going. The future is customers serving themselves and paying through a checkout. It'll make shopping easier for the customer and more cost-effective for the company."

"So what's that got to do with us?"

"I represent a company that's planning to open supermarkets right across the West Riding. They've had an eye on your store for some time and would like to make you an offer for your business."

"Well, I'll be damned," said Betty.

"It's a generous offer, but you'll obviously need time to think about it. So I'll leave you this letter and my card and I'll call back in a week's time, if that's all right with you. Should you have any questions in the meantime, just give me a ring at this number."

After the man let himself out, Tommy picked up and read from the typewritten sheet, letting out a gasp as he came to the price they were being offered. "We could retire very comfortably to our dream cottage in the Dales on that, Betty love."

"But what would our customers think if we sold out? They like being served and having a chat while they shop. We're part of their lives. They'd hate a soulless store where they have to help themselves, and there's no one to pass the time of day with."

"Well, we don't have to worry about it right now. There'll be time enough to think about it later, so we'd better crack on."

* * *

The slow decrease in the proportion of wool grease in sewage discharged at Esholt during the previous decade accelerated during the sixties as processors in Bradford succumbed to international competition. Having acquired the machinery and learned the skills from Britain, clothing manufacturers in the Far East were able to take advantage of cheap labour to price Yorkshire mills out of the market. One by one, the multi-storeyed stone edifices, once a symbol of permanence and prosperity, fell silent. Around the city, tall chimneys issued their last whisps of smoke to become blackened fingers of rebuke to a dying era. The writing was clearly on the wall for a sewage treatment works uniquely designed to cater for the height of Bradford's wool bonanza. As income from bi-products declined, the increasing cost of treatment was becoming a burden on the rates, a situation that could not be allowed to continue unchecked. There was even serious talk of Bradford eventually relinquishing control of the treatment works for which the city had fought so hard and paid such a high price.

* * *

Much as Helen would have preferred a quiet and simple wedding, even a civil ceremony, she did not want to hurt her parents who had been building their hopes on a big day. So it happened that a good proportion of Selkirk folk turned out to see her arrive outside the Parish Church in a plain cream dress, to be accompanied down the aisle on the arm of her proud father. After the ceremony, bride and groom made the short journey to their reception on a decorated farm cart pulled by two resplendent draught horses. A five-course meal, speeches and toasts preceded a traditional ceilidh band, during which the couple managed to make a discreet exit by taxi, bound for a honeymoon hideaway near Melrose.

No one that night could have imagined they would be filing into the Parish Church just days later to say farewell to Gordon following a massive heart attack at his farm. Distraught mother and daughter walked behind the ornate coffin, borne by her three sons and son-in-law into the churchyard, which had so recently been the scene of family celebration. In the generous eulogies that followed, all agreed that the Ettrick Valley had been cruelly and prematurely robbed of one of its most distinguished sons at the age of sixty-seven.

There was to be further mourning in the tight-knit farming community with the death, the following year, of Gordon's elder sister Fiona at the age of seventy-five. With her daughter away in Glasgow, Elspeth could only take solace from helping her sons to carry on her husband's work on the farm, acknowledging their enthusiasm for the more intensive methods then in vogue.

* * *

Tommy took the call from the British Consul in Calais. His son James, who now owned his own lorry, had been detained by the French authorities on suspicion of drug smuggling and was in need of money and clean clothing. Peter was quickly despatched via the Dover ferry, finding his brother incarcerated by French Customs. James swore his innocence, saying he had been on a routine cross-channel job in his cab, picking up a trailer at Calais to bring it back to England. Apparently French Customs and police had been keeping an eye on the trailer all the way from Italy, suspecting it was carrying contraband. At Calais they discovered a large quantity of cocaine in a consignment of household goods and were waiting to pounce on whoever made the pick-up.

"I had no idea what was in the trailer," James protested to his brother. "It was just another routine pick-up job as far as I was concerned."

"I'm sure they'll realise you're innocent once they've carried out their investigation. We're on your case so don't worry. The Consul will keep in touch."

Within days of Peter returning to London, the detention of his brother in France had become something of a cause celebre in the British tabloids, which did not help the situation by printing lurid, stereotypical headlines about Gallic jurisprudence. On advice from the Consul, Tommy hired a French lawyer to protest his son's innocence and highlight his previously unblemished character. But the investigation continued to drag on slowly, increasing the family's fears about the outcome. Then, to everyone's immense relief, British police managed to track down the intended recipients of the trailer's contents and arrested a gang in the Midlands. One gang member testified to James' innocence in the hope of being dealt with more leniently.

Tommy travelled to Calais to greet his son as he was released from detention and shared the ferry journey back to England in his liberated cab. "That's it. That's the last time, I drive to the Continent," said James, enjoying a coffee in the ferry's lounge bar. "I've lost a mint through this nonsense. From now on I'm sticking to inland haulage only, if I've still got a business."

"Don't worry about that, son. Your mother and I will see you back on the road. One day you might be able to run your own fleet of lorries; there's so much more going by road nowadays."

"We can help James back on his feet," Tommy told Betty the following Sunday as they drove north along the A65 on their way to view a cottage in Clapham. "We'll be able to afford it after the sale."

"I'm still in two minds about selling," said Betty. "But I must say, it's not an offer to be sneezed at. Neither of us is getting any younger."

Her heart leapt as they drove into the pretty village, bisected by a stream and with a lovely stone church at its head. A tour of the bijou cottage set in a colourful garden of hollyhocks and roses made up her mind, and she gave her decision over a cup of tea in the tiny village cafe.

"I think we should sell," she told Tommy, to his evident relief. "I just love the cottage and I love it here, it's so peaceful. There'll be lots of things I can do to help in a village like this," she said, anticipating his concern that she might find life in the Dales too quiet.

"We'll have the car as well, so we'll be able to go places," he told her. "There's even a railway station, so we can get to Bradford or Morecambe in no time. Let's go and tell them we like the cottage and we'll put in an offer. We'll speak to the supermarket chap tomorrow."

"We'll have a lot of unhappy customers once they find out," said Betty. "But if the world moves on, I suppose we have to move with it."

* * *

Dubbed by some the 'Harrods of the North', Brown Muff's department store seemed to present a disdainful face to the brash new concrete and glass shopping development now encroaching on its traditional location in Market

Street. Brown Muff's store, like its rival Busby's, Bradford's other celebrated department store on Manningham Lane, confirmed the city's wealth and status for the chauffeur-driven shoppers from Ilkley, who viewed the drive towards modernisation with disdain. They liked to be recognised by shop assistants and to receive personal service for spending not inconsiderable sums of money in the various departments. Sheila Ackroyd took great pride in welcoming and assisting her regulars, as she called them, skilfully helping them to make up their minds about expensive purchases. Her value as a floor supervisor at Brown Muff's was recognised in her remuneration, allowing her to make valued visits to her brother and sister-in-law in London as well as helping her parents to view their retirement plans with equanimity. She had a more difficult relationship with her brother James, who she felt had been too quick to take advantage of their parents' windfall to expand his business.

Satisfied they had done their best for their staff, whom they had been promised, would be offered jobs in the new supermarket, Tommy and Betty bade an emotional farewell to their many loyal customers at a special evening organised in their honour at St. Augustine's Church hall. They were surprised and delighted to be greeted by some of the new Asian shopkeepers they had befriended on their regular trips to market, and accepted more lunch and dinner invitations than they would ever be able to fulfil.

"It's a good job you're driving. We're both a bit giddy," Betty told her daughter later as they headed out of town towards Esholt.

"It was a grand do, lass," said Tommy. "I never realised we had so many friends."

"You get out of life what you put into it," said Sheila. "You both gave them years of your lives. They were simply saying thank you."

"Anyway, it's all change now," said Betty. "I don't think I'd enjoy the new set-up. It's a good time to stop and let the youngsters take over."

"I reckon it's the Asians who'll be taking over," muttered Tommy sleepily. "They're born shopkeepers, just you watch."

"Well, it's all behind us now, love. In a couple of weeks we'll be in our little cottage with not a supermarket in sight..."

"Dad's out for the count, Mum," interrupted Sheila, looking in the rear view mirror at the reflection of her father slumped asleep on the back seat.

* * *

For the first months of their marriage, Helen and Greg seemed a typically happy couple. They knew some of the same friends from work and shared their leisure time between socialising in the city and trips out to Loch Lomond and The Trossachs. The fact that Greg's job necessitated travelling to other branches raised no suspicions until Helen overheard a conversation in the washroom at work. It was all round the office, apparently, that he had been seen in the company of a young female at a recent business convention. When Helen told him what she had heard, he blamed jealous colleagues for spreading lies about him.

Weeks later, after receiving his telephoned apology for having to work late, she called at his office on her way home from a friend's house only to find it securely locked and in darkness. She was waiting up for him when he eventually arrived home in the early hours.

"Sorry I'm late, darling. I thought you would be in bed."

"I wouldn't be able to sleep — how did you get on at the office?"

"Fine. You can get so much more done when there's no one about to distract you."

"Well, there were no lights on when I passed by your building tonight and your car wasn't in its usual spot, Greg. So where were you?"

"Are *you* checking up on me now?" he bellowed, suddenly red-faced with anger. "I suppose you've been listening to the malicious gossip being put about. If you must know, I had to grab something to eat."

The final unravelling came a few weeks later when one of Helen's colleagues walked into a Paisley lounge bar to find Greg with his arm around a female almost half his age. The game was up. To avoid an angry confrontation, Helen simply wrote him a note saying their marriage was over and moved out of their flat. She was offered and accepted a transfer to London, leaving her husband to face the opprobrium of her friends in the office.

* * *

"I'll be able to pay them back," James reassured his sceptical sister. "I've got three wagons on the road now, and I'm having to turn work away. Road haulage is big business and growing all the time."

"Well, see that you do. Mum and Dad worked hard all their lives and deserve a good retirement on the money they put aside over the years."

"I still need someone to run my office if you'd only think about it," coaxed James. "We'd be a family business."

"Absolutely no chance," Sheila told him. "We'd fight like cats and dogs. No, you crack on with it and good luck to you. But don't forget our mum and dad. They would also like to see you once in a while."

* * *

Peter checked that the children were sound asleep and helped himself to a beer from the fridge. He switched on the television and settled down to watch his newly adopted team, Arsenal, playing at home. He would normally have been among the crowd at Highbury, but tonight he had agreed to babysit so Jessica could spend an evening with girlfriends at Kingsbury. Once they had become accustomed to the dense urban sprawl, Peter and Jessica both enjoyed the convenience and cultural opportunities of living in London.

The doorbell rang halfway through the News at Ten on ITV. She must have forgotten her key, thought Peter as he walked along the passageway and opened the front door.

"Good evening, sir. Am I Speaking to Mr Peter Ackroyd?" asked the uniformed police officer.

"Yes," confirmed Peter, wondering why he was receiving such a visit late at night. "Do you mind if I come inside, sir?"

asked the police officer, stepping over the threshold and following Peter into the lounge.

"Please take a seat, sir. I'm afraid I have some bad news concerning Mrs Ackroyd." Peter switched off the television, suddenly overcome with nausea and breathlessness as fear of the impending revelation gripped his heart. "Your wife was involved in a road accident this evening."

Peter sank heavily back into a chair. "Oh God, please no," he choked, his voice breaking with emotion. 'How is she?"

"She's been taken to the accident and emergency department at Northwick Park Hospital. I'm sorry; I don't know her condition, but I am able to take you there now."

"The children. I'll need to ask a neighbour to sit in until I get back."

"Leave that to my colleague, sir. She'll arrange a babysitter."

Peter grabbed a coat and quickly briefed the woman police constable about which neighbour to approach before stepping into the back of a police car for the short ride to the hospital. Once there he introduced himself at the reception desk and was quickly ushered into a side room where he was soon joined by a fresh-faced junior doctor in a white coat.

"I'm afraid your wife suffered severe head injuries in the accident and is still in surgery," he was told. "She may be in there for a while yet, but the duty nurse here will keep you informed about her progress."

"When will I be able to see her?"

"We'll let you know as soon as possible. Now please excuse me, I have to get back. We're experiencing a heavier than normal workload tonight."

Peter was offered and accepted a hot sweet tea before being directed to a public telephone. The ringing tone sounded for fifteen seconds before Sheila's voice came on the line.

"Sheila, it's Peter. Listen, it's bad news, I'm afraid. Jessica's been hurt in an accident. She's in hospital where I'm ringing from. Do you think you could come down to help with the children?"

"How…how is she?" stammered Sheila, her mind racing, trying to fully comprehend what she was hearing.

"We don't know yet. Can you tell Mum and Dad, but try not to shock them."

"I'll get the first train in the morning, but ring me as soon as you have more news." Sheila replaced the receiver and sat motionless as the full gravity of the situation started to sink in.

Back in the side room time passed very slowly for Peter as he prayed for Jessica's recovery and waited for more information. He was going over the events of the evening once again in his mind when a consultant entered the room wearing a grave expression that warned him to prepare for the worst. The consultant told him the surgical team had done their very best to save Jessica, but her injuries had been too severe. In spite of their combined efforts, she had slipped away from them without regaining consciousness.

Peter felt himself go cold and limp as the shock of his wife's death swept through him. He heard voices, but not what they were saying, as he tried to grasp some meaning in what was happening to him. He must have asked if he could see her and been told she would be taken to the chapel of rest in due course. In a daze he was accompanied back to the reception area and telephoned Sheila with the shocking news.

Peter spent the hours and days following Jessica's death in a state of semi-detachment from everything around him. As he and Sheila made arrangements for the funeral, it surprised him that people were able to go about their normal business while his world was in ruin. In contrast to their wedding day, the sun shone for the large turnout of Peter's family and friends who gathered at St. John's Church in Shotley Bridge to say farewell to Jessica and lay her to rest in the valley of her childhood.

The subsequent inquest heard evidence from eye-witnesses to the accident who said that as Jessica set off from a green traffic light, a car jumped the red lights to her right. The joy rider, who was also badly injured, had taken a car without consent, having no driving licence or insurance. The youth, who had a string of previous convictions for motoring offences, showed no remorse at a later court appearance and received the maximum custodial sentence for causing death by dangerous driving.

Sheila resigned her job at Brown Muffs' and took on the role of step-parent to Sandra and Paul, while keeping alive their memory of the mother so cruelly and suddenly taken away from them. She helped her grieving brother to cope with his mental pain and gently reminded him that he still had an important responsibility for the future of two young lives. Slowly Peter pieced his life back together with the loving support of family and friends, taking succour from a rehabilitating visit to his parents building a new life for themselves in the heart of the Yorkshire Dales.

* * *

Bradford's inexorable decline as a wool-processing centre, coupled with the radical redesignation of local government, were to bring an end to Esholt's unique chapter in the city's historical record. The realignment of local government boundaries in 1974 also relieved local authorities of their responsibility for sewage disposal, which in Bradford was placed under the control of the Yorkshire Water Authority. Denied income from wool grease by-products, the new Metropolitan District Council was happy to devolve basic sewage treatment and disposal to the new body, which would have to meet the heavy cost of upgrading Esholt's ageing infrastructure for its vital, if more mundane role. Gradually, parts of the Esholt works fell silent as processes ceased and buildings were abandoned, some to be preserved for posterity, others to be demolished to make way for the installation of the new treatment plant. From the vantage point of the Leeds-Liverpool canal towpath, retired former workers taking the air would pause and gaze with sad nostalgia at the slowly transforming scene.

Half a mile away, Esholt villagers had become used to the television crews and technical paraphernalia sent there regularly by Yorkshire Television to film the village pub for the new Emmerdale Farm. Less welcome were coachloads of viewers, eager to see the location of their favourite soap opera and enjoy a pint at The Woolpack, confusingly calling itself The Commercial. Last to complain about the hordes of star-struck drinkers was the pub landlord, whom it was claimed 'had never had it so good'.

Chance Encounter

The black-cab driver barely uttered a word during the one-mile journey, his mood matching London on this grey, cold and damp January lunchtime in the City. Peter was grateful for the quiet interlude away from his busy desk, so he could get his thoughts in order for the coming meeting.

Since Jessica's tragic death two years earlier, he had striven to honour her memory by devoting his time to their two young children, ensuring for them the best possible start in life with the generous help of his unmarried sister, Sheila. He had shunned the frantic social life led by many of his colleagues and resisted being drawn into a new relationship, in spite of the many expressions of interest shown by the opposite sex. So today's assignation felt curiously risqué, potentially inviting the disapproval of Sandra and Paul, who still revered the memory of their mother.

The taxi pulled into the kerb outside a pub Peter knew was unlikely to be frequented by other City traders. He paid the driver and strode into the bar, anxiously casting his eyes around the warm, smoky interior. Helen was sitting at a table for two in the corner of a small side room occupied by only one other couple deep in conversation. She was wearing a formal navy blue suit complemented by red earrings, which offset her auburn, shoulder-length hair. She looked every inch the City trader, unlike the first time he had seen her at her office Christmas party. Since that afternoon, three weeks ago, he had been unable to get her out of his mind.

"I'm sorry I'm late," he greeted her, kissing Helen lightly on the cheek.

"I've only just got here myself," she replied in a soft Scottish accent, unwinding a scarf from around her shoulders. "We had a last minute panic when the screens started to go red. The boss got the jitters, but it settled down."

"Down's the word," he agreed. "There's not much good news coming out of the markets with the war in the Middle East. What would you like to drink?"

As Peter moved across to the corner bar to order a Saint Clements and a spritzer, Helen appraised this tall, intelligent man: lightly tanned, lived-in face under thinning, sandy-coloured hair, noting for the first time his north of England accent. She was attracted to the laughter lines around his mouth and his blue eyes, which conveyed a look of mild surprise. She guessed he was in his late thirties.

"That was a crazy party," he said as he put the drinks down. "I expect it got wilder after we left."

"There were one or two empty desks the next morning. It's a good job it wasn't a normal trading day. Even the boss looked distinctly green about the gills!"

"I think he fancies you," teased Peter. "I don't think he was very chuffed when I whisked you away before the end. I hope it didn't cause a problem."

"No, not at all. He's a bit of a Lothario, but all the girls are up to him."

"Anyway, you looked fantastic in that black dress. It's hardly surprising half the office was after you."

"Of course, it might just be they value my intellect and success as a City trader," she laughed.

"I don't doubt that for a second. But I think I'll just stick with my memory of that black dress, if you don't mind," said Peter, receiving a playful kick under the table for his trouble.

"By the way, I don't think I thanked you for taking me home after the party," said Helen. "Sorry I couldn't invite you in, but my mum was staying and she keeps her beady Scottish eyes on me."

"My sister lives with us, so I quite understand. But apart from being Scottish, I really know next to nothing about you. Tell me..."

"No, you first. Tell me about yourself."

As the small room began to fill up, Peter had to raise his voice to tell Helen about his childhood in the grim industrial West Riding of Yorkshire. Ackroyds had worked in wool for generations. He was the first member of his family to go to university and then via banking to a job in the City. He felt it had put a bit of a barrier between him and some of his northern relatives, who now considered him a bit posh. Helen listened attentively when he spoke about his twelve years of happy marriage to Jessica that had ended so tragically. Since then, he had brought up their two children, Sandra aged thirteen and Paul eleven, with the help of his sister. Jessica's death had made him reappraise the London rat race and now, at forty-one, he was starting to consider moving back north to spend more time with his family.

"Funnily enough, I've been thinking along similar lines," said Helen, clearly moved by Peter's narrative. "I've enjoyed my seven years in London. I have an excellent salary and good social life, but..." she tailed off, thoughtfully.

"But...you're not happy?"

"Well, I've started to think about green hills and wide open skies again. After all, money isn't everything, is it? Sometimes I feel I need to get a *real* life, if you see what I mean. Sometimes I wonder what I'm missing, not having a nice home and children. I was married too, but it didn't work out."

"That explains it. I couldn't believe you'd stayed single."

"Well, I grew up on a farm in the Borders and went to school in Edinburgh, then Glasgow University. To a girl up from the country it was quite a shock believe me. I probably enjoyed student life too much, but I managed to get my degree and learned this trade in Glasgow. I was very naïve; I fell for this charmer who worked in the same office. Unfortunately, he didn't understand the meaning of the word monogamy, so we split after just a few months. There were no children, thank God. Since then, it's been 'once bitten, twice shy'."

Peter was so engrossed in Helen's story that he didn't notice the queue beginning to form at the food counter. It took him a few minutes to place their orders before returning to tell her how much her background interested him.

"Well, I don't usually tell my life story to complete strangers. But, for all we've just met, you really don't seem like a stranger to me at all."

"Then I'd like to take you out to dinner, as I'm sure there's lots more to talk about," said Peter, sensing his moment had arrived. "Are you free this evening?"

"No, I'm taking mum to the theatre tonight. She just loves going into the West End when she comes down to London. But I'm free the rest of the week. I can do Friday."

"Perfect, you're on."

Helen watched Peter squeeze his way through to the bar, surprised by her need to be so open with him. Was it his air of quiet integrity, his refreshing lack of cynicism? Both were elusive qualities in the City. Her extrovert behaviour belied the quieter, thoughtful person within, who looked for confidence and maturity in others. She decided she wanted to know a lot more about Peter Ackroyd. As she waited for him to return, her attention was drawn to the newly installed colour television on the wall opposite. On screen a group of cloth-capped characters were arguing outside a typical northern village pub named The Woolpack.

"I always feel a bit nostalgic when Emmerdale Farm comes on," said Peter, setting down their sandwiches and fresh drinks. "They film it in Esholt, the village I grew up in. That's the actual pub I used to go to with my father and brother. It's really called The Commercial. They rename it The Woolpack for the soap. It's a popular name in Bradford, once the richest and proudest wool city in Britain. But then, like all Yorkshiremen, I always say there's nowhere quite like Yorkshire."

"Did you say Esholt? I remember my gran telling me about a place that sounded like Esholt, when I was little. She was born in Yorkshire, you see, but she rarely talked about it. I think she was involved in some sort of scandal there."

"What was your gran's name?" asked Peter, thoroughly intrigued by what Helen was telling him.

"Her maiden name was Storey — Constance Storey. I believe she was engaged to a soldier who was killed in the Boer War. Then she met my grandfather, a Scottish sheep farmer called Donald Jameson. They were married in Queen Victoria's Golden Jubilee year, and my gran settled on a farm in Selkirk. That's where my family still live today."

"Did you ever find out what the scandal was about?"

"No, not really. But piecing together the few bits my mother told me, it seems gran had some connection with the landed gentry at the end of the last century. It was all very hush-hush for some reason. Anyway, she died when I was only seven. I just remember her as a rather formal old lady dressed in black. She was a bit intimidating, but always very kind to me."

As Helen's story unfolded, Peter became increasingly aware of a possible millions-to-one coincidence. "It's amazing our paths should have crossed this way," he said, glancing at his wristwatch. "Much as I'd love to hear more, I'm afraid I have to get back to the office. Let's continue this on Friday."

"Yes, I'd completely forgotten the time; always happens when I get into an interesting conversation."

"Same here. So, I suggest the Maison Blanc in William Street, if that's all right. I'll meet you there at eight on Friday." Helping Helen on with her coat, he added, "I've really enjoyed this lunchtime."

"Me too," she said, with complete sincerity.

They emerged together on to the grey London street, both feeling strangely elated, Helen walking off with a cheery wave while Peter hailed a cab. As his taxi edged through the inevitable traffic, Peter recalled Humphrey Bogart's famous line from Casablanca: 'Of all the gin joints in all the towns in all the world she walks into mine'. In a city of over seven million people he had found Helen, whose story pointed to their common heritage; a real-life soap opera played out against the backdrop of deep social divisions during the turbulent decades of the great industrial revolution in the wool capital of Britain.

* * *

In discreetly lit alcoves of the cellar restaurant, tiny flames flickered through deep-red glass candle-holders on each table. French waiters dressed in black shirts and trousers with long white aprons attended diners with Gallic élan as Peter greeted Helen's arrival with a kiss on both cheeks.

"Oh, very French, in keeping with the ambience, I suppose," she quipped as a waiter took her coat and ushered them to a table. "This is very nice."

"I've been really looking forward to this evening, ever since our lunch," he confessed.

"I hope it didn't interfere with your work."

"Well, as a matter of fact, I found it quite hard to concentrate at times. I couldn't get you out of my mind."

"Did you want me out?"

"Just the opposite," he said and was about to continue when a waiter arrived to take their orders.

"Sorry to tease," said Helen once they had ordered. She reached across the table and placed her hand on his. "It's just my crazy sense of humour. I've been really looking forward to this as well."

"Why don't we go mad and have a glass of champagne to celebrate?" said Peter.

"Celebrate what in particular?"

"Celebrate our good fortune in finding each other. We seem so right together and I've only known you such a short time."

"Well, as I said before, it's been a case of 'once bitten, twice shy' as far as men are concerned. But this feels different. So, yes, I'd love some champagne."

"You know, it's the most amazing thing," he said later, opening a bottle of Bollinger and charging two flutes, "but I think our ancestors were linked somehow. I'm going to do some research; I believe our families used to live a stone's throw from each other. Our getting together like this could be a million-to-one chance."

"Oooh, sounds spooky. Anyway, good health."

"Good health," he repeated as they clinked glasses, taking a sip from their effervescing champagne and looking directly into each other's eyes.

After a leisurely meal, during which they continued to explore common interests, people and places, Peter paid the bill as Helen was helped into her coat. Feeling light-headed from the champagne or general euphoria, they made their way into the night and hailed the first available taxi.

"Fancy a nightcap?" asked Peter as he paid off the taxi outside her apartments.

"I've got liqueur if you'd like some in your coffee," Helen replied, surprising him with her unexpected invitation. "Mum's gone back to Scotland, so you won't have to run the gauntlet. And, by the way, I don't make a habit of inviting strange men in for a nightcap," she laughed as she pushed open her front door and directed him to her lounge.

"I'm not sure if that makes me strange or not," said Peter, falling in with Helen's sense of humour.

"Make yourself at home while I make the coffee. The liqueur's in the cabinet over there."

"Won't your sister worry if you're not home?" she asked him later as they drank their coffee on Helen's deeply cushioned sofa.

"Not at all, I warned her I might be late."

"Oh you did, did you, just how late?"

Peter pulled Helen to him and kissed her long and determinedly. She returned his passion, pausing for only a moment for air before resuming their embrace. Helen luxuriated in the feel of Peter's caresses as they expended their passion, but restrained him as he sought to take matters further.

"Steady tiger, we need more time," she said breathlessly, stroking the side of his face. "I do like you very much, but I just need to get to know you better that's all."

"I know it must seem a bit sudden, but I fell in love with you the moment I saw you at that party," he told her. "One thing is for certain, I want us to see a lot more of each other from now on."

"Me too. That's exactly how I feel as well," said Helen. "But now I must get my beauty sleep, so forgive me if I let you out. Give me a ring at the office tomorrow." He held her close as they kissed in the doorway before making his way into the night.

"Wow," said Helen to herself as she closed her front door. "He may be a thirty-something father of two, but he certainly ticks all my boxes."

Desperate to find out more about the history of the former Esholt estate and the family who lived in the hall, Peter enlisted the help of his father who took the train into Bradford and spent time searching the city archives. Tommy also got back in touch with an old acquaintance in Esholt village who was something of an amateur historian. Reading through his father's research notes later, Peter's eyes lighted on a passage he had hardly dared hope for. In the second half of the nineteenth century, a scandal surrounded the sudden dismissal from Esholt Hall of a young chambermaid called Anna Storey. She subsequently gave birth to a baby girl, but never revealed the name of the father. That baby girl, he reasoned, must have been Helen's grandmother.

"Have I got news for you," Peter announced a week later as Helen invited him into her flat for the dinner she had promised to cook for him. "But I'll keep it until we're eating." She released herself from his embrace, protesting that the food would spoil, and invited him to open and pour the wine he had brought with him.

"So what's this news then," she asked as they sat down to eat.

"Well, it seems your gran was the result of a liaison between her mother and someone unknown. Anyway, the exciting bit is that your great gran, a housemaid, was sacked from Esholt Hall by the Stansfield family. And someone there supported her financially afterwards. It was all hushed up because of the scandal. At the same time, my great grandfather, Josh Ackroyd, was helping to build Bradford's first sewers to rid the river Aire of the pollution that so infuriated the very same Stansfields. What do you make of that?"

"It's a small world," said Helen. "If you wrote that stuff in a book, nobody would believe it."

"So what you're saying is I might have blue blood in my veins," she joked later as they settled on the sofa with digestifs. "I'm not sure I should be dallying like this with a member of the hoi polloi."

"I may be hoi polloi, but at least I know who my grandfather is," countered Peter, earning a cuff on the ear for his trouble. They broke into spontaneous laughter, falling back on the cushions and locking lips in a long embrace. He eased up enough to tell her, "I love you." Helen pulled his head down to breathe in his ear, "I love you too and I want you to make love to me." Peter gently eased his arms under her and with their lips still joined, carried her into the bedroom.

* * *

At the first opportunity Peter, accompanied by Sheila and the children, drove Helen up to Yorkshire to meet his parents. On the way they discussed their mutual disenchantment with the rat race and their desire to leave it for a better quality of life. Sandra and Paul were getting on well with Helen, happy to accept her as a stepmother. Sandra was a bit concerned about leaving all her friends behind in London, but Paul regarded the move as a big adventure. Sheila admitted she would miss caring for the children on a day-to-day basis, but she was delighted Peter and Helen had found such happiness together and looked forward to seeing them all regularly when she relocated back to the north and possibly her old job.

Helen exulted over the verdant Dales as they drove along twisting narrow lanes between moss-covered, dry stone walls. "I really have got the bug for big city living out of my system," she confessed, "especially when I see a village as pretty as this. It's like something out of a travel brochure."

"This is Clapham where my parents retired for peace and quiet after a busy life in Bradford," Peter told her. "They'll be dying to meet you after all I've told them about you."

"Only the best bits, I hope," she quipped.

"Hello Son…and this will be Helen we've been hearing all about," greeted Tommy at his front gate as Betty emerged from the cottage doorway. They warmly embraced Helen and Sheila, Peter and his children before inviting them inside to a table spread with a cornucopia of home baking.

"You'll be peckish after your long drive," said Betty. "I'll pour the tea and we can talk while you eat."

When another car pulled up outside they were joined by James and Elsie, occasioning another round of hugs and kisses before the room echoed with the hubbub of familial conversation. Helen drew gasps of amazement when she recounted the story about her antecedents from Yorkshire and expressed a strong desire to see where her grandmother came from. James immediately offered to drive her, Peter and the children to Esholt the following day.

Look, it's that pub on TV," shouted Paul as James drove past The Commercial into Esholt village to show Helen where he and Peter used to live.

"Gosh, this place is much prettier than I expected, so many trees," she observed as they made their way past the site of the giant precipitation tanks and former acid plant to descend Gill Lane towards Esholt Hall. "I never imagined a sewage treatment works in such a lovely green valley as this. It's really beautiful."

"And that's where your great grandmother was in service," said Peter as the imposing stone frontage of the hall came into view. Helen's eyes filled with tears as she felt an involuntary surge of emotion just gazing at the sunlit eighteenth century facade across a wide swathe of lawn.

"The Stansfields made a huge personal sacrifice to give this up," she said. "But I suppose it was a choice of their heritage or the future of Bradford."

"They did, in more ways than one," said Peter, adding that the former family home now stood as living witness to Bradford's heroic struggle to emerge from early Victorian squalor into a model of urban self-improvement.

Helen stepped out of the car and, holding Peter's hand, stood silently for several moments, taking in the view around her. Then she gave him her opinion that Yorkshire would be a great place to bring up their children.

"I feel I've come home," she told him. "Let's go and give the good news to your parents."